ALSO BY JUDITH HENRY WALL

Handsome Women
Love and Duty

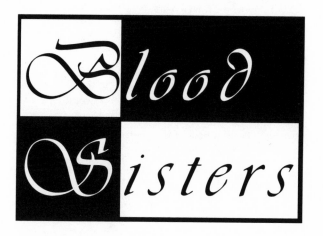

Judith Henry Wall

VIKING

VIKING
Published by the Penguin Group
Viking Penguin, a division of Penguin Books USA Inc.,
375 Hudson Street, New York, New York 10014, U.S.A.
Penguin Books Ltd, 27 Wrights Lane,
London W8 5TZ, England
Penguin Books Australia Ltd, Ringwood,
Victoria, Australia
Penguin Books Canada Ltd, 10 Alcorn Avenue, Suite 300,
Toronto, Ontario, Canada M4V 3B2
Penguin Books (N.Z.) Ltd, 182–190 Wairau Road,
Auckland 10, New Zealand

Penguin Books Ltd, Registered Offices:
Harmondsworth, Middlesex, England

First published in 1992 by Viking Penguin,
a division of Penguin Books USA Inc.

1 3 5 7 9 10 8 6 4 2

PUBLISHER'S NOTE
This is a work of fiction. Names, characters, places, and
incidents either are the product of the author's imagination or
are used fictitiously, and any resemblance to actual persons,
living or dead, events, or locales is entirely coincidental.

LIBRARY OF CONGRESS CATALOGING IN PUBLICATION DATA
Wall, Judith Henry.
Blood sisters / Judith Henry Wall.
p.   cm.
ISBN 0-670-84114-5
I. Title.
PS3573.A42556B57   1992
813'.54—dc20   92-54078

Printed in the United States of America
Set in Garamond #3
Designed by Claire N. Vaccaro

To my children—
Laura, Doug, and Richard,
whom I love more than anything

Special thanks to Shelba Bethel, M.D., of Norman, Oklahoma; Eva Hodges of Denver, Colorado; and Nancy and Richard Lea of Fort Collins, Colorado.

And my continuing gratitude to Pamela Dorman of Viking Penguin and Philippa Brophy of Sterling Lord Literistic.

Prologue

JUNE 1966

Had Libby died, they would have been able to make a saint of
her and burn candles on the altar of her memory. Perhaps an
annual meeting on her birthday to offer a toast, visit her grave,
and fondly say their "remember whens" is all that would have
been necessary.

And if she had turned her back on her three best friends,
they could have put the Libby years behind them, revised their
common history, and decided that Libby hadn't really been all
that important to them after all.

As it was, they hung in limbo.

That last night, she had been in white. Libby often wore
white. The snow princess. The twirling ballerina on the
jewelry box.

3

Even when she wasn't dancing, she was a dancer. Her posture, her every movement spoke of grace, training, discipline.

That night, at the anniversary party, her hair was even pulled back in a severe ballerina bun. Such wonderful hair. Heavy, black, shining. When she wore it loose, it hung down her back in a smooth, satin curtain—perfect hair that men stared at and women envied.

Her lipstick was too red. Helen remembered that. A slash of red against pale skin.

Helen remembered it all with the perfect recall saved for those moments in life that mean change—the death of loved ones or presidents, war declared or love rejected. That night Helen remembered with special clarity because it was the last time any of them saw Libby.

They were at Lenny and Bonnie's new downtown apartment. The aroma of Lenny's chicken curry simmering on the stove mingled with the smell of varnish and fresh paint.

Libby was late. Breathlessly, she made her entrance, posing in the entry hall, blowing kisses to the three men in the living room, then swooping into the kitchen to pluck baby Beth from her infant seat, spinning around the room with the baby held high in the air.

Libby's full skirt billowed out behind her, sinewy muscles straining in her bare arms as she held Helen's baby high in the air. "Beautiful, beautiful baby," she sang out. "Aunt Libby's beautiful little baby doll."

At first glance, the white dress was demure, with its high neck and princess waistline. But the back was a V almost to her waist, revealing a surprising expanse of skin, and in front, the outline of her nipples showed through the gauzy material. The men tried not to stare. Helen couldn't blame them. Helen had seen those nipples bare many times and been only passingly

4

interested, yet barely visible through pristine white cotton, they were erotic.

Small rosy nipples, the size of quarters—on two perfect mounds.

"Jesus, Libby, why the peep show?" Bonnie demanded, her own dark hair pulled back in a no-nonsense ponytail.

Jen glanced at Libby, wrinkled her brow in a puzzled frown, and returned her attention to her own baby.

The men began talking too loudly about golf. The U.S. Open. Arnie was lookin' good.

Nervously, Helen watched Libby with her daughter. Libby didn't know about babies. Beth wasn't old enough to be held like that. Her neck was too wobbly. Libby was spinning too fast. Finally, Helen stepped forward to intercede. "I want to feed her and get her to sleep before dinner," she explained as she cuddled Beth against her shoulder.

"You're a good mother," Libby said matter-of-factly, her hands behind her back, feet in third position as she watched Helen stir formula into rice cereal and attempt to poke it into Beth's mouth.

"So are you, Jen," Libby said, smiling at Jen sitting across the round kitchen table, her back to the men in the living room, as she adjusted blouse and bra so she could nurse her daughter. Jen's lovely, smooth face was intent on her baby daughter, her hair as sleekly blond as Libby's was black. Jen, the beauty queen turned mother. "You're both such good little mothers," Libby went on. "And Bonnie mothers Lenny instead of a baby. Remember how we swore we were going to be different? To be famous. They were going to write books about us in fifty years—we were never going to be ordinary?"

"Everyone is ordinary," Jen said, holding her nipple between two fingers and expertly guiding it into her baby's mouth.

"Individually, maybe," Libby said. "But together, we were special."

Helen felt herself nodding. Yes, they *had* been special together. But that time had passed. Now instead of four little girls, there were three couples, two babies—and Libby. The couples were celebrating five years of marriage. Libby had been the maid of honor to all three brides. And she still was. Alone. Clinging to memories of the way things were supposed to be.

Libby began to dance again, eyes closed, swaying to a music that had nothing to do with the sounds coming from the stereo in the front room. The distant Front Range was framed by the bay window behind her, the slopes shrouded in purple shadows, their peaks silhouetted against a pink and gold sunset. Libby's shoes made swishing sounds on the freshly varnished floor. Helen caught a whiff of her perfume. White Shoulders. Always.

"Hey, Libby, where'd you get the grass?" Lenny asked, leaning against the doorjamb between the kitchen and living room.

"No grass," Libby hummed, her arms floating over her head like water lilies in a pond. Bonnie, sitting with Jen at the kitchen table nursing her bourbon and water and a cigarette instead of a baby, shook her head at her husband, shushing him.

Libby twirled her way to an easy chair in the living room and sank into it. She leaned her head against the high back, her arms hanging limply over the sides of the chair, her eyes closed.

Jen gave the baby to Ted, and Helen motioned for her husband to take over feeding Beth.

"You okay, Lib?" Jen asked, kneeling beside her. Bonnie and Helen shared the footstool. The women looked at each other. Libby's skin was ashen. Beads of perspiration stood out above her lip.

Helen turned and gestured to her physician husband. Alex came to feel Libby's forehead, check her pulse.

Lenny and Ted, with his tiny daughter in his arms, watched from across the room, worried frowns on their faces.

Tears rolled down Libby's pale cheeks. Jen put her arms around Libby's shoulders. Helen and Bonnie each took a hand. "Don't cry, honey," Jen whispered. "We love you."

It seemed an act against nature to see Libby cry—like water flowing uphill.

Libby hadn't believed in tears. Even in grade school, she'd had little patience for them. *You can't be in our club if you cry.*

But the club was no more, and Libby was crying.

Libby had been the spark that made their girlhood exceptional, the hub around which their lives turned so effortlessly for all those years.

How they had loved Libby and her magic. When they were little, the magic always began with the words " 'tend like"—as in " 'tend like we are Amazon warriors" or " 'tend like we are princesses locked in a tower."

When they were older, they shared dreams and secrets by candlelight. Libby had a thing about candles. And stemmed glasses. They drank Dr Pepper from wineglasses, sitting in a circle, with a candle in the center. Circles and candles had mystical properties, Libby informed them. She went to the Episcopal church with her father rather than Unitarian services with her mother because she liked the ritual, the chants, the candles, the mystery.

Libby fueled their imaginations and sparked their fancies. With Libby, they didn't just go on a picnic to the park, they went on an expedition to the Sudan. Bicycles were never just bicycles, they were steeds. Head scarfs became veils. Headaches became brain tumors. Mean teachers were Soviet spies. Dime store rings were priceless jewels.

They took turns being men during playacting. Men were either villains or heroes. But then women were either witches or virgins. Completely good or unrelentingly bad.

Sometimes they played convent, dressing themselves in bathrobes, with towels on their heads, chanting prayers and lighting candles as penance for extraordinary sins. Bonnie liked to be the mother superior, Jen a novitiate. Helen remembered one time when Libby was an ancient nun on her deathbed, saying Hail Marys and farewells.

In high school, Libby's brand of fun bordered on the bizarre—like pretending that one of them was deaf or blind or royalty or crazy. They would go into restaurants and stores with little scenarios all worked out. Once, when they had led a blind Jen onto a bus, an old man exposed himself. Jen squealed, "He's got his thing out!"

"For Christ's sake, Jen," Libby said with disgust. "You can't see him. You're *blind*."

So, Bonnie and Helen took up the clamor until the bus driver came back and made the man get off the bus.

Even in college, Libby made up scenarios. She convinced Helen's blind date that he was about to go out with Bing Crosby's illegitimate daughter. They passed Bonnie off as a Hungarian freedom fighter whose family had escaped from Budapest with only the clothes on their backs.

In the seventh grade, Libby had written their song—about loyalty and forever friends. The last time they sang that song together had been at Jen's wedding rehearsal dinner—as a joke, after all the toasts. But shoulders square, Libby sang it for real.

Helen had kept her eyes on her plate, embarrassed for Libby. They weren't kids anymore. The time for her body-and-soul brand of sisterhood was over. The rest of them were getting married and would stay in Colorado forever.

Only Libby was going to follow through on their old dream. New York. *Mecca.* Fame and fortune.

They had talked about it for years. Libby would dance her way to immortality. Bonnie would be a famous journalist. Jen's face and figure would appear on the covers of fashion magazines for years to come. And Helen—they weren't quite sure in what arena Helen's light would shine. Perhaps she would marry dethroned royalty or a literary giant and hold soirees in her Fifth Avenue salon. Perhaps she would be book editor for the *New York Times.* But one by one, Helen, Jen, and Bonnie had backed out of the dream. And they felt guilty, envious, even fearful for their friend. Libby was a world-class dreamer. But Libby's dreams had never been tested.

"If she had found someone to marry, she'd be staying here, too," Jen had rationalized.

"She didn't want to find anyone," Bonnie had countered. "The rest of us were too cowardly to test our wings."

And as the years went by, Helen wondered from time to time if all the effort to continue their friendship was worth it. Maybe after Libby had disappeared, they should have just gone their separate ways. Except that they were haunted by the memory of four girls laughing and sharing secrets and having fun and knowing that what they shared set them apart, that life was more exciting because they had each other.

Helen

and Her

Friends

One

During their freshman year at East High, the student body, with heads bowed, prayed every morning for the war in Korea to come to an end. No one smarted off or made stupid noises. Boys from East High had died.

Eisenhower was a runaway winner in the high school's mock election, a portent of the real election to follow. Of course, his wife, Mamie, was a Doud from Denver, but the real reason everyone liked Ike was because he promised to end the war.

Bonnie—in spite of having an older brother at boot camp —was one of the few students sporting an "I Rely on Adlai" button. But, then, Bonnie liked being different. She smoked, wore cowboy boots instead of saddle oxfords, had her ears pierced like the Mexican girls, and refused to wear starched petticoats under her gathered skirts.

Helen, who worked as hard at being conventional as Bonnie did at being different, had her first real crush that year—on her history teacher, Mr. Simons, who wrote in her yearbook that she was not only a brilliant student but a beautiful person. *A beautiful person.* That wasn't the same as being a beautiful girl.

That same year, in December, Libby's dance teacher arranged for her to audition for a professor in Boulder, a Russian who had trained with the Bolshoi before the Second World War. The professor had watched dispassionately, his face betraying nothing. But then, in an unheard-of gesture, he invited Libby to dance with his university classes twice a week.

The following summer, Jen and Ted started sneaking down into a basement storeroom of her house every chance they got. She wouldn't let him look at her small, taut breasts, only reach under her bra and touch them. And she closed her eyes when she touched his penis as it grew hard in her hand. They kissed for hours. Until their lips were swollen, sometimes even bleeding.

That fall, when Ted got his driver's license, they drove down mountain lanes that seemed to have been created for courting. In the backseat, they took off their clothes. Ted put his finger in her. And rubbed his penis against her belly. He wanted her and Jen loved it.

In November, he produced a condom and begged with tears in his eyes to go all the way. He loved her more than anything. She was making him crazy. He couldn't think about anything else. He couldn't study. Couldn't sleep. And after all, they were going to get married.

Married. Well, that made it almost all right.

But not all right enough that Jen ever told anyone. Not even her three best friends.

It was Libby who guessed. They were in Jen's basement admiring a litter of new kittens. Libby couldn't have a cat. Her brother had allergies.

"You and Ted are doing it, aren't you?" Libby asked.

Jen wanted to deny it, but she could feel her face and neck growing hot and red. She looked away. "He loves me," she said. "We're going to get married someday."

"And you'll end up going to luncheons like your mother. Is that what you want?"

"Maybe Ted can go to New York, too," Jen suggested.

"And give up a ready-made partnership in his daddy's law firm? Do you use birth control?"

Jen nodded. "He uses a rubber."

"That's not good enough. You need a diaphragm."

"Sure," Jen said, giving the kitten back to its fretting mother. "Doctors just love prescribing diaphragms for sixteen-year-old girls."

"You can say you're eighteen."

"What if the doctor doesn't believe me?"

"I'm sure some doctors are smart enough to realize that if a girl is asking for help with birth control, she needs it."

Libby took care of it. She found the doctor and made the appointment. She drove Jen to Golden to visit a middle-aged female family doctor, who practiced in an office in her home. Without a word of chastisement, the tiny physician fitted the pretty blond teenager with a diaphragm and gave her instructions for its use. The doctor made her insert and take out the device three times until she was satisfied that Jen had mastered the technique.

"There's no such thing as a diaphragm baby," the doctor said. "But you've got to use it. A diaphragm won't do you any good in the drawer."

On the drive back to Denver, Jen reached across the seat

to touch Libby's arm. "Thanks. You're the best friend I've ever had."

The round, white-plastic case looked like a compact. Jen opened it and stared at the rubber circle inside. It looked like a huge condom.

Someday, she would probably marry Ted and have his babies. But in the meantime, Jen wanted to be young and have fun. And just in case she and Ted fell out of love, or if there was another war and Ted got drafted and never came home, or if he didn't get a football scholarship at CU and had to go some faraway college to play, Jen wanted her options open. Maybe she would even become a famous New York model, like Libby said.

They stopped at a drugstore on the north side of Denver for Jen to buy spermicidal cream. The pharmacist stared hard at her face before he rang up the purchase. She felt her cheeks grow warm and fought the urge to run out of the store.

"I wish Ted and I had waited," she said when she got back in the car.

Libby was wise enough not to comment.

The topic of conversation was Bonnie's walk. They were gathered in Helen's cluttered bedroom with its collection of Elvis pictures lining one wall, a huge bulletin board filled with assorted memorabilia dating back to grade school hanging over the bed, and a plate of oatmeal cookies that Helen had just baked sitting in the middle of the floor.

According to Jen, Bonnie had a sexy walk.

"What a stupid thing to say," Bonnie said, nibbling on an oatmeal cookie, nodding her approval to Helen. Helen was the official cookie baker of the group. She'd used raisins, dates, and walnuts in this batch.

"No, I'm serious," Jen said, blowing on her freshly painted fingernails. "Libby walks like a princess reviewing her guard. Helen's always in a hurry. I kind of bounce along. But you saunter. Like Lauren Bacall. Boys think that's sexy."

"No boy in the history of the world has ever thought I was sexy for any other reason than my bra size," Bonnie said.

But later, in the privacy of her own bedroom, Bonnie examined her walk from all angles in her dresser mirror with the help of a hand mirror to check the rear view. Did she really have a sexy walk? Did she even *want* to?

She already knew there was something about her that made boys exchange secret glances when she walked by. She had always assumed it was her breasts, which had erupted quite dramatically from her chest by the end of the sixth grade and assumed their present D-cup proportions by the beginning of the eighth. The idea that there was something else about her person that was noticed by the opposite sex was at least interesting.

Bonnie found most boys repulsive, but a few were her buddies—Libby's brother for one. A year older than his sister, Carl was sweet. And smart. He and Bonnie used to work on the school paper together, but he had cystic fibrosis and hardly ever came to school anymore. Libby thought Bonnie was just being nice when she played cards with Carl and told him all the gossip from school. But Bonnie liked him. A lot. He had a crush on Jen, though. And he was dying. That made him kind of like a saint.

Bonnie's other male buddies either had bad complexions or belonged to the Chess Club or both. She smoked with them in cars during lunch. But she wouldn't have considered going out with them.

The boy who lived next door to Bonnie attended the Colorado School of Mines in Golden. Craig Odom. They started hanging around together. Bonnie acquired a certain mystique as a girl dating an "older man." And when Craig gave her his old East High letter jacket, the boys at school were more respectful.

Their dates were stiff and uncomfortable. Bonnie would ask Craig about his classes, his family, his hobbies. Sometimes there were awkward silences.

But after the dates, they had long, into-the-night telephone calls that were relaxed, more companionable.

Craig was excited about his future as a mining engineer. He thought there was still significant silver to be mined from the Colorado Rockies. He was going to invent economically efficient retrieval methods.

"And I'll write about it and make you famous," Bonnie promised.

"Do you think we'll still know each other then?" he asked.

"Do you want us to?"

"Yeah. I do. A lot."

It was during one of these late-night phone calls that Craig admitted he wanted to put his mouth on her tits. That thinking about it made him crazy.

Bonnie wasn't sure if she felt mad or just embarrassed. She didn't hang up. She let him elicit a promise of "maybe someday" from her.

And then, the ice having been broken, a few nights later Craig told her over the phone that he was dying to have sex with her. That he thought about it constantly.

Bonnie was shocked. He'd never even tried to kiss her.

Then he said the worst thing of all—that he was in love with her. *Jesus.*

Libby said Bonnie would feel terrible afterward if she went all the way with Craig.

"How would you know?" Bonnie demanded as they sunned themselves by the country club pool, where Jen's folks were members.

"Because anything that you really shouldn't have is a disappointment when you give in," Libby explained, as she rubbed baby oil on Bonnie's back. "It's like eating a bowl of chocolate chip cookie dough. When you finish, you wish you hadn't. You feel sick and have to diet for a week."

"Sex isn't fattening," Bonnie observed. "Don't you ever want to just do it and get it over with so you don't have to worry about whether to stay a virgin or not? I'm so curious and sometimes at night I feel so open, I think I'm going to turn inside out if I don't get a boy to fill me up. Then in the daytime I get around boys and can't stand them. Except Craig. He's not so bad. And your brother is nice."

"Just look around you, sugar," Libby said, her voice gentle, her fingertips soft as she smoothed the oil on Bonnie's shoulders. "Do you think the filling up made our mothers happy? Do you know of any married woman who lives an exciting life? We can't settle for a life like that just because everyone else thinks they're supposed to."

"But eventually we're going to have sex," Bonnie insisted, adjusting her straps and leaning back onto the chaise.

"I suppose so," Libby said, staring at Helen and Jen swimming laps in the pool. "Maybe it'll be okay when we're older and don't run the risk of some boy telling everyone in the locker room. But sex makes a boy think he owns a girl. If you start screwing Craig, then you'll be his girl friend and have to sit by the phone in case he calls. You'll be afraid he'll tell his buddies that you let him do it, afraid of him dropping you and having to tell the next boy that you're not a virgin, afraid of getting pregnant, afraid he won't like your haircut or your new dress.

And you'll be like Jen and put your friends second. She's spending the afternoon with us only because Ted is playing golf with his dad."

"Do you think Jen and Ted go all the way?"

"If they don't, they will pretty soon. You don't spend that much time alone in a car with a boy without having sex with him eventually."

"I think I'm already afraid of making Craig mad," Bonnie confessed.

"And do you like feeling that way?" Libby asked.

Bonnie looked away. She didn't, of course. "But sooner or later, we're all going to fall in love and get married," she insisted.

Craig was nice enough, but not by any stretch of the imagination could Bonnie see the two of them riding the Orient Express while she pursued an elusive celebrity for an exclusive interview. For by then, her success with the East High newspaper had convinced her that she wanted to be a journalist. A *real* journalist. Not a woman who wrote up the weddings and garden club stuff like Miss Collins at the *Post*. Bonnie wanted front page. Wire service. Writing a best-selling autobiography when she was old, telling of her fabulous life. Libby kept pointing out that that kind of journalist didn't live in Colorado. Bonnie supposed she was right.

Even on the nights they double-dated, after the couples had parted, Ted would find a shadowed place for some quick sex before he took Jen home.

And the next morning, Jen would prop a leg up on the lavatory and remove the gooey diaphragm, wash it, and return it to the plastic case, which she kept hidden in the bottom of her scarf drawer.

Jen and Ted screwed their way through high school, while their parents, who played bridge and golf together at the country club, thought it was just wonderful their children were going steady. Jen spent a lot of time practicing her future signature. *Mrs. Theodore Echols.*

If she didn't marry Ted, she still wanted to go to New York with her friends. And spend some time in Europe, maybe find an elegant, foreign man to kiss her hand and treat her like a princess. But she knew the course she was following with Ted eliminated the prospect of European adventures and certain other of life's possibilities.

Jen admired Libby's aloofness about sex. Libby wasn't going to let a relationship with a male interfere with her goals. Boys noticed her, but she didn't seem to care whether they hung around or not. Often if a boy dropped by her house, she instructed him to play checkers with her brother while she went off to make phone calls or do homework.

Jen knew she herself cared too much. And even though she hated the sneaking and lying and diaphragm, the screwing itself was wonderful. She liked it best when they made it last and last, devouring each other with kisses, dirty talk all mixed up with whispers of love and forever and making babies someday. Jen even liked it on freezing cold nights in the backseat of Ted's Chevy with the windows all steamed over. For warmth, they used an old down comforter Ted kept hidden away in the trunk.

She wondered if married sex in a double bed could ever be as much fun.

During the girls' second semester at the University of Colorado, Ted informed Bonnie that he had arranged a blind date for her with one of his teammates—Leonard Brewster, a split end with lackluster talent and no pro prospects. Like Ted.

"Jocks don't like smart women," Bonnie protested. "Their egos are too fragile. Their minds too small."

"Jen's smart," Ted pointed out.

"But her vision is flawed," Bonnie said. "She has this huge blind spot."

"Eight o'clock. Wear your hair down. And if you're not there, I'll start a rumor."

"What rumor?"

"That they're silicone." Ted crossed his eyes as he stared downward at her chest.

"Yeah, I got them from the same doctor who fitted you with a pecker," she called over her shoulder as she hurried off to botany lab. "And I'll wear my hair any damned way I please."

Saturday night, when Bonnie arrived at The Sink, she was surprised to see the good-looking, sandy-haired guy from the back row in her news-writing class sitting in the booth with Jen and Ted.

Ted winked—her hair was down. She wanted to give him the finger but restrained herself in front of Leonard Brewster. Ted called him "Lenny."

"I liked your story about the ten most boring professors," Lenny said. "The whole campus was talking about it. I'll bet the guys you wrote about were really pissed off."

"You know who I am?"

"Yeah. From my news-writing class. I saw you with Ted and Jen one evening and asked Ted to fix us up."

He'd asked for the date. Ted hadn't twisted his arm. He'd read her story.

"So, you got a *real* major, huh?" she asked.

He grinned. "Not all football players major in recreation."

She grinned back. "Too bad." He had great dark eyes with thick lashes like a woman.

"You want a glass for your beer?" the waiter asked as he set two longnecks on the table in front of them.

Bonnie shook her head no and fumbled for the bottle. It was hard to look away from his face. A sweet face. *Jesus.* And on that gorgeous body.

He arranged their next date before he said good night at the dormitory door. Next Saturday night. Seven o'clock. She wouldn't have to wait in agony for a phone call.

She couldn't sleep. The room was so quiet. Jen had checked out for the night, supposedly to go home, but she was really off screwing Ted in some motel, which she did a lot. Jen said that when she wasn't screwing Ted, she was thinking about screwing him.

Bonnie wondered what it would be like to want someone all the time. To have someone to want all the time.

Should she allow herself to think about screwing Lenny Brewster?

No. Not a good idea. What if it never happened? It would hurt too much if she had allowed herself to fantasize it.

But when she closed her eyes, she realized the thought was already there.

She tiptoed across the hall to Helen and Libby's dark room. Bonnie knelt by Helen's bed. "Come over and talk to me," she whispered in her ear.

They drank warm beer and talked into the night. "You honestly think this is the real thing?" Helen asked Bonnie. "You just met this guy."

"I don't know. But I feel so nervous and sweaty and scared and excited. No other boy has made me feel like this."

"I wish Libby would fall in love," Helen admitted. "I don't

think any of us are going to New York or anywhere else with her. And if she doesn't fall in love, we're going to break her heart."

"Yeah, I'd rather some boy do it than us."

Libby wasn't like the rest of them, Helen thought, back in her own room, shivering in her cold bed. Libby didn't seem to need a man to love her. And she wanted only one set of friends, one dream for the future.

Helen would always love Jen and Bonnie and Libby best of all. But she wanted other friends, too.

All of their Delta Gamma pledge sisters, and the members, too, vied for Libby's attention. In a group, Libby was the hub. Libby could turn an ordinary gathering into a party. She'd clap her hands for attention, then have people choose sides for charades, teach them how to polka or, for no reason at all, organize a parade through the campus with streamers on the cars and everyone waving out the windows like homecoming queens.

Everyone in their DG pledge class became good friends. But when Helen went someplace with just one of the girls, she felt almost disloyal to Libby and didn't always tell her. She especially liked Gloria Addison, the pledge class president. Gloria had lost her parents when she was fourteen and lived near the campus with her grandparents. Gloria had lived abroad and had read more books than even Helen. She had a wonderful laugh and lots of friends. When she invited Helen to go skiing with her, Helen told Libby she was going home to Denver for the weekend.

"Why can't I mention the skiing trip to Libby?" Gloria demanded.

"It might hurt her feelings," Helen tried to explain.

"That's *creepy*, Helen," Gloria said.

Jen went off with Ted all the time, and if Bonnie started

going with Leonard Brewster, that would leave only Helen to
carry on with Libby's dream.

She looked over at the sleeping form in the other bed. Did
Libby really close her eyes at night and not think of a man's
arms around her? But why would she pretend such a thing if it
wasn't true?

$\mathcal{T}$ w o

By her junior year, Libby was a campus celebrity. Elizabeth Ballard, the dancer. The university's public relations department published a wonderful four-color poster showing a swanlike ballerina being lifted high over the head of an enormous uniformed lineman complete with pads and helmet. The caption said: "The University of Colorado—from fine arts to football, we've got it all." Libby was the ballerina. The campus bookstores sold out of the posters, and a second printing was ordered. Helen had one framed and hung it over her bed. She often found herself studying the musculature in Libby's back and limbs, her long graceful neck, the purity of her profile. The lineman's thick hands on her diminutive waist were almost obscene.

Libby performed for donors at university galas. She made a

special appearance with the Denver ballet. To the delight of a packed field house, she did a high-energy cancan as part of a half-time presentation at a basketball game. The cheers and whistles were deafening.

The school paper did a full-page picture spread on her. School children from all over the state were bused to the campus when she appeared in *Peter Pan*. The governor and his wife came to Boulder when she danced the lead in *Firebird*. She was Maria in *West Side Story*. Her singing voice was thin, but she was hailed as the most talented dancer ever to come through the university program. Everyone predicted great things for her. The frontispiece in the 1959–1960 Buffalo yearbook featured a full-length, diffused picture of her on *pointe*.

Libby never discussed the men who drifted through her life except in the most perfunctory terms. Her friends speculated that she screwed her dance professor. Zubov, the Russian. An elegant man with a wonderful accent and sad eyes. But Ted insisted that Zubov was gay.

Zubov devoted himself to Libby's instruction. He spent long evening hours alone with her in the dance studio in the Theatre and Dance Building. Jen went with Libby one evening and marveled at the whole process. Just the warm-up exercises took almost an hour. And perfecting each movement required painstaking effort. Zubov danced by her side, demanding. Always demanding. Making her do it again and again, bringing her to the point of tears, then backing off and cajoling. She had to work harder than the others. Only she had a chance. Only she had the heart and talent of a true dancer. They had forgotten that Jen was even there.

Zubov danced a special pas de deux with Libby at her last CU performance before graduation. Her parents were there. And her brother, Carl.

Helen clapped till her hands hurt. The audience refused to

sit down. Even Ted and Lenny took up the cry of "Bravo!" and punctuated it with piercing whistles.

Tears rolled down Evelyn Ballard's cheeks, but Libby's father seemed unmoved. But then, he'd never really approved of his daughter's dancing. He thought she should be getting a degree in nursing or elementary education.

Carl was crying, too. It amazed Helen at times to realize that Carl loved Libby. Libby was a better friend than she was a sister.

Helen watched as Jen changed places with Ted to give Carl a hug. "Isn't that sister of yours incredible?" Jen said, and hugged him again. Carl looked like he had just been given the Holy Grail.

Family, friends, dance majors, and faculty gathered at the union for an after-performance party. Most of their Delta Gamma sorority sisters came. "I wish I had a film of them dancing together," Helen said with a sigh. "I'd watch it over and over for the rest of my life."

"I couldn't take my eyes off Zubov's face," Jen admitted. "I had to watch him watching Libby. God, it was beautiful."

"Still think he's queer?" Bonnie asked Ted with an elbow jab to his ribs.

At that moment, Libby and Zubov entered the room. Zubov was elegant in an exquisitely tailored silk suit. Libby was a princess in ivory chiffon. Once again, the cheers erupted.

Zubov bowed then lifted Libby high over his head in a splendid, graceful motion. One last lift.

With her hands on his shoulders, Libby smiled down at her teacher. So radiant. So pure.

Of course, Zubov loves her, Helen thought. *How could he not love her?*

But Libby loved only her three friends.

By the time her acceptance to graduate school at NYU had arrived in the spring of 1961, Helen was engaged to Alexander Compton Radcliff. A second-year medical student at the CU Health Science Center campus in downtown Denver, Alex was from Kansas City, but he'd always planned to attend college in Colorado, where his family vacationed. Alex loved Colorado with the zeal of a convert.

Alex had been a fraternity brother of Helen's cousin Bill. But when Alex called to ask her out the first time, she couldn't remember him. He sounded nice enough, though, and she was tired of never going out. After the rush of her freshman and sophomore years, she had slowly settled into that dateless state that plagues unattached junior and senior women. Alex was coming to Boulder for the annual Colorado-Oklahoma football clash, a big party weekend. His old frat always had big bashes after the games.

The idea of going to the football game with a boy, eating hot dogs and drinking beer, then dancing away the evening at a frat dance sounded collegiate and nice.

She remembered him as soon as she opened the door. The good-looking guy that Bill had roomed with as a freshman. She wouldn't have dreamed in a million years *he* would have called her. This guy had big brown eyes, a cleft in his strong chin, and a beautiful, sexy mouth. And was a doctor in the making. For an instant, Helen crawled inside her mother's skin. *Perfect. Absolutely perfect.* Her GP father would be thrilled.

Helen wished she'd worn a skirt instead of jeans. And spent more time taming her hair.

He was much better looking than she was.

Helen was often compared to June Allyson, who was always

cast as a nurse, nun, or steadfast wife. Her screen husbands were Jimmy Stewart or Van Johnson—not Gregory Peck.

And here stood a young Gregory Peck.

Smiling.

"I kept trying to remember if you were Bill's friend who kept the boa constrictor in his closet or the one with the Adam's apple," Helen said all in a rush. "I'm not sure I would have agreed to go out with you if I'd known you were the good-looking one."

"Well, now that I'm here, may I come in?"

Helen stepped aside, aware of the dust on the furniture, the clutter of books and notebooks on the table. The four girls had rented an apartment for their senior year, but Jen usually slept over at Ted's, and Bonnie at Lenny's. Libby and Helen didn't bother much with housekeeping.

"What kind of doctor are you going to be?" she asked.

"OB/GYN."

This gave her further pause. Stirrups. Pelvics. A man who planned to earn a living dealing with women's most intimate parts.

"Would you like a beer?" she asked.

He smiled again.

No point getting worked up about this one, Helen told herself as she fetched two beers. The man was out of her league.

It was a clear, crisp day, the mountains forming a lovely backdrop to the stadium. They tucked a stadium blanket around their knees and shared a thermos of coffee.

Colorado actually beat the mighty Sooners. Afterward, they dropped by the apartment so Helen could change. All during the game Helen had mentally discarded one garment after another until she finally settled on a Pendleton plaid skirt, silk blouse, and her best cashmere sweater—with a good leather belt from Jen's collection. And a couple of combs to hold back her unruly hair.

They met Libby in the hallway on her way out. She was wearing a baggy sweatshirt over a leotard. Her legs were encased in heavy, moth-eaten leg warmers. A pair of well-worn ballet shoes was slung over her shoulder. With a freshly scrubbed face and hair in braids, she looked twelve years old. Alex had seen her picture in the paper. The ballerina. Libby smiled sweetly and rushed off. "Zubov is waiting," she said over her shoulder.

"Zubov is her dance professor," Helen explained. "He's in love with her."

"I can see why," Alex said, his gaze following the departing figure.

The streets were choked with game-day traffic, so they left Alex's car in the parking lot and walked across campus. The evening was crisp and beautiful. The campus was brilliant with fall foliage and beds of colorful mums. The mountains were shades of purple in the setting sun. Helen felt good. Too good.

Calm down, she told herself. *Wait and see if he calls you back.*

Alex asked Helen what she was going to do after graduation. She told him about her plans for graduate school. English lit. She did not, however, say anything about her application at Columbia. Or NYU. After all, she had also applied at CU—as a hedge against losing her nerve.

He told her about the clinics. He was seeing patients now. General medicine. He wouldn't be doing much OB/GYN until his residency, which would come later. He'd gone to school on an ROTC scholarship and owed the army four years of military service in return.

The party was too noisy for much talking. They danced to Buddy Holly, Fats Domino, and Elvis. Between dances, they sat close and drank a lot of beer. During the occasional slow dance, he grew hard against her belly, making the crotch of her panties grow moist from nervousness—or something else.

When he said good night, however, he kissed her rather gently. She didn't know whether to be disappointed or pleased.

He didn't call the next day. Or the next. Helen hated the way her heart jumped when the phone rang. And the painful disappointment because it wasn't him.

The following Sunday, Helen was still asleep when the phone rang. She broke out in a nervous sweat. He only had a minute. He was doing something called "externing" at General Rose hospital.

He wanted her to drive down to Denver.

"We can do something corny like go to the zoo and eat pizza. I'll warn you now, I'm on a limited budget. If you're going to keep company with me, you can put your ball gowns and diamond tiaras in storage."

If you're going to keep company with me. Helen sighed and sank back in her pillow.

Except, could she trust a man who had taken a week to call? Had he been trying to make up his mind? Breaking up with another girl? Going down his list?

Hooking up with a physician-in-the making meant wrapping her life around his. Like her mother had done. The doctor's wife.

And she really wanted to go to New York. For so long, she had planned on it. Graduate school. Somewhere that women were expected to excel just like men. She'd earn a Ph.D. *Doctor* Helen Donaldson.

Of course, she could get a less prestigious Ph.D. at Boulder. Maybe it didn't matter *that* much where she got it. And anyway, Jen and Bonnie probably weren't going to New York. Jen was still saying maybe—for a year or two, but Helen doubted if she'd leave Ted even for a week or two. And Bonnie said she would go only if she could talk Lenny into it.

But if Jen and Bonnie didn't go, that meant Helen was the only one keeping Libby's dream alive.

Helen spent more time analyzing her new relationship than she did studying. She was falling in love. She found herself contemplating a whole new category of passages in her literature books.

Dame Edith Sitwell claimed that the fire of the heart and the fire of the mind could never be one. Helen wondered which won out in Dame Edith's life. The heart or the mind?

And dear Miss Emily Dickinson couldn't live with the man she loved. Was it fear or self-preservation or wisdom that kept her from him?

But in Alex's arms, Helen didn't care about wisdom or her own ambition. All she cared about was the next kiss and the incredible feel of his body making love to hers. She found herself sneaking looks at Jen's bridal magazines.

Libby insisted that it was time for Jen to get a portfolio together, and took her to a photographer in Denver. The pictures were stunning. Dozens of them. Wholesome. Seductive. Regal. Aloof. Cute. Every kind of Jen imaginable—all flawless. Ted hated them. Jen felt like they were of someone else, but she stared at them endlessly. Did she want to be that perfect person born of the camera's eye? Did she want to make a conventional life as a lawyer's wife or risk all and try for the life Libby had designed for her?

Libby painted wonderful scenarios of what that life would be like in New York. And other people encouraged Jen, telling her that she was as beautiful as Suzy Parker, whose perfect oval face graced countless magazine covers. Now she was making movies. Starring with Louis Jourdan. But Jen knew that being the next Suzy Parker took more than looks. It took luck and desire. Wanting it more than anything.

Ted wasn't interested in New York.

"I want you to stop filling Jen's head with all that crap about New York," Ted told Libby one night on the dance floor at the Denver Country Club. Her parents had reserved three tables at the regular Saturday night dinner dance. It was Jen's twenty-second birthday.

"Why?" Libby asked. "So you can make her queen of the suburbs with beauty shop hair, driving her station wagon to club meetings? In five years, the Jen we know wouldn't even exist. She won't like sex. She'll hate you for messing up her perfect house."

"I can give her a damned good life," Ted insisted. "She can go to the beauty shop every day if she wants to. Now shut up and dance."

Ordinarily Ted loved the feel of Libby in his arms. She was small and delicate. He'd often wondered how it would feel to make love to her. A man would have to be exquisitely tender. Not like the lusty romps he enjoyed with Jen.

Tonight, Ted was not feeling tender toward Libby. This New York nonsense had gone on long enough. Jen was still in shock over those damned pictures and saying stupid things like maybe she should try it for a while. After all, she owed it to Libby. Just a year or two, while he was finishing up law school. Maybe he'd even like to give New York a try. He could be a famous New York lawyer with celebrity clients.

It was weird the way Libby could talk Jen into things.

"God, men are so stupid!" Libby was saying, pushing on his left hand, trying to take the lead away from him. "You love Jen because she's beautiful and exciting and sexy. And you can hardly wait to turn her into a housewife. Why can't you let her come and go? When you see her, it would be like heaven."

"People get married and have kids and *change.* And everyone has to make choices. If Jen wants to go to New York with you, I'm not going to sit around waiting for her to drift in and out of my life."

"You just want to own her!" Libby challenged. Her chin was lifted, her angry eyes hard and alien in her porcelain doll's face.

Was she really a virgin, Ted wondered.

One of the other first-year law students insisted that Libby didn't go all the way but she gave great head. That she really *liked* to give head. Ted seriously doubted the guy had ever even taken Libby out. He was too much of a loudmouth. Still, it was quite an image. *Libby with a cock in her mouth.* Ted felt his own cock stirring at the thought.

"Yeah," he said. "I want to own Jen. Have her all to myself. Just like you want. Only you can't give her babies."

She bit the back of his hand. Hard. Leaving a deep imprint of small perfect teeth.

Lenny followed Ted into the men's room. Ted ran hot water over his hand and rubbed at the angry red teeth marks. They'd leave bruises. *Cute.*

"A souvenir from the goddess, I see," Lenny said.

"You saw?"

"Yeah. I was watching. We all watch her, don't we? You and Alex and I. What did you do to deserve that?" he asked, nodding toward Ted's hand.

"I got Jen."

"She hates us, you know. Alex, too. Weird how we all pretend to be such good friends."

"Yeah. Weird."

For Christmas her senior year, Ted gave Jen an engagement
ring. The solitaire diamond was almost a carat and a half. Maybe
she had never really believed in New York anyway—any more
than she had believed in becoming a spy or a duchess or any
of the other roles they had played.

She told Libby first. "Be happy for me," Jen pleaded.

"Of course, I am, honey, if this is what you really want,"
Libby said, with tears in her eyes. Her heavy hair hung over
her shoulders like a veil. *Sister Libby.* She looked out of place
in her mother's maple living room.

"It is," Jen said passionately, accepting Libby's congratula-
tory hug, hugging back too hard. And hugging again. Libby's
body felt like that of a child. She always seemed so strong, but
she wasn't strong at all. "I wanted the other, too," Jen whispered. "But I couldn't have both."

"I know. Don't cry. We'll always be friends. Blood sisters.
Remember?"

"Then you forgive me?"

"What is there to forgive?"

"And we'll always love each other."

"Always." Libby took Jen's face in her hands and gently
kissed her on the mouth. "Always," she repeated. "You are so
beautiful. How could I help but love you?"

Blood sisters. When they were in the sixth grade, they had
actually let Libby slice open their thumbs with a razor blade—
by candlelight in Bonnie's basement, shadows flickering on bare
concrete walls.

Solemnly, they had rubbed their thumbs together, mingling the blood, swearing to be sisters until the day they died.

But it had only been a game.

Bonnie got her ring on Valentine's Day. Lenny said if she accepted his proposal of marriage, it meant she would love him forever and check his spelling for life.

Alex proposed at the end of March. Helen didn't make him promise they would live in a university town so she could earn her Ph.D. All she said was "yes."

$\mathcal{T}hree$

Helen and Alex had the first wedding. And spent an idyllic week-long honeymoon in Santa Fe. During the long drive and over dinner, they talked endlessly about the future. He wanted to be the world's best doctor and make lots of money. She wanted to continue her education. And children—they both wanted children more than anything. Their lovemaking was tender. Alex promised to love her forever, never to hurt her. Back in Denver, in Alex's tiny apartment, Helen's wedding dress was put away, the honeymoon photographs printed and admired. Helen fell into a funk, finding it difficult to tear herself away from morning quiz shows and afternoon soap operas to pack away wedding gifts and start getting organized for their move to San Antonio, where Alex would do his internship at Brooke Army Medical Center.

Married to Alex. What she had wanted more than anything. She should be more joyful, more excited. The blushing bride. She didn't know what to say when people asked her how she liked married life.

But things would be better when they got settled in San Antonio. When Alex had regular hours. And she had a teaching job next fall—junior high English. Graduate school was on hold for now. Without knowing how long they would be in the state, she didn't want to start a graduate program at a Texas university. And it seemed like a good idea to get some money in the bank in preparation for the lean residency years they faced when Alex finished his military service.

Ted and Jen got married next, in an impressive ceremony at Montview Presbyterian with banks of flowers, a string quartet, the mayor and lieutenant governor in attendance. Helen had tears in her eyes as she stood with Bonnie and Libby at the altar rail, watching Jen come down the aisle. No bride had ever been more beautiful.

After the wedding reception, Alex and Helen drove up to Lookout Mountain. His idea.

Alex was silent on the way up the mountain, taking great care with his driving in the wake of all the wedding champagne.

His silences always made Helen nervous. And made her babble. *Hadn't Jen been gorgeous? The food and music fabulous? Were he and Lenny still going fishing next Sunday? Maybe she and Bonnie would go shopping. Bonnie still hadn't found the right shoes for her wedding.*

Was Alex as frightened as she was by the changes in their relationship in just one short month? The difference between courtship and marriage—she hadn't expected it to be so marked and quick.

But tonight, she was feeling sentimentally passionate. The words of the wedding ceremony had brought tears to her eyes.

She did believe in marriage. It was just going to be harder than she thought. Not automatically wonderful.

The city of Denver sprawled below them, bejeweled in nighttime splendor. The lighted dome of the state capitol building shone in the distance like a gold beacon. Behind them were the mountains—huge, eternal, humbling.

"The mountains brought us together," Alex said as they stood on the precipice. "If my parents and I hadn't fallen in love with the Colorado Rockies, it never would have occurred to me to come to school here. I probably would have gone to Missouri."

"The mountains keep me from getting lost," Helen mused. "As long as I can see the Front Range, I know what direction I'm going in. I hate foggy days and stormy nights. I get lost. I need to see mountains to know where I am, who I am."

"I'll keep you from getting lost on foggy days. I have a compass in my head."

"Why did you marry me?" she asked abruptly.

"Because I fell in love with you."

"But what made you fall in love with me? What made you finally call me back? Why didn't you find someone as gorgeous as you are? Do you have any idea how distracting it is to know that everyone is thinking, 'Well, Helen is *attractive*, but she's not in his league?' "

"I don't have a league, Helen. And from the first moment I saw you, I knew you were special."

"But what made you more attracted to me than someone else?" she persisted.

"You were so up front about liking me and wanting me. I liked that. You don't play games."

"Then I can tell you that I'm scared to death. What happened? We said 'I do' and started being old in the same breath.

40

God, I look at you in that tacky recliner, reading the evening paper, and feel like I slept through the second act. And I get into bed and want to say, 'Not tonight, dear, I have a headache.' What the hell happened?"

Suddenly she was crying. He held her. Soothed her. Helped her into the backseat.

"Remember the parking lot at the hospital?" he asked.

"Yes, let's do it like that," she said as she peeled away her underwear.

With the voluptuous skirt of her bridesmaid dress wadded between them, he entered her. "God, you're so hot and wet."

"Because I want you so. I love you, Alex. I love you."

In a tangle of arms and legs and tulle, kissing endlessly, they pumped away at each other. But too hurriedly. And the armrest was digging into the back of her head.

Alex collapsed on her, moaning.

It was better when they got home. Naked in bed, they kissed and fondled with deliberate leisure. She loved the feel of him, the smell and taste of him. And she loved wanting him to the point of pain.

She began to come almost as soon as he entered her. An endless orgasm that left her weak and moaning.

"Better?" he asked.

She snuggled up against him. "Much." And it was, for now. She needed him too much to feel secure.

Bonnie was married in an off-white satin suit and her grandmother's pearls. Lenny wore a navy suit. They stood under the tree in the backyard where the tire swing once hung. Her errant hippie brother even drifted in for the ceremony, his hair in a ponytail, on his way to Alaska.

41

"You're the most beautiful bride of all," Helen told Bonnie. "You look the most like yourself."

Bonnie was radiant. She and Lenny smiled and giggled like two children.

After their honeymoon, camping on the Great Divide, they would move to Stockton to run a weekly newspaper. "It's not for life," Bonnie had explained. "But we'll learn a lot. And the owner was willing to take both of us."

Libby disappeared after the ceremony. Helen found her in Bonnie's bedroom, lying on the bed, sobbing.

"I've lost you all," she said. Her face was flushed, her brow hot and moist, her nose running.

Helen found some Kleenex and held her and said they all loved her, but she didn't deny Libby's words.

Libby was leaving the next day for New York. She and her father. He was driving the station wagon already packed with her possessions. Libby would follow in her almost new T-bird, a graduation gift from her parents.

Professor Zubov had arranged for her to live in the apartment of an elderly émigré who had once danced with the Ballets Russes.

Helen couldn't imagine Libby alone in New York. Without her friends.

"But Lenny, we have to go to press tomorrow," Bonnie said, not trying to hide the exasperation in her voice. "You promised in the last issue to run a profile of Coach Schaeffer. And what about last night's game? Have you written the copy on it?"

"I interviewed Schaeffer," Lenny said defensively. "I just haven't had time to write it."

He hadn't had time because he'd gone fishing with some of

the high school football players. In the three months they'd been in Stockton, Lenny had made lots of friends. He'd joined the Chamber of Commerce and Lions' Club. He'd been invited by the local radio station to do a sports show on Sunday afternoon. And he attended high school football practice every afternoon. All under the guise of public relations.

"How about I just talk the stories, and you can type them?" he suggested, coming to stand behind her and rub her neck.

"Lenny, I don't have time. I've got two weddings and three club meetings to write up—plus going over the ads with Miss Holt."

"Come on, Bonnie. I've got the stories in my head. And while you're finishing up here, I'll buy a couple of steaks and a bottle of wine."

"We can't afford either," she grumbled. His rubbing felt good. She'd been hunched over her desk since eight this morning. She all but lived in this seedy old office, while Lenny did "public relations." And sold ads. He did do that—a new one just today from the dry cleaners. He'd convinced Mrs. Clark that she needed to use the coupon approach to get people to bring in their cleaning. Twenty-five cents off with their coupon clipped from the *Eagle*. He was working on Mr. Jenkins at the hardware store. That coupon would entitle shoppers to a free pocket flashlight with any purchase over twenty dollars.

"If we can't afford steak and wine, I'll buy beer and fix my special hamburgers," he said, kneading up and down her upper arms. "And make brandy alexanders for dessert. We've already got the brandy. You'd have to edit the stories and fix the spelling anyway. You might as well type 'em right in the first place."

"Ever heard of a dictionary?" Bonnie retorted.

Lenny rubbed for a minute more then began to pace about her desk. "Schaeffer's been here for five years. His dad was a high school coach up in Nebraska, and he played his college ball at NU. But before that he was a high school standout at some little town—I've forgotten the name. All-state his senior year. He's a tough coach, very demanding. But the guys really respect him. I wrote down a couple quotes from his players. And yes, I made sure their names are spelled right."

It was almost ten when Bonnie finished up—tired, hungry, and angry. She was going to have it out with Lenny when she got home. He wasn't carrying his fair share. The newspaper was supposed to be a partnership.

The hamburgers were ready to grill. The table was set. Their new Henry Mancini album was playing. Lenny greeted her with a hug and a Coors. "You go take a quick shower and put on your robe. I'll have the burgers cooked in a jiffy."

They ate by candlelight. The hamburgers were served open-face, smothered with sautéed onion, mushrooms, and peppers, topped with melted Swiss cheese. For the vegetable, there was creamed fresh corn. Lenny liked to cook. Which was fine with Bonnie.

But a home-cooked meal a couple of times a week wasn't a fair trade for all the work she was doing at the newspaper.

Still, a home-cooked meal by candlelight with Lenny at his charming best just might be. And the brandy was having its warming effect.

Bonnie didn't have on anything under her robe. Which made her feel sexy. She let it gape a bit in front. An invitation.

Lenny reached across the table and pulled her robe aside. "Oh, baby," he said softly. "I still get off on them."

Four

The spring of 1963, Ted graduated from law school, and Alex was sent to Saigon. Helen moved in with her parents and got a job teaching English at East High. It was a strange adjustment to be a teacher in the building that harbored so many memories of her adolescence.

Ted and Jen made the short move from Boulder to Denver, buying what Jen's mother referred to as a "starter home" in a new neighborhood populated by other young couples just starting out. Someday she and Ted would have a grand house in a prestigious neighborhood, but right now Jen adored her little house with chintz curtains, braided rugs, a deacon's bench on the front porch.

That fall, Lenny was offered an entry-level sports reporter

job on KROC-TV in Denver, and he and Bonnie resigned their positions at the *Stockton Eagle*. Bonnie was hired at the *Post* to write women's news. She had not been able to make a credible newspaperman out of Lenny or a credible newspaper out of the *Stockton Eagle*.

The five friends huddled together after the Kennedy assassination. The men cried, too. So hard to believe. So hard to understand. Their Camelot president.

Helen couldn't get a telephone line to Saigon. All the international circuits were jammed with calls, an operator told her. Apparently a lot of other people needed the reassurance of their loved one's voice.

They tried to call Libby in New York, but her telephone number was no longer in service. Her mother didn't have a new one. Evelyn had tried to call her, too.

The three women watched the funeral together in Jen's new living room. Brave Jackie marching behind her husband's casket—they cried for her as much as for him. And the Kennedy children. And themselves. It was a difficult time.

Helen missed Alex terribly. He called that evening, after trying to get through for days. "Are you okay?" he asked through the static.

"No. What about you?"

"Pretty devastated. It makes me want to be home—with you. You are my home, babe."

The U.S. military was in South Vietnam in an advisory capacity, but Americans were getting killed. Ted said that Johnson was hell-bent to get the U.S. involved in a real war. After four years of ROTC, both he and Lenny would have reserve commissions, thank God. Of course, their unit could be called, but they were protected from the draft.

The threat of war took up a great deal of conversation time

when the five friends gathered, but they talked about Libby, too. Was she succeeding or failing? She never answered their letters. Her mother always said she was doing fine, with lessons every morning and practice every afternoon. They hoped she'd found new friends. Surely, she would come back for a visit soon. Carl was in a wheelchair now. The prognosis wasn't good.

"I think you should go see her," Carl told his mother.

Evelyn Ballard looked over her reading glasses at her son in his wheelchair, a knitted shawl draped around his thin shoulders like an old man at the end of his life. It was the spring of 1964. She wondered if it would be his last. And he was only twenty-six.

Too weak now to take more than a couple of steps by himself, Carl spent his days in the wheelchair or propped up on the family room sofa. Except for Carl's worst days, Fred got him out of bed in the mornings and dressed him. Even put his shoes on. Fred's whole purpose in life was to keep his son alive.

"Me? Go to New York? Why, that's about the craziest thing I've ever heard of," Evelyn said as she folded Libby's letter and put it back in its envelope—if one could call two lines a letter: *Note the new address. I'm all right. Kisses to you and Carl.* Not a word about her dancing, how she was paying her bills, what her life was like, places she had been, people she had met.

Her new address was on Bleecker Street. They didn't know if she lived alone or if there was a telephone where she could be reached.

Libby didn't write at all to her friends. Helen and Bonnie called Evelyn from time to time to ask about her. Jen stopped by—which made Carl both happy and sad. Jen represented everything that life had denied him.

47

Evelyn never admitted to her daughter's friends how little she knew about Libby's life. "Everything is fine," she always told them. "Libby is dancing and sends her love."

"You could go for her birthday," Carl was saying, taking a breath every couple of words. "Surprise her."

"Libby doesn't like surprises," Evelyn said, sorting through the rest of mail. Bills. Advertisements. A letter from her sister in Florida that would be full of gossip about people Evelyn didn't know.

"What if she's lonely and broke and too proud to come home?"

Evelyn stared at him. "I can't, son."

"Why not? Because Dad would never hear of it?"

"Well, he wouldn't. Plane tickets are expensive."

"Dad got to see New York when he took Libby up there," Carl persisted from his side of the table, today's stack of newspapers in front of him, every page already examined, the crossword puzzles already worked. Carl loved newspapers. Fred made a special trip downtown every morning to get him the *New York Times* and the *Washington Post*. Carl could have been a journalist—like Bonnie. He had worked on the school paper with Bonnie at East High the last year he had been able to attend. "Shouldn't you have a chance to go someplace, too?" he asked.

"I've been someplace."

"Yeah. To Florida for Uncle John's funeral. Where else have you gone?"

"I went to Omaha with Jen and her mother," Evelyn reminded him. "And we took lots of vacations with you children."

But never any farther than Estes Park or Central City. And not for years. As Carl's disease progressed, they needed to stay close to the oxygen tank in the front bedroom, close to hospitals and doctors and respiration therapists.

"What's the worst thing that could happen if you bought a ticket, packed a bag, and announced you were going?" Carl asked, pausing a minute to catch his breath. "He'd carry on a while, insist you were bankrupting him, but I'd be the one who'd have to listen to him. You'd be in a cab on the way to the airport."

Could she do that, Evelyn wondered. It wasn't like she had to be here to look after Carl. Fred was retired from the bank now and did most of the looking-after. Even slept with him every night. She and Fred used to take turns. Now, Carl slept downstairs in the front bedroom with his father, and Evelyn had moved into the upstairs bedroom that was Libby's. She had taken down her daughter's dance posters and hung a delicate floral wallpaper. She made a new dust ruffle and pillow shams for the twin bed and matching curtains for the windows and brought in the reading lamp and end table from Carl's old room. Even bought a four-by-six oval braided rug at Sears. The room was pretty. Like a little sitting room. All her own. It pleased her immensely. She was fifty-six years old, but having a room of her own made her feel independent. She was saving Green Stamps for a little television set to put on the dresser.

"What's the point?" Fred had asked. "No one is ever going to see the room."

"*I* see it," she told him.

Then he grumbled a bit about wasting money. Evelyn hadn't bothered to respond.

She wasn't as afraid of her husband as she had been. Sometimes she couldn't remember why she had been that way. Maybe because he was older. And so stern. It took her years to understand that he hid behind that stern face.

When Libby's dancing progressed to the point where she wanted two and three lessons a week, Fred put his foot down. A foolish expenditure.

Evelyn understood. He wanted to save money. He worried about their medical insurance running out. About losing his job.

She sold the rent house she had inherited from her mother and put the money in a special account for Libby's dancing lessons—the bravest thing she had ever done.

But to go to New York. . . .

"Your father said it was a terrible place full of pickpockets and trash."

The motor of Carl's chair whirred softly as he guided it around the table. He put his hand on his mother's arm. "You and I both know there's more to New York than pickpockets and trash. I want you to see and hear and smell it for me. Will you do that, Mom?" He paused again, taking several breaths. "And bring Libby home if she needs to come. It's been three years, and I'd like to see her again."

"But . . ." Evelyn stopped, unable to say what was on her mind.

"But what if I die while you're gone?"

She put his hand to her lips and kissed it. He could say the word out loud, but his parents could not.

"If I do," Carl said, "you just come out to the cemetery and sit beside my grave and tell me all about it."

He would have been a handsome man. The evidence was there—good bone structure, perfect brow line, a full mouth. But his eyes were sunk deep in their sockets. His body was emaciated, his skin ashen, his lips and fingernails tinged with blue.

"Do you have any idea how much I love you?" she asked.

"Yes. And isn't it strange? I ruined your life. All of your lives."

"Oh, my dear boy, you've been the very best part."

But sometimes Evelyn speculated about what life would have been like without Carl.

And Libby.

Libby, the healthy child, had also brought her share of heartache. Libby had always thought her parents loved Carl more than they loved her. She may have been right about her father, but a mother loves her children equally—at least that was what Evelyn used to tell herself. Now, she was no longer sure. Of their two children, Carl was easier to love. Libby was a challenge.

She and Fred had so much more invested in Carl—emotionally, financially, physically. Without them, he would probably have already died. They had to watch him every minute and rub his back and chest by the hour to loosen the mucus that clogged his lungs. Fred had a theory that if they kept Carl alive long enough, someone would come up with a cure. He even thought the boy might outgrow the disease that thickened his body's secretions, making breathing an agonizing chore. No one with cystic fibrosis ever lived past young adulthood, but maybe if it was possible to keep Carl alive past some magical cut-off date, he'd be all right. Perhaps growing up itself would be the cure.

Evelyn could have let go years before. Carl's suffering filled her with too much pain. And not just his physical suffering—which was considerable. But when she watched her son looking out at the world from his diseased body as other children ran and played, as other children grew up and fell in love, as she watched Carl fall in love with beautiful, healthy Jen of the shining blond hair and radiant smile, it broke her heart.

But Fred wanted Carl to live at any cost. His whole life was wrapped up in the boy. They played chess by the hour. Never missed a televised sporting event. Memorized sports trivia.

Fred had had little time or patience for his daughter, even though Libby was a determined child who wanted her due. It almost seemed like the first words out of Libby's mouth were,

"That's not fair." And it wasn't. Carl got more attention and more toys and games to while away the hours of his existence. Carl was coaxed to eat the food on his plate, Libby was ordered to. They couldn't go on family excursions unless Carl was well enough. If Carl didn't like a television program, the channel was changed.

And like other brothers and sisters, Libby and Carl were often deliberately hateful to each other. Carl would tell on Libby when she came in late, when she neglected her chores. Libby teased him about Jen and threw away newspapers before he could work the crossword puzzles. Fred always took Carl's side. Evelyn never said anything.

Libby couldn't have been more than six or seven when she stood in the middle of the living room, hands on her hips. "I'm going to find myself a family that loves me," she announced.

And she had. She found Jen and Bonnie and Helen.

The address was in Greenwich Village on a charming street with trees and well-kept houses all connected to one another. People were sitting on stoops or walking their dogs, enjoying the bright spring day. The box for number seven said "Ballard." Timidly, Evelyn pressed the button.

"Yes?" a man's voice said on the speaker.

"I'm here to see Elizabeth Ballard."

Evelyn jumped when a loud buzzer abruptly went off, unlocking the interior door, which she pushed open. She climbed up three flights to number seven.

A tall, graying man in a nylon athletic suit answered the door. Behind him was a room with tall, arched windows, white walls, and large cushions scattered about the polished wooden floor.

"And who might you be?" he asked.

"I'm Libby's mother."

He stared a minute. "Yes. I can see it. The same eyes. The jaw."

The man extended his hand. He was past fifty. Maybe as old as Evelyn herself. But handsome. A very good haircut. A tiny Errol Flynn mustache. "And does 'Libby's mother' have a name of her own?"

"Evelyn Ballard."

"I'm Edward Rasmussen. Do come in. I'll tell her you're here."

Libby appeared, wearing jeans and a man's undershirt. The arm holes came almost to her waist. She was bone thin, her breasts almost flat.

"Mom?" she said, walking slowly across the room. "I thought he was kidding. It's really you. What are you doing here?"

"It's your birthday. I wanted to see you. I was worried. You never call. Your letters don't say anything." Evelyn's hands fluttered helplessly. She shouldn't have come. Libby didn't write of her life because she had things to hide. "Carl sent you a belt," she went on, her voice too high. "He tooled it himself. And we made you fudge."

"Fudge? You know that dancers don't eat fudge." But Libby smiled. And gave her mother a hug. "You look great, Mom."

A shaving mug and brush sat on the shelf in the tiny bathroom. A man's silk bathrobe hung on the back of the door. But that man was too old. And Libby didn't get involved with men, did she?

Should she leave, Evelyn wondered as she stared at herself in the bathroom mirror. She should wear makeup more often. It made her look younger. But she didn't feel young. She felt old and very confused.

They took her to dinner at a tiny restaurant below street level with exorbitant prices for plates of pasta with fancy shapes and names. Evelyn's stuffed ziti tasted like macaroni stuffed with cottage cheese—with too much garlic in the tomato sauce.

But Evelyn had never tasted anything as fine as the burgundy wine Edward selected. She never drank wine anymore. Hadn't for years. She and Fred used to drink a bottle of wine as a prelude to sex. So long ago. Before Carl.

She knew she'd get a headache, but she kept drinking, closing her eyes to savor each sip, willing her uneasiness away. Edward seemed like a nice man. Maybe an older man was what Libby needed. A fatherly man who would look after her. A May-and-December marriage to settle her life.

"How long have you and Edward been going together?" she asked.

They laughed at her. *Going together.* Libby was Rasmussen's mistress. She even used the word. Like out of a novel. His home and wife were in Upper Montclair. He had five grown children and three grandchildren and even showed Evelyn their pictures.

"What about the dance company?" Evelyn asked Libby. "What about Professor Zubov's friend? What happened to her?"

"She died," Libby said. "And I still dance in the corps. For next to nothing. I was sharing a rundown two-room flat with two other dancers and assorted rodents when Edward came along. He pays for things, don't you, Edward darling?" She stopped playing with her food long enough to pat his cheek. She was smiling, but her eyes were cold.

Her daughter didn't even like this man, Evelyn realized.

The next morning, Libby went off to her lessons, and Edward came for Evelyn. For the next three days, her daughter's lover showed Evelyn the city. The first day, they did the tourist things—the U.N., the Statue of Liberty, the Empire State Building. Evelyn recognized Times Square from the newsreels that

played at the end of World War II. A sea of overjoyed, celebrating people, kissing and hugging, the air alive with confetti.
And to think that she was actually standing in the middle of
where that scene had taken place! Evelyn bought dozens of
postcards to take Carl and kept a list of things to tell him.

The next day, they walked through Central Park and visited
Chinatown and Little Italy.

And finally, Edward took her to the museums. She liked
the Museum of Natural History. The art museums were intim-
idating. She didn't know the proper adjectives to whisper in
front of a Renoir or a Sargent.

"Why are you doing this for me?" she asked over lunch in
a chic French restaurant near Central Park.

"It pleases me," Edward said.

"I don't understand any of this—why you're being nice to
me or why you support my daughter."

"I'm being nice to you because I like you. You're refreshing.
And really quite lovely."

Evelyn couldn't look at him for a minute. *Lovely.* Such a nice
word.

She took a sip of wine and leaned her head against the back
of the high banquette. When she got home, she was going to
start having a glass of red wine when she read at night.

Two women wearing slouch hats like 1940s movie stars were
speaking French at the next table. "And the other question?"
she asked. "Why do you support my daughter? Surely you could
find a girl more caring than Libby."

"Libby was the damsel in distress. I was the rescuer. It made
me feel good. But now, she needs me. And that makes her not
like me very much. I have too much power over her life. And
I suspect that the only thing that Libby enjoys about men is
controlling them."

"Are you in love with her?" Evelyn asked.

"No. It's foolish to waste love on people who can't give it back. But I am smitten by her."

"What about your wife?"

"We came to terms years ago. Libby is not the first. Actually, though, I'm very devoted to Grace, but her face and body remind me how old I am. It scares me."

"I would think that Libby's face and body would make you feel even older."

"Only afterward," he said as he refilled her wineglass.

When the cab stopped in front of the apartment building, Edward didn't get out. "I'm going home tonight," he explained. "Being with you makes me want to be nice to my wife."

He took her face in his hands and kissed her. Not a romantic kiss. But his hands and lips felt warm and nice. His cologne smelled of spice and fresh wood shavings.

Mother and daughter had dinner alone—by candlelight, sitting on cushions, eating Chinese food from white cardboard cartons and drinking wine from stemmed crystal goblets.

Libby drank a lot of wine but hardly touched her food. She was discouraged, she admitted. She had no hope of advancing out of the corps. No praise from her teachers. Other dancers as good as she had been dropped to make room for others more promising.

Evelyn had never seen her daughter like this—deflated, her narrow shoulders slumped forward, dark shadows under her eyes making her look older, less pretty. And so thin. What was that disease she had been reading about? Girls who didn't eat.

"What will you do?" Evelyn asked.

"Keep trying," Libby said with a shrug. "In Colorado, I was the only one who was good. Here, everyone is. And I'm not getting any better. That's the worst part. I think I've peaked."

How strange to have Libby confiding in her. Evelyn was

touched. But so sad for her daughter. "What about Edward?" she asked. "He won't let anything bad happen to you."

"Edward *is* something bad. It didn't have to be like this, you know. I could have made it. It wasn't supposed to be this way. That's why I had friends. The four of us were going to be together. We were going to help each other."

Libby hugged her knees to her chest, her eyes full of indignant tears.

"Oh, Libby, honey, you can't blame them. Young girls fall in love. Surely you didn't think you could have them to yourself forever."

But Evelyn understood. Libby needed someone to blame. Had she and Fred done this to their daughter? Had they been so intent on caring for the dying child that they had forsaken the well one? Now, Libby was no longer well.

"I don't want anyone back home to know about Edward," Libby said. "You won't tell, will you? I'd die if you did."

"Only Carl. He wants you to come home. He wants you two to make friends before he dies."

"But I can't go back there," Libby said, shaking her head back and forth. "Not as a failure. Not to watch Carl die. I hate Denver. I hate people feeling smug about those damned mountains. And as long as I'm here, there's always the possibility that something good will happen."

Libby fell asleep on the cushions. Evelyn covered her with a blanket, then poured another glass of wine to take with her to the bedroom where Edward and Libby made love that wasn't love.

In the morning, they put off saying good-bye until the cab was outside.

"It took a lot of courage for you to come here," Libby acknowledged.

"Think about coming home, honey. You could always teach, you know."

"No, I couldn't. But thanks anyway."

"I love you, Libby."

Libby hesitated. "I love you, too."

Evelyn managed to hold her tears until the cab pulled away from the curb. Her poor little girl. What would become of her?

Five

The following winter, Carl showed his mother an obituary in the *New York Times.* "Isn't that the man you met in New York?" he asked.

Evelyn carried the newspaper to her room. Prominent real-estate developer Edward Rasmussen had died at age fifty-eight of a heart attack. A noted philanthropist and patron of the arts, he had served on the Board of Trustees of Harvard University and on the boards of an impressive list of financial and charitable organizations. His wife was a Du Pont. They had three daughters and two sons. The family requested that in lieu of flowers memorial contributions be sent to the Carnegie Hall Foundation. The accompanying picture was not a recent one.

Evelyn sat there for a long time in her pretty bedroom, the folded newspaper on her lap. Edward Rasmussen had given her three of the nicest days in her life.

And now, what was going to happen to Libby? And why hadn't her daughter called to tell her the news?

Two weeks later, they put Carl in the hospital. Evelyn called Libby. "We'd like to have you here, honey."

"You'll have to send me money for a ticket."

Evelyn would have preferred a simple good-bye at the cemetery with only a reading and a prayer, but Fred had insisted on a full-blown funeral.

And it hadn't been so bad, she decided. The young minister allowed that there was a lot that they didn't understand about life and death. He didn't claim that God had a special mission for Carl, only that Carl had been brave and loved.

Helen, Bonnie, and Jen cried. Libby did not.

And she hadn't cried when Carl drew his last breath. But she did when she walked into his hospital room and saw her brother's welcoming smile through the plastic window of an oxygen tent.

Those last days, she joined her parents at his bedside, sometimes reaching under the tent to stroke Carl's hair. Talking was difficult for Carl. He needed all his air and strength for breathing. So Libby carried on one-sided conversations about whatever came into her head. New York cabbies. Uncle John's snoring. Their childhood battles. "We weren't very nice to each other, were we," she said. "I'm sorry about that now. It wasn't your fault."

Libby's friends all visited Carl at the hospital, Jen almost every day—even after Carl had become comatose. Libby had been cool to them.

60

Bonnie's and Jen's husbands came with them to the funeral. Helen's husband was still in Vietnam, but soon he, too, would return to finish his training at the university medical center.

Ted was working in his father's law firm. An oversized man, he would be fat like his father someday.

Bonnie's sandy-haired husband was a sports reporter on television. Lenny Brewster. Carl had gotten a kick out of watching him. Bonnie had brought him with her to the hospital once. Poor man. He didn't know what to say to a dying young person. But then, none of them did. Except Jen. She didn't pretend. She told Carl how special he was. How she would never forget him. How she hoped they'd meet again in another life. She even said she loved him.

Her friends hovered around Libby after the graveside services. She allowed them to court her. Yes, they could take her to dinner next week. Evelyn wondered if they had any idea that Libby blamed them for her failure.

Libby wasn't going back to New York. She had no money. No career. No laurels. Nothing.

Fred asked Evelyn to drive when they went back to the cemetery late that afternoon. She tried to remember if she had ever driven before with her husband in the car. Fred sat slumped over against the door, his hands buried in his coat pockets.

The air was clear and cold, the winter-white mountains standing sentry in the distance.

Just the sight of the raw earth made the tears start again. Her head throbbed from crying. She felt dry and empty inside. Cried out. But still the tears came.

The gift and the curse of Carl had dictated their lives. Now they had to find out what was left. Fred, it seemed, had already decided.

He sank to his knees and placed his hands palm down on the mounded earth. "I wish I were buried in there with you, son," he sobbed. "My poor boy. My poor, poor boy. Without you there isn't anything."

"You have a daughter," Evelyn reminded him, her hand on his shoulder. *And a wife.*

"And what good is she?" Fred said, allowing Evelyn to help him to his feet. "Will she ever give us grandchildren to ease our loss? Will she care for us when we're old and sick? Will she love us? She didn't even cry for her own brother."

"Maybe she doesn't love us because we used up all our love on Carl."

"And maybe she isn't capable of love. Get her out of the house, Evelyn."

"She has no money, Fred."

He leaned on her as they walked back to the car. Fred had been strong for Carl. Now, he was weak and old.

Libby joined them for a silent meal of leftover funeral food. Then they said polite good-nights. Evelyn had moved into Carl's upstairs room, allowing Libby to reclaim her old bedroom. She pulled the covers up under her chin and stared into the darkness a long time, thinking of her husband downstairs, alone and grief-stricken in the bedroom they used to share.

Should she go to him?

But if she went tonight, she would have to face the same decision again tomorrow night and the night after. And she didn't want to give up her solitude.

Her decision made, she was able to sleep for a time—a luxury after so many sleepless nights.

But she woke in the night crying.

Carl, her baby. Her precious son. She would never see him again. Never touch him. Never hear his voice.

She had given him life and kissed him in death. She, too, had loved him more than anything.

Libby reluctantly decided to teach dancing to young children —what she'd always said she would never do. But if that was to be her fate, she would do it with style. Helen admired her for that. Libby was no longer the fun-loving person they had grown up with, but she still had spunk.

Libby's father begrudgingly cosigned a note, allowing her to buy a run-down Victorian house in a downtown neighborhood for a song. She convinced the State Historical Society to declare the street a preservation district, thus allowing her to borrow from a special fund for renovations.

The results were stunning. Soon, the building next door was being restored by the grandson of the building's original owners. And the one on the other side by a gay couple. Libby had started a trend.

She loved her building but hated encouraging little girls with no talent, and being nice to pushy mothers. She made pets of a few of her students and left the others to teenage assistants. Still, mothers brought their daughters to her. Libby had developed a haughtiness that impressed people and made rich ladies court her. Even she dared to be optimistic. Maybe the school was going to succeed.

With her friends, she was reserved. While they opened their arms to her and seemed genuinely pleased she had returned to them, they did not hover around her. If she decided not to join them for an evening, they were sorry but did not beg.

Libby did join them at the airport to welcome Alex home, but it was Jen and Bonnie who made the banners and bought the balloons. Libby brought a single white rose to present to a weary but ecstatic Alex after he swept his wife into his arms.

Helen had been a nervous wreck for weeks before and couldn't stop crying when Alex finally arrived, when she could feel the solid, living reality of him in her arms.

"I hope we made a baby," she told him that first night as they held each other, satiated, blissful, full of hope and love.

"Me, too," he said. He turned on the lamp and took her face in his hands. "Let's be happy, Helen. Let's be the happiest people in the world."

They moved into an apartment by the medical center, and Alex began his OB/GYN residency. He'd seen enough medical trauma in Saigon to last a lifetime. Deliveries and women's surgery sounded like heaven.

Libby brought them a bottle of wine and basket of fruit for a housewarming gift. "Don't you think she's changed?" Helen asked Alex when she'd left.

"Not really," Alex said. "She's still trying to run the show. She's just more subtle than she used to be."

"I think she's confused. She can't decide if she loves us or hates us."

When Libby offered to train the annual bevy of Denver debutantes for their moment in the sun, every mother signed up her daughter. Libby taught the debutantes to walk with heads high and shoulders back and to curtsy like princesses. She ordered a deb with bleached hair to return it to its original color. She made one girl exchange her sequined gown for a more youthful one. Helen, Jen, and Bonnie looked on, pleased. Libby needed to be in charge. The debs were good for her.

The next year, Libby started her debutante class early enough to be in on the dress-selection process. The *Post* society editor referred to her as the "deb queen."

Her success with the debs brought even more mothers with

their young daughters to her school. More than ballet lessons, they wanted Libby to turn their awkward little girls with scuffed toes on their shoes and scabs on their knees into poised and polished young ladies.

The school could have been a success, but Libby had a disdain for business. She hated paper shuffling. Hated bankers, accountants, lawyers, the IRS. She would toss mail in a basket unopened. She didn't return phone calls.

Even Bonnie admitted that what Libby needed was a nice, normal husband to take over the business end of the school. Professor Zubov was still Libby's sometime escort, particularly to concerts and galas. In evening attire, Libby and Zubov looked like royalty. Pictures of them together appeared regularly on the society page. But there were other men in her life. Libby always seemed to have a man in tow to fetch her drinks and watch her face while she talked. If she went out with the same man twice, her friends held their collective breath and waited.

Once, she brought a violinist with the Denver symphony to one of their gatherings—an elegant man who reminded them of Zubov. Libby had insisted that he bring his violin and play for them, which he did—so poignantly that it brought tears to Helen's eyes. Libby rewarded him with a kiss. A rather wonderful kiss, actually, her body pressed close, her eyes closed. And she had whispered something in his ear that made him close his eyes and sigh. They never saw him again.

Another time, she brought a lumberjack she'd picked up earlier in the evening at a highway tavern. At least, he said he was a lumberjack. From South Carolina. A gorgeous hunk of a man with curly blond hair and bulging muscles. "I'm right honored to meet Miz Libby's friends," he told them. Libby actually seemed charmed when he told them he was a convicted felon and had spent half his life in prison. Logging with prison crews on state property was how he had learned his current profession. But after he slipped up with a quote from Oliver Wendell Holmes, he admitted he was really a history professor at Northwestern on his way to the slopes. Libby was livid and insisted that he leave. While the rest of them just laughed it off, she left instead.

Once, Helen suggested Libby bring Zubov. But she never did. Alex thought she could at least bring someone who played bridge.

"Do you suppose any of these guys ever try to get into her pants, or do they just know by the holy aura surrounding our Libby that the gods would strike them impotent if they tried?" Lenny had pondered after Libby and a nonverbal cowboy from West Texas were the first to leave one of Helen's kitchen-table dinners.

"Naw. She's just one of those girls who saves herself for marriage," Ted offered, ignoring his wife's frown and holding out his plate for a second slice of Helen's apple-crumb pie, "just like Jen and Helen and Bonnie," he added with a wink, garnering an elbow in the ribs from his wife. "Great pie, Helen. I wish you'd give Jen lessons."

"If I cooked like Helen, you'd weigh three hundred pounds," Jen retorted.

"I don't know why you're so convinced she's a virgin," Bonnie said to her husband, pouring herself a second cup of coffee. "For all you know she and the cowboy are getting it on even as we speak."

"What do you think, Alex?" Helen asked her husband. "Does she or doesn't she?"

Alex shrugged. "I don't think it matters. Virgin or not, Libby's different. She could never *belong* to a man, sexually or any other way. That would be like expecting a butterfly to land on only one leaf."

"Oh dear God, the boy's talking in similes," Bonnie teased. "I hope there's a cure."

"Alex is right," Helen said. "Can you imagine Libby washing her husband's BVDs or matching up his socks?"

"Hey, I match up my own socks," Lenny said.

Helen and Jen had the thrill of being pregnant at the same time, with Bonnie a tolerant bystander and Libby trying hard to pretend she wasn't repulsed by their swelling bodies. Bonnie and Lenny were waiting to have children; maybe they never would. But for Jen and Helen the need to have a baby was as deep and real as anything they had ever experienced. And pregnancy was the most fascinating thing that had ever happened to them. They discussed every symptom, every ache, every apprehension. They shopped for maternity clothes and layettes together. Helen was a little jealous of Jen's unlimited budget, but she refused to let that get in the way of her delight in sharing her pregnancy with one of her best friends. Libby and Bonnie gave a joint baby shower, inviting old friends and new. At the shower, Jen and Helen made Bonnie take a picture of them in all their pregnant glory, back to back, bellies protruding proudly.

The babies were born two weeks apart, effectively turning the Echolses and the Radcliffs into homebodies. The anniversary party that year at Lenny and Bonnie's new downtown apartment was the first time the group had tried to get together in months.

Libby acted so strangely—dancing around like she was in a trance, then collapsing in tears, with no one having a clue as to what she was upset about.

Bonnie put her to bed for a while. Alex ran to the hospital for a tranquilizer.

Later, she tried to eat a few bites but complained of dizziness.

Alex and Helen took her home, ending the party abruptly, no glasses raised to five years of marriage.

And then, suddenly, inexplicably, shockingly, Libby was gone. *Vanished.* With her clothes still hanging in her bedroom closet. Food in the refrigerator. Unopened mail on the kitchen table.

Helen didn't realize she was gone until the Monday after the party. The dance school pianist had called Evelyn Ballard. Children were waiting. Libby wasn't at the school. She wasn't upstairs in her apartment.

Evelyn called Jen. Jen called Bonnie and Helen.

Tiny hairs stood up on the back of Helen's neck. *Disappeared.* People didn't just disappear.

The men weren't back from fishing. Alex had called earlier from a gas station in Fraser. Problems with Ted's Jeep. Helen fell asleep on the sofa waiting for him. When she got up in the night to feed Beth, Alex was sprawled across the bed, still wearing his fishing clothes.

She waited until morning to tell him. "No one knows where Libby is. She didn't show up for her classes yesterday, and her mother is worried sick. I think I am, too."

"She's probably just decided to go someplace on the spur of the moment," he said, pulling off his clothes to take a shower.

"Without telling anyone? Without canceling her classes?"

"She's not the most responsible person in the world," Alex reminded her. But he didn't sound convinced.

"But she was acting so weird the other night. I should have called the next day to check on her."

Alex closed the bathroom door. Soon the elderly plumbing noisily came alive. Helen hoped he didn't use all the hot water. She needed to do a load of diapers.

Alex was the last one to see Libby. He had driven her home

from the party and given her a sleeping pill. Helen followed in Libby's Thunderbird. He was waiting for her when she drove up.

"What's the matter with her?" she asked on the way home.

"She hates her life," Alex answered.

"But what else can she do?" Helen asked.

"Move away. Find new friends who don't know she was supposed to be the world's greatest dancer."

And if she moved away, they'd all breathe a sigh of relief, Helen had thought guiltily.

Libby's car was gone, too. And her overnight bag. Still, they decided not to worry. She'd probably slipped off someplace to brood. Or party. Helen wondered sometimes if Libby wasn't into one-night stands. Sex with no commitment.

But days went by, and the police were called. They began to investigate, ask questions. Did she have any enemies? What about the men in her life? What did she talk about at the party? Had she ever talked about taking her own life?

"You mean *suicide?*" Helen gasped.

"Yes, ma'am," the youthful detective said. "You said she wasn't herself."

"Libby would never do that, would she, Alex?"

Alex wasn't sure.

If Libby had chosen to vanish, she'd done a good job of it. The police investigation revealed that no checks had been written on her bank account since she disappeared. No recent payment had been made on her building. No recent charges on her Diner's Club card. No one had seen her since the anniversary party—not the neighbors or the neighborhood grocer or the bartender in her favorite bar. As far as her parents could determine, she was not with relatives or friends, either in-state or out. Evelyn even called the ballet company in New York.

Jen and Helen made phone calls to college chums. And tried to call Zubov. But he'd gone for the summer, the secretary in the dance department office told Jen.

Suddenly, Helen needed to be in touch with Bonnie and Jen constantly. Had they heard anything? Had they thought of anyone else to call? They relived every moment of the anniversary party over and over again, searching for a clue. What could Libby have been so upset about?

"Lenny's really concerned," Bonnie said over Saturday morning coffee at Jen's kitchen table. "He can hardly talk about it. He thinks something awful could have happened to her."

"Ted, too," Jen said. "And that scares me all the more. Ted is not the sort to worry needlessly."

"Alex keeps talking about how reckless she was, how something bad was bound to happen to her," Helen said.

"But we would have heard if she'd gotten hit by a train or had a wreck," Bonnie insisted. "Jesus, it's been three weeks. If she's alive, she's got to know we're worried sick. To say nothing of her mother."

After a month, her parents moved Libby's things out of the school and her apartment and turned the building back to the bank. The bank was about to foreclose anyway. Libby was four months in arrears with her mortgage payments.

Bonnie wrote a series of articles for the *Post* about Libby's disappearance—with pictures. Libby on *pointe*. The poster of her and the football player. Libby and Carl as children. Her worried parents in front of their house.

How could someone simply vanish without a trace, the three women kept asking themselves. They didn't know whether to be worried or angry. Had she left on purpose? Or had something happened to her? Had she picked up some man who slit her throat and stole her car? Sometimes cars tumbled off mountain roads and weren't found for months.

"I keep thinking we're to blame," Helen said. "She wanted more from us than we gave her."

"Don't you think we need to know what happened to her before we start blaming ourselves?" Bonnie chided.

Gradually the intensity lessened. They began to accept the possibility that they might never know what had happened to her. The police put Libby's file in their stack of unsolved cases. The women visited and phoned each other less frequently. And the three couples didn't get together anymore. Helen wasn't sure why. Maybe the men had gotten tired of the talk about Libby.

Even after a year had gone by, Helen still jumped when the phone rang. Still had strange, disturbing dreams. Libby calling to her. Libby stealing Beth away in the middle of the night. Libby dancing on the edge of a cliff.

Six

Bonnie recited the words with her face uplifted. "Equality of rights under the law shall not be denied or abridged by the United States or any state on account of sex."

Helen and Jen exchanged glances.

Bonnie was into causes lately. The last one had been the fund drive for a Denver women's shelter. At least she wasn't espousing a new theory about Libby. She'd come up with more than her share of those in the last year and a half.

Helen had hoped for some girl talk. At this point in her life, she worried more about Beth's diaper rash than the status of women.

She had envisioned a lovely Sunday brunch with her friends. She'd been planning it all week, deciding on the menu, shopping, cleaning house. She made crab and pasta salad, sesame rolls, and apricot mousse for dessert—all from her own recipes. They would drink wine and have a nice long visit while the babies napped. Alex would either be at the hospital or out golfing. Sunday, she was discovering, was not a time for family togetherness.

Mandy napped, but Beth refused to sleep and had demanded constant attention for the past hour, dirtying her diaper, crawling off and on Helen's lap.

Finished with her recitation, Bonnie was looking expectantly at them.

"Did you write it?" Jen asked.

"Of course not!" Bonnie said. "It's the Equal Rights Amendment. It will change our lives. If I did embroidery, I'd have made samplers for us to hang on our walls." Then she had the good grace to offer a sheepish grin. Bonnie had never so much as sewed on a button, much less embroidered.

"How will it change our lives?" Helen asked, allowing Beth to slide from her lap and wondering if she had given up the right to change when she became a mother. Of course, her life would be different next year when Alex finished his residency and they moved to Boulder. They would live in a nice house instead of a shabby apartment. She could go to graduate school at CU. Boulder was more relaxed than Denver. No Junior League, Symphony Society, debutante balls. If they stayed in Denver, she would have felt pressured to turn herself into a proper society matron—just like Jen.

And she might be pregnant again. That would change things, too. Maybe they could talk about that after Bonnie finished with her amendment. Except, she really should tell Alex first.

"Our lives will change because we can stop being second-class citizens," Bonnie was explaining.

Jen laughed. "So, if we get an amendment, do we start suing our husbands when they won't change messy diapers?"

"Come on, Jen," Bonnie said, pausing to light a cigarette. "What about inequities in divorce laws and inheritance laws? What about firing a woman because she's pregnant? Or passing her over for promotion so the job can go to a man. At the *Post*, men get the promotions, and they get to write the real stories. Most of the writing I do is fluff. Brides and teas. For that I have a degree in journalism?"

"So, what are we supposed to do?" Helen asked.

"There's a new organization being formed to lobby Congress to pass the amendment and get the states to ratify it. It's called the National Organization for Women. NOW. I want you both to join."

"Oh, Bonnie, I don't have time for another club," Jen said.

"This isn't a *club*, for Christ's sake," Bonnie said. "Don't you two care about sexual politics?"

Helen busied herself clearing away dishes. *Sexual politics.* She certainly understood those. She clipped coupons from the newspaper to save nickels and dimes, and her husband had come home the day before yesterday with a secondhand Jeep for his fishing trips. She demanded to know what made him think he had the right to make a major purchase without consulting her. Because he put in sixty or seventy hours a week supporting this family, he had informed her.

She couldn't decide if she would have been better off biting her tongue and saying nothing about the Jeep. After all, it was an old one—dented, in need of paint. As off-the-road vehicles went, she supposed it was a real bargain. And Alex did work long, hard hours. Probably she should have just smiled sweetly and clipped another coupon.

That's what her mother would have done.

Helen wondered what Jen and Bonnie would do if Ted or Lenny came home with a Jeep. But there was no time to discuss it. Already, Jen was looking at her watch. Her parents and in-laws were coming to dinner. And Bonnie had a story to write.

The three of them didn't get together very often, and when they did, there never seemed to be enough time. And Helen hadn't seen Ted and Lenny in months. They didn't do couple things much anymore. Helen missed that. She wondered if the men had had a falling out. Alex said no, that he simply preferred to socialize with other doctors and their wives. But they hardly ever did that, either.

Helen's life had become so routine, she got excited when a downstairs neighbor invited her to take an evening class on cake decorating at the community college. *Cake decorating,* when she used to write essays on Milton!

Milton. She still remembered. *Such sights as youthful poets dream on summer eves by haunted stream.* But her present self didn't want to write essays on Milton or anyone else. She'd wanted to get out of this apartment and away from her child one night a week even though she loved that child more than life itself. And she'd wanted to decorate cakes ever since she was a little girl begging for a slice with a rose.

Helen spent most of her time with a human being whose total vocabulary consisted of "no" and "dada." Sometimes she didn't see her husband for twenty-four hours at a time. She would cook wonderful meals to make the evenings they could be together special. But Alex talked all day to patients, nurses, medical students, other physicians. When he came home, he wanted to carry his meal into the living room, where he could enjoy it with his newspaper and some mindless television. Sometimes Helen objected. Sometimes she went with him. Often she begged. "Talk to me, honey. I'm starved for some

adult conversation." And he would oblige, folding the newspaper, turning down the television, and tell her about his day,
sharing hospital gossip, listen to her recitation of Beth's new
accomplishments, what the pediatrician had said, what she had
heard on the news. Masters and Johnson. Movie star and Jackie
Kennedy gossip. Vietnam. It was a real war now. Would Alex
have to serve again even though they now had a baby?

But Alex seldom initiated conversation. Even Helen's parents had abandoned her, moving to Arizona to spend their
retirement golfing in perpetual sunshine, leaving her to the
scrutiny of her in-laws, who now spent winters running an art
gallery in Aspen.

"I want you both to come to a local organizational meeting
for NOW," Bonnie announced as she poured the last of the
wine. "You need to be a part of the women's movement. It's
your duty as educated woman."

Beth came toddling out of the kitchen dragging a mop.
Buster, the newly acquired yellow Labrador puppy, followed
after her, barking at the mop head. Beth's shirt was too small
for her, and her belly button protruded above her diaper.

Helen reached for Beth and pulled her shirt down over her
round belly. She should have bought that little outfit at Penney's
for Beth to wear today. But she had thought of the bills at home
in the basket on the kitchen counter and talked herself out of
it. Now she was sorry. *My baby needs clothes, and my husband
bought a Jeep.*

A Jeep for his damned fishing.

If Alex had a couple of days off, he headed for mountain
streams.

He used to go with Ted and Lenny. Now he went with two
inhalation therapists named Paul and Joe. Helen knew their
names but had never met them.

Not that Alex didn't love his wife and daughter, but Helen realized that he was bored by them.

He adored taking pictures of Beth. And he rocked her to sleep at night, tenderly carrying her to her bed, kissing her before he tucked her in. But fifteen minutes of entertaining her was his limit. "What do you want me to do with Beth?" he would call out. Of course, he did change messy diapers. In Jen's eyes, that made him a hero.

Precious Beth, whom Helen loved so fiercely that she worried there might not be any love left over for another baby. Did she need to do this for her daughter, get an amendment passed? *Equality of rights that couldn't be abridged or denied?*

"Best friends?" Jen asked in parting as she put her arms around the two of them.

Helen and Bonnie returned her embrace. It felt good.

"Do you think she's still alive?" Jen whispered.

Helen winced. She thought that, for once, they had avoided the topic of Libby.

"If she is alive, she hates us," Bonnie said, digging for her keys. "I'd almost rather think of her dead."

"We didn't have the anniversary party this year," Jen pointed out needlessly.

"Next year, I think we should have it," Helen said.

Bonnie arrived home from Helen's in time to put in a couple of hours working on a free-lance story about the maternity leave policies of Denver employers. After changing into jeans and one of Lenny's old shirts, she pulled off her earrings and put them away.

Grouped around the jewelry box on her dresser was her collection of framed pictures. Her parents. Her brother, Buddy, at fifteen. Lenny's parents. She and Lenny as bride and groom. Lenny in front of their honeymoon tent.

And a picture of four best friends.

They had been at The Sink, celebrating their last night as undergrads. Jen had brought her camera and asked one of the waiters to snap the picture. They scooted close together in the booth, big smiles on their faces, mugs of beer in front of them on the graffiti-carved table. Bonnie was wearing a ponytail. Helen had attempted a Jackie Kennedy pageboy. Jen's blond hair hung in a heavy braid over one shoulder. Libby's dark locks were tucked up under a beret.

It was typical of Jen to have had four enlargements made and put them in four identical pewter frames decorated with the Delta Gamma crest.

Bonnie picked up the picture and touched each young face in turn—faces made ready for the camera, smiles exaggerated, chins uplifted.

After leaving The Sink, they had driven up into the Flatirons and sat in the open door of Bonnie's van to share another six-pack, the lights of Boulder stretched out below them.

They were a little sad. Their four years of college were spent. Soon they would go their separate ways. "But we'll stay friends forever," Jen said. "We'll just have to work at it a little harder."

"And here's to forever friends," Libby said, jumping up, raising her beer bottle high over her head. "Let's turn this wake into a celebration."

She searched the dial on the van radio a couple of times, and then turned the volume on high for Chubby Checker and "The Twist." Libby had led the way in a wild, gyrating twist around the van, atop a rock wall, up and down the deserted road. Then it was their beloved Elvis with "It's Now or Never." Connie Francis singing "Everybody's Somebody's Fool." Patsy

Cline's absolutely perfect voice with "I Fall to Pieces." One last night of youth, the university and its memories below them, already a part of their past.

Bonnie carried a cup of coffee to her typewriter and shuffled through her notes. The telephone company let women work until they delivered. The schools made pregnant women quit at three months. She had tried to get Helen to protest that policy, but she had meekly left her job teaching high school English to sit in her apartment for six months with nothing to do but eat too much and shop for booties with Jen.

Helen and Jen irritated Bonnie. Libby had expected too much out of life, but Helen and Jen didn't expect enough. Both of them were willing to be defined by their husbands. *But I'm one to talk,* Bonnie thought, drawing deeply on her cigarette. She had given up her position as managing editor of the *Stockton Eagle* so Lenny could launch his television career.

She hadn't been hard to convince, though. Running a small-town paper was supposed to be a shared dream. But it had been a stupid idea. Bonnie could see that now. Lenny was no newspaper man. And the Stockton paper was little more than a weekly advertiser. The editorial content was weighted heavily to weddings, club activities, and Lenny's coverage of high school sporting events. And it was out on the plain. They had both missed the mountains. Stockton would never feel like home.

Bonnie had framed the last story she wrote for the Stockton paper and had it hanging over her desk. The headline read TUPPERWARE BRIDAL SHOWER HONORS GERTRUDE SCHWARTZ.

Her job at the *Post* wasn't as grim as she had painted it for Jen and Helen. She did have to write fluff, but she was getting other assignments, too, like the stories about Libby and a series on women in prison. They knew she could write.

And she was getting better. Writing well excited her. Like the story she was working on. It was an okay idea that was turning into a damned good story.

She worked through the rest of the afternoon, checking the clock every so often, anticipating the evening ahead. Lenny had promised to be back from the meeting of state high school football coaches at Fort Collins in time to cook the fresh salmon she'd bought for dinner.

They did dinner well. He cooked the main dish. She made the salad and set the table. They would gossip and share their day while they worked side by side, while they ate by candlelight, while they finished off the bottle of wine. Such times made Bonnie euphoric. Everything was just fine. Separating their careers had been a good idea. In Stockton, she had been starting to feel like Lenny's mother.

But recently, they did well to have dinner together once a week. The news department had moved Lenny from mornings to evenings. If he wasn't at the station, he was off covering some sporting event, giving a speech at a high school banquet or playing with the news department team at a benefit basketball game. Lenny loved the attention, the success. And Bonnie was trying to be a good sport.

At five-thirty, she turned off her typewriter and turned on the television. She listened to the evening news while she changed into a sweater and knit pants, brushed out her hair and added a dusting of blush to her cheeks.

But during the sports segment, the sportscaster accepted Lenny's phone-in report from Fort Collins. The coaches had voted to require more thorough preseason physical examinations for high school players.

Lenny was still in Fort Collins. *Damn!* Why hadn't he called?

Bonnie changed into her bathrobe, fixed herself a bowl of cereal and opened a bottle of beer.

Lenny smelled of bourbon when he crawled into bed. "Did you see my ten o'clock report?" he asked as he snuggled up next to his wife.

"No."

"Damn! I wanted to know what you thought of my interview with Bud Wilkinson. He was the speaker at the luncheon this afternoon."

"I thought you were coming home for dinner."

"Change of plans."

"Don't they have phones in Fort Collins?"

"Ah, come on, Bonnie. I knew when you saw the evening news you'd figure out I was still up there. Wilkinson said it was one of the best interviews he'd had in years."

He was pleased with himself. And wanted to make love. "Not tonight," Bonnie said.

Jen put Mandy in her playpen and stood with her hands on her hips, proudly surveying her immaculate home. The table, already set for this evening's dinner with both sets of parents, glistened with her wedding crystal and silver. Even the leaves of the house plants shone.

Jen couldn't understand why Helen didn't do more with that dreary little apartment. Even Bonnie had gotten into decorating. She and Lenny had completely redone their vintage downtown apartment, and Lenny had refinished a wonderful old sideboard for the dining room. Lenny was great around the house. He even cooked and did laundry. Of course, Bonnie worked. That made their household different. Jen didn't expect Ted to do housework. She just wished he were neater. Jen loved her big, cuddly husband—her Teddy Bear. He was fun at parties. Fun in bed. But she had to follow around picking up after him. Dirty underwear. Shoes. Scattered newspaper pages. Beer cans. He never put anything away. Never closed a cupboard or closet door.

She remembered Libby saying that, while men had occasional moments of elegance and sensitivity, basically they were uncouth and selfish. Only during courtship did they stop belching, picking their teeth, and constantly arranging their crotch.

"And during courtship, women get all caught up in narcissism," Libby went on, sadly almost. "No mirror has ever reflected as flattering an image as that seen in the eyes of a lusting man. And the fact that he chose *her,* that he wants *her,* makes her feel beautiful. Desirable. Like a princess. Her femininity confirmed. She isn't making love to him—she's making love to herself. Which may be lovely. Maybe even the very best sort of loving. But temporary. Why do women never understand that when the proof of it is all around them? Take away the shining armor, and men are either boring, insensitive, or unfaithful. Sometimes, all three."

"So, armed with these beliefs, what do you plan to do? Remain unmarried for the rest of your life?" Jen asked.

"Of course," Libby said with a shrug of her slim shoulders. "Didn't you guys ever listen to me? I don't believe in marriage."

"Yeah, but no one believed you," Helen said. "We all said that. I remember we used to play like we were nuns in a convent. But I don't think I ever seriously thought I wanted to grow up and be one."

"Then you should have said so," Libby said. She was wearing a white sweater with jeans, sitting very straight, in a wicker rocker in front of the broad bay window in the apartment over her school. The window framed a wonderful view of the state capitol building, its gold dome blinding in the sunlight. The sunlight made Libby's sleek black hair shine a brilliant navy blue. Her body was drawn in tight, as though she were wrapped inside an invisible cocoon.

Then she let it go. Relaxed. Smiled. The moment had passed. "I so seldom get to see all of you together anymore," she said. "I want to make the most of it. Jen, open another bottle of wine. Bonnie, turn up the music. And Helen come here and let me brush your hair. Maybe I can fluff it out a bit. Why in the world do you insist on cutting off all that glorious hair?"

Jen stared out the kitchen window, remembering. The Beatles singing "Lucy in the Sky with Diamonds." Touching. Laughing. Libby had once again been the queen holding court. Commanding. Smiling at their stories.

But time was ticking away. There were nervous glances at watches. Husbands would be wanting dinner. In the old days, they would have spent the night. Talked till dawn and slept until noon.

Libby made it easy for them. She had waved them away with a kiss and hug, sending them home to their husbands, demanding only a promise that they all come back together Sunday after next.

Had they? Jen couldn't remember. Probably not.

Libby made them uncomfortable. At times, when some of her old moxie came bubbling to the surface, she would laugh and tease, and they could pretend that she was just as before. But a cynicism would slip out, revealing a crack in Libby's facade and a glimpse of the confused child who hid behind it. And her three best friends had cast their lots with the enemy. They loved their men in a way that Libby could never understand. But her words were not without glimmers of truth.

Libby. Where in the hell was she? There was a hole without her that refused to be filled in. If she was dead or if she had turned her back on them and run off to Tibet to live with a guru on a mountaintop, it wouldn't matter nearly so much. It was the not knowing that gnawed at Jen.

Of course, after a year and a half, thoughts of Libby had

become a once-in-a-while thing. Seeing Bonnie or Helen made them surface. Maybe that was why they didn't enjoy each other as much anymore. If they didn't see each other, they wouldn't have to think about Libby. They wouldn't have to wonder why she was gone, if her disappearance had something to do with them.

Jen pulled the playpen into the kitchen so she could chatter with Mandy while she cooked. She put a bib on her daughter and gave her a teething biscuit.

Jen hovered for a minute, watching while Mandy unceremoniously plopped down on the padded surface and with great seriousness turned her attention to the biscuit. Jen leaned over and touched her child's soft, blond head. "Mama's precious baby girl," she cooed.

She turned on the radio and pulled a recipe from her file box. Rosemary chicken with olives, made with cream of mushroom soup—one of her standbys for company fare.

Helen and Bonnie didn't file recipes. Helen had hers loose in a drawer or tucked in the pages of her cookbooks—of which she had an absurd number. And she had recipes in her head—none of which called for cream of mushroom soup. Bonnie liked to say that Helen could cook "by ear." She could taste something in a restaurant and duplicate it—even improve on it—in her own kitchen. Of course, the kitchen would look like a disaster when she finished, and she would have forgotten to do the laundry or dust the furniture, but the food would be incredible.

Bonnie didn't believe in cooking anything complicated enough for a recipe. She prepared macaroni and cheese out of a box or threw pork chops in a skillet. Lenny was a better cook than his wife, and Bonnie actually boasted about it. His shrimp creole was fabulous. When he and Bonnie entertained, the usual party format got reversed. The women would take their drinks into the living room while the men leaned against the kitchen counter, drinks in hand, talking sports with Lenny while he bustled about. When Libby was still with them, she would drift back and forth between the men and women, drinking too much wine. Ted and Lenny were forever after her to tell who she was screwing, if she'd ever screwed, if she was ever going to screw. She'd laugh at them. Sometimes the old sparkle was there. She'd clap her hands imperially to put an end to arguments or organize a game of charades or bridge. But most of the time she was subdued—always smiling, but a sadness lurked in her great, dark eyes.

And suddenly, she wasn't there anymore. Jen still couldn't get over it. Just thinking about it made the flesh prickle on her arms.

Now, there were no parties with the men. Only the women carried on. And not as well as before.

Helen was right. They needed to have the anniversary party this year.

They went to Bonnie's NOW meeting the Wednesday evening following Helen's Sunday brunch.

"No mistaking that for a Junior League Meeting," Jen observed on the way home. "Army surplus stores must be making a killing on fatigue pants."

"And what's with the nursing mothers?" Helen demanded. She hadn't realized that nursing one's baby in a public meeting was a political statement. She wasn't sure just what the statement was, however.

"What about the *purpose* of the meeting?" Bonnie demanded.

"Women will never have equal rights," Jen predicted. "If

women make more money, men will make less. If women get better jobs, some men would have to be sacrificed. I don't think men are going to voluntarily give up their position in the workplace just to be fair—any more than whites are willing to move over for blacks."

"So what are you saying?" Bonnie asked. "Not to bother?"

"No, I suppose we have to bother," Jen acknowledged. "But I don't think we should expect too much."

While Alex took his shower, Helen straightened up the kitchen, then tiptoed in to stare at her child. Alex came in behind her, a towel wrapped around his middle.

"Pretty cute, huh?" he whispered into Helen's hair. "Beth and I did better tonight." His arms came around his wife's waist, and he rubbed against her to show that he wanted to make love.

When Helen emerged from the bathroom, a finger of Jim Beam waited on the bedside table. Alex was sitting up in bed, leaning against the headboard, his dark hair combed in damp waves, his chest bare. She had always wondered about the wisdom of loving a man more beautiful than she was. And now she was even less beautiful. Frumpy.

"I talked the guy I bought the Jeep from into taking it back," Alex said as she settled in beside him. "You were right. I had no business spending money on a Jeep when we're living hand to mouth. I'll wait until I'm in private practice to buy a fishing wagon."

Helen was stunned. *He took back the Jeep? And admitted she was right?*

Not knowing how to respond, Helen took a sip of whiskey, but her stomach protested, and she put the glass back on the table. "Maybe I was overreacting," Helen heard herself saying. "You do work hard. I suppose you should be able to do what you like when you have a day off."

"You work hard, too," Alex acknowledged. "And never spend a dime on yourself or get a day off. I haven't been very considerate, have I?"

Helen started to cry. Alex reached for her, pulled her face to his shoulder. "Don't cry, honey. Please, don't cry. Tell me what I can do to make you happy."

Tearfully, she told him about the cake decorating class, realizing while the words came pouring out that they weren't what he wanted to hear. She was supposed to say that she was just tired from carrying groceries and laundry and a baby up and down two flights of stairs, that it would be different when they had a house and some money. "I'll have Beth fed and ready for bed," Helen promised. "All you'll have to do is play with her for a while and give her a bottle. Maybe rock her. She loves for her daddy to rock her."

"Cake decorating? I think it would be great for you to take a class, but Christ, Helen, why don't you enroll in something meaningful? Go to one of the consciousness-raising things I've been reading about. Work on your master's degree."

"Cake decorating is all I can handle right now." She reached for him before he could say no. Hushed him with her tongue.

Then he was tugging the tie of her bathrobe. "Play with me a lot," she whispered. "Let's make it last."

She stroked his strong, male back, felt the muscles of his buttocks lengthen and contract as he pumped away at her— going too fast. Too hard. Not making her feel like she needed it to feel.

"Let's stop and touch some more," she begged. "I want it to last forever." But already he had entered his final frenzy. "Oh, God," he moaned, collapsing on top of her.

He apologized. "I'm sorry, baby. I know you wanted more. But you felt so damned good. . . ."

Helen wondered if that meant it was her fault. If she didn't feel good to him, maybe he could last longer and help her come, too.

They lay in each other's arms for a time, Alex dozing off. Then he woke and knelt beside her on the bed to examine her more thoroughly, confirming what he had apparently detected during their lovemaking.

"You're pregnant," he said flatly, flopping heavily back on his pillow.

"I thought so," Helen said, her knees still up, her belly tender from his probing, her vagina still open.

"Why didn't you say something?" he asked.

"I wasn't sure what you'd think. I know we agreed to wait until we had some money and a decent place to live, until we'd had some time to enjoy being a family with just Beth."

"How do you feel about it?"

"Confused. Kind of stupid. The one night I didn't wear the diaphragm. . . ." Pulling down her nightgown, she rolled onto her side.

"Two babies. That's a lot of responsibility. What about graduate school?"

"I don't know. Maybe I can't do it all. But I wouldn't trade Beth for anything."

"I know, honey," he said, folding her once again into his arms. "You're a terrific mother. I never tell you that. We're both so tired all the time. But you're wonderful. And Beth— she's so perfect. So silly."

Helen felt her eyes fill with tears, her throat constrict. He appreciated her and loved their baby. That made her love him so much it hurt. She buried her face against his neck. "We are so lucky," she said. "So lucky."

"Another baby," he said softly. "How about that?"

Helen couldn't remember the last time they'd made love a second time. But he was hard again. Gloriously hard. Whispering how much he wanted her. This time, he made it last, not allowing her to come until she was crazy with wanting. In the back of her mind, she worried that Beth would wake up and spoil it. *Please, don't wake up. Please. Mommie needs this.*

As she came down from her beautiful, long, glorious orgasm, she heard Beth whimpering. "I'll see about her," Alex said, kissing her eyes, her forehead, her lips. Helen turned into her pillow, limp with passion and love.

She folded her hands across her belly. *A terrific mother.* Of course, she could love this baby, too. She was full of love.

Seven

"Mommie, Ben pooped his britches," Beth called from the family room.

Helen paused in her chopping. She should have put him on the potty chair after lunch, but she hadn't been able to face thirty minutes of sitting on the side of the tub, trying to convince a two-year-old to "poopie in the potty like a big boy." *Not today.*

She picked up a stalk of celery and resumed chopping, her movements smooth and automatic. Normal. She supposed she even looked normal. *Thirty-one-year-old, slightly overweight woman in jeans and a sweatshirt working in her cluttered kitchen.*

Even the stew she was preparing was normal.

But she didn't feel normal, so why was she going through the motions?

Because last night she had taken the stew meat from the freezer, and today it needed to be cooked.

But that was before she found the picture.

"Mommie, he *stinks!*"

"In a minute, Beth," she snapped. "I'm busy."

She glanced at the clock. She had just enough time to get the stew in the Crockpot before she took Beth to her afternoon play school and dropped Ben off at the baby-sitter's.

Then could she stop acting normal?

She hadn't acted any other way in so long. Good old Helen. Never loses her cool.

She was supposed to be meeting Bonnie and Jen at the Howard Johnson's halfway between Boulder and Denver. To plan this year's anniversary party.

She paused, remembering another anniversary party. Four years ago. *Alex taking Libby's pulse. Alex taking Libby home.*

She wouldn't go, Helen decided. She'd call the restaurant and leave a message for Jen and Bonnie.

Then what would she do?

She took a deep breath and scooped the sliced celery into the pot with the meat and potatoes. *Stew.* Alex should be delighted. Good, old-fashioned food. Last night, she had made hot German potato salad with a dressing made of bacon drippings, poppy seeds, vinegar, and sugar. "How come you never make plain old-fashioned potato salad?" he asked. He left out the words *like my mother used to make.*

"Do you like *this* potato salad?" she asked.

"Sure. It's terrific. But it's not the same."

"I didn't mean for it to be the *same,*" she countered, whisking the bowl from the table.

Then he lost patience with Beth for refusing to eat her piece of chicken. With Ben for banging on the metal tray of his high chair with his spoon. He asked Helen when she planned to start graduate school. He'd been asking her ever since they moved to Boulder last spring. There was still time to apply for admission to the spring term.

"Why do you keep asking about graduate school?" Helen demanded. "Do I seem stupid? Are you embarrassed by me?"

"Of course not," he had said, his tone overly patient. "But it's what you've always said you wanted to do. On our very first date, you said you wanted to get a Ph.D. and teach. It's hard for me to understand how someone with your brains can settle for being an ordinary housewife. I thought you'd be a professor by now. Have a career. Have something to talk about in the evening beside kid rashes and potty training."

After dinner last night, Alex made a point of shuffling through the basket of unpaid bills. "Think you'll find time to pay these before they turn off the water and lights?" he asked.

Last night, she dismissed her husband's behavior as the result of a bad day. Too many whiny patients. He got that way sometimes. Today, as Helen replayed the scene, she got a different reading. Maybe bad days and whiny patients had nothing to do with his moods.

Helen placed two peeled carrots on the chopping board and sliced away with her knife. Why hadn't she just told him she didn't want to go back to school? The time for sonnets and symposia had passed in her life. She liked watching "Mister Rogers' Neighborhood" with her babies. She liked thumbing through *Better Homes and Gardens* or reading paperback mysteries at her kitchen table while good things bubbled on the stove or baked in the oven. She liked her homey kitchen and her big old, never-quite-tidy house. And if she ever did anything out of the ordinary, it would have to do with cooking. That was what she was good at. Terrific, actually. And this embarrassed her husband. He didn't want her to enter the Pillsbury Bakeoff for fear she'd win.

"Mommie, Ben wants his diaper changed."

"Coming." Helen grabbed an onion.

Alex wanted a wife who was interesting and exciting, maybe a bit glamorous. Helen was none of those things. She had worn the sheer black nightgown he'd given her for her birthday exactly once—on her birthday. He didn't seem to understand that she couldn't feel passionate and self-conscious at the same time.

And she wasn't as good a bridge player as he would have liked. Every time they played, on the way home, he "discussed" alternative ways she might have played various hands.

Alex used to say that Libby was brilliant at bridge. "The Bridge Witch," he called her, saying she knew what was in the other three hands before they'd sorted their cards. If she didn't have a date, the seven of them would play, with one table bidding for the dummy.

Libby.

She had found a picture of Libby this morning. Helen closed her eyes, seeing it again.

Maybe it wasn't what she thought. Maybe she was jumping to conclusions.

But a bad taste rose in her mouth. She felt ill. Physically ill.

She picked up another onion and began hacking away. Too hard. Too fast. Too furiously. Not paying attention.

Her previous butcher knife had fallen into the bottom of the dishwasher, and the handle had melted. This one was new and as sharp as a surgeon's blade.

And suddenly the blade was grating across the bones in her hand.

Helen's scream brought the children running into the kitchen. Buster followed, barking.

It took a few seconds for the pain to begin. She stared as the thin red line cutting diagonally across the fleshy part of her palm began to open, as the blood began to spurt out. Had she really done that?

To the bone. *Jesus.*

Blood went everywhere. God, so much blood. All over the chopped vegetables, the chunks of beef, the counter, the sink. Helen grabbed a dish towel and pressed it against the flow. Her stomach convulsed. Her head went light. She slumped against the counter. *I will not pass out.*

She stumbled into the bathroom. "You guys go watch television," she told the children. "Mommie needs to find a Band-Aid."

She shut the bathroom door behind her and sat on the toilet seat. The dish towel was blood-soaked. She pulled a hand towel from the rack.

She applied pressure and tried to plan.

"Hey, Mommie, what're you doin' in there?" Beth's voice came from under the door. She did that, putting her lips up the crack to make sure her mother heard her.

"Mommie," Ben's voice was beside his sister's. "I got poopie." He was crying. He hated having his diaper full.

Buster whined his confusion at the strange goings-on.

"Go watch television," Helen said as firmly as she could with a quavering voice.

"I want to see," Beth said.

"I want to see," Ben parroted.

Helen looked. Gushing. The blood was actually gushing. *Jesus.* She clutched the towel more firmly against her hand and awkwardly dropped her head between her legs at the same time. What if she passed out? Would she bleed to death? The sobering thought helped clear her head.

She pressed harder with the towel, then wrapped another hand towel tightly on top of it and got shakily to her feet.

Opening the door and stepping over the children and dog, she walked unsteadily to the phone in the hall.

Helen dialed Marilyn, her next-door neighbor. No answer. Then she remembered that Marilyn's mother was visiting from Oklahoma City, and they were going shopping.

She sat on the bench and put the phone on the floor so she could dial with her head down.

She tried the only other neighbor whose number she knew by heart. Jo Ann. The line was busy. Helen pulled out the phone book but the numbers swam in front of her eyes. She tried Information for another number but couldn't make herself remember it long enough to dial.

She dialed Alex's office instead.

"Annie, this is Helen Radcliff. I need to talk to my husband."

"He's with a patient, Mrs. Radcliff. May I have him call you?"

"No. I need to talk to him now. Right now."

It was more than a minute before his voice came on the line. "Helen, what's wrong?"

"I need you. I cut my hand. Real bad."

"Does it need stitches?"

"Yes. There's a lot of blood."

He sighed. "I have a full office and a patient in labor."

Helen didn't bother to comment.

"Can't you drive yourself to the hospital? Or get Marilyn to bring you. I'll arrange to have someone to look at it."

She hung up on him.

The second towel was already soaking through. She must have severed something important.

Ben and Beth were holding hands. No shoes. Ben's shirt

was covered with his lunch. He was standing with legs apart, his diaper full and hanging.

"Get your coats, kids. We have to go get Mommie's hand fixed."

She needed to look for their shoes. Get some diapers out of the laundry basket. Someone at the hospital would have to change Ben.

Could she drive like this?

The phone rang.

"Helen, for Christ's sake, do you want me to come home?"

"Yes," she said as she sank back down on the bench.

"Is it bad?"

"I told you it was. Do you think I would have interrupted an examination if I didn't need you?"

"No, of course not. I'm sorry. Hang on, honey. I'll be right there."

She didn't remember much else. She was aware of Alex arriving. Of a careening ride to the hospital. She tried to ask him what he had done with the children but couldn't form the words. Surely someone would change Ben.

And suddenly it was the next day. A hand surgeon had come up from Denver to repair severed tendons. Doctors' wives got special treatment. Ordinary people who severed their tendons were taken to Denver.

"The kids?" she asked her husband.

"Mother is with them."

"Where?"

"At the house."

"*Our* house?"

Alex nodded.

"But it isn't clean!" Helen protested. "You know that I clean for a week before she comes."

"Well, next time clean before you try to cut your hand off. My mother is *helping* us," Alex said very evenly.

"I want to go home."

Alex all but fought with his mother to get her out of the kitchen. "But I thought I'd mop the floor," she protested. She'd already changed the shelf paper and polished the copper bottoms on the pans. Helen would be livid.

"You go give the kids a bath," he insisted. "I'll finish up here."

Helen had wanted to get up, but Alex insisted she stay in bed. She was still a bit woozy, and he felt like babying her. He'd bought her flowers. Served her dinner in bed. He'd take her up some cocoa later, and cuddle with her after the kids said good night. He'd been pretty moody lately, and he needed to let her know that he knew it.

She used to bitch at him about how much time he spent away from home fishing. They never argued about that anymore.

He was too busy building a practice to fish as often as he would like. And when he did go, Helen didn't seem to mind. Maybe she needed time away from him as much as he needed it away from her and the kids—and away from the telephone. Only when he was with his fishing buddies, wading in swift-running mountain streams, could he completely relax.

Helen seemed to assume that they'd go on family fishing trips when the kids were older, that he'd want to make fishermen out of his children, but Alex wasn't so sure. It wasn't something he wanted to share with his family.

What he wanted to share with his family was life here in this house. Or a better house. His practice was growing. He could afford to give his family a nice place to live, a rich life.

Helen wasn't holding up her end of the bargain. Their home life was too haphazard. Alex didn't care how she managed it—hell, she could hire a full-time maid if that's what it took—but he wanted their lives to be more orderly. He wanted tidy rooms, well-behaved children, and a competent wife. Granted, Helen was a fabulous cook. But their meals around the big round table in the kitchen were a circus, with Ben in his high chair spilling or dropping his food and Beth refusing to eat anything green or brown. Alex had found himself screaming at his daughter the night before last that chicken breasts were white, God damn it! "Not the outside," Beth had whined.

Alex preferred the nights they hired a baby-sitter and went out to dinner. The best times with his wife were over a glass of wine in a nice restaurant. Helen could still look pretty when she put her mind to it. They could still talk for hours. And have good sex afterward.

But they didn't go out—just the two of them—as often as they should. Usually when they went to the trouble to hire a sitter and dress up, they went to a party, or out to dinner with another doctor and his wife.

His and Helen's life was too conventional. And Alex blamed Helen. They didn't take trips for more than a weekend because she didn't like to leave the kids. She preferred their big old house and didn't want to build a new one. He wanted her to spend more on clothes, to wear smart shoes, to join something, to get involved. He wanted her to *entertain*—not just have folks over for dinner.

Helen had never bought chairs for the dining room table. Guests still sat in the kitchen. Ben and Beth used the dining room as a play room. A blanket covered the table, making a "fort" underneath.

Alex had always assumed that Helen would be a different

sort of woman than their mothers were. A new breed. He had supported her decision to stay home with the children while they were young. But now he worried that she'd be there forever.

Most physicians' wives didn't work. But in Boulder, they tended to be involved women who were civic- or ecology-minded, did serious volunteer work and skied, played tennis, golfed, even climbed mountains. Helen claimed she'd do more when the kids were older.

Alex couldn't understand how she was satisfied with so little. Even if she didn't want to work toward a graduate degree at this point in her life, she could take a few classes. Teach freshman composition. Keep her hand in.

Or write a book. Helen was always reading mysteries. He'd suggested several times that she try writing one. God knows, she was smart enough. But if she ever wrote a book, it would probably be a cookbook.

And if she was going to settle for being a full-time homemaker, why didn't she do a better job? Why wasn't she as compulsive about housework as she once had been about her studies? Here was a woman who had graduated *summa cum laude,* and now she just sort of wandered through life, folding half a load of clothes, leaving the rest piled on the bed while she went off to give the kids a bath or talk on the phone. Dealing with the pile of clean clothes on the bed was a regular part of their nighttime routine. The whole house was never clean at the same time. One room of the house would be tidy, the next room a disaster. If he ran his practice like she ran their house, they'd all starve.

Helen thought he was always comparing her with his mother. But that wasn't true. Sometimes Alex longed for his mother's chicken-fried steak and cream gravy, but his mother carried cleanliness to the extreme. Her house smelled of Lysol. She followed people around cleaning up after them. She whisked their plates away almost before they had taken the last bite. She usually had a sponge or rag in her hand, cleaning— always cleaning.

Jen was a little bit like that. Mrs. Clean. Compulsive. Ted said she wouldn't go to bed at night until the house was tidy. He could be standing there with a bottle of wine to carry up to the bedroom, and she would be fussing about getting fingerprints off the front of the refrigerator.

Alex preferred the way that Bonnie had turned out. She had a career, hired out the housework, and didn't own an apron.

What if Libby had gotten married? What kind of wife would she have been? Alex couldn't imagine Libby cooking or changing diapers. She was different. She was the most exciting woman he'd ever known.

Alex was just finishing up the dishes when his mother returned to the kitchen. She reached for an apron and the mop.

"No," Alex said, taking the mop away from her.

Wilda looked puzzled. "But it won't take me very long. I can be finished by the time the news comes on."

"Nope. You've done far too much already. Let's go tuck the kids in. I'll come back later for Helen's hot chocolate."

They watched the news with Helen on the bedroom television. More on the Kent State tragedy. Wilda said that college students should be given lessons in patriotism. Helen didn't comment. She had hardly spoken all evening.

Helen's hot chocolate still sat on the bedside table when he got out of the shower. Alex crawled into bed and nuzzled her neck. Her body stiffened.

He rolled away from her. "Christ, can't I even kiss your neck? How many times do I have to tell you I'm sorry? I should have known you wouldn't call me out of an examining room unless it was an emergency."

"I know you're sorry," she said. Side by side, the lamp still on, they stared at the ceiling.

"How's your hand?" he asked.

"It aches, but not too bad. I'm getting up tomorrow. Your mother can go."

"She's worried about how you'll do housework and take care of the kids with a bandaged hand."

"I'll manage. Beth can help."

Alex knew he'd have to all but push his mother out the door. But Helen sounded quite firm. She wanted to reclaim her turf.

"Have I ever told you how much I appreciate all you do for me and the kids?" he said, wondering if he should risk an affectionate pat.

"Sometimes. But you wish I'd do something other than raise two kids and do a half-assed job keeping house. You thought you were marrying someone special, but you judged me by my friends. *They* were special. I'm just good old Helen."

Then she started to cry.

Alex felt a flush of irritation. *Now, what in the hell brought that on?* "You want to tell me what's the matter?"

"I found a picture of Libby."

Libby.

"So?" he said, keeping his tone a careful neutral.

"Yesterday morning. I was looking for our birth certificates—for those insurance policies. There was a box of your army stuff. All my letters to you. Letters from your folks. Pictures of them. My picture. And one of Libby. She was sitting on the front porch of your folks' cabin. When did you take her there?"

Alex swung his feet to the floor, and sat on the edge of the bed, his back to her. His skin, still damp from the shower, felt cold and clammy.

"When?" Helen asked again. Her voice was very small. She was afraid of the answer. He was afraid to give it.

"A long time ago." He was starting to shiver.

"Why?"

"Don't, Helen. None of it really matters."

"You had her picture in Vietnam, didn't you?"

"I don't think so. It just must have gotten mixed in. I had other pictures, too. Of the whole gang."

"Libby never went with us to the cabin. Hiking and wiener roasts weren't her style. Jesus, Alex, my best friend. How could you?"

Alex went to his bureau for a T-shirt. Then he stood by the window, looking out into the night. He wished he still smoked. He used to smoke in college. But doctors who tell other people not to smoke can't themselves indulge.

"Talk to me, Alex," she demanded from behind him. "You took her up there. When? Why? Did you make love to her? Were you in love with her?"

"We were all a little in love with Libby," he said to the window. "All six of us. Sometimes it got a little out of hand."

"Was I second choice?" Helen was crying hard now. Sobbing. Alex was afraid his mother would hear.

With a sigh, he went back to the bed and tried to hold her, but she pulled away. He had to settle for holding her unbandaged hand. Her fingers were limp.

"No, baby. You were always the only one for me. Always. I just had to make sure. It was all a long time ago. Don't dredge up something from back then to fuck up our lives now. Please."

"I thought she loved me. I thought you both loved me. Oh, God, Alex, I hurt so much inside."

Her hair was mussed, her face blotchy, distorted with pain, no longer young. Not the face of the bright, passionate girl who had come so readily into his arms.

Helen had been the kind of girl a man marries. Libby had been the sort a man sold his soul for. Alex used to wish she'd die and leave him in peace.

"Please, Helen, let me hold you. The last thing in the world I wanted to do was hurt you. What happened then has nothing to do with us now."

He was crying, too. But she turned her back to him, her shoulders shaking, her sobs muffled in her pillow. Every time he tried to touch her, she shrugged him away.

After a while, she accepted his offer of sleeping pills. He waited until her breathing was deep and even before he tiptoed up to the attic. It was freezing cold, and the dust made him sneeze.

He had to look a while before he found the right box. Helen had left the picture there, on top, in the folder Libby had put it in. A slim leather folder. Soft dark green leather tooled in gold.

He was sure he'd thrown it away. He had meant to. Before he'd ever left Nam. So stupid. He never meant to cause Helen pain. Never.

Libby was flirting with him on the other side of the camera's lens. She was sitting sideways, looking over her shoulder, her wonderful black hair loose down her back. He'd looked at that picture a thousand times.

Helen's picture was in another folder with one of his parents. Her senior yearbook picture. She looked like a college girl.

Alex carried the photograph of Libby downstairs.

The kitchen smelled of Lysol. His mother had come back downstairs and mopped the floor. He felt a rush of rage. *Damn her.*

Alex took the picture from its folder and tore the picture into tiny pieces and washed them into the garbage disposal. Then he took the lock of black hair that was hidden behind it and caressed it between his fingers. He used to bury his face in that hair when he took her from behind. Hair that smelled like that same perfume. Always. Sometimes a woman would walk by wearing Libby's perfume, and Alex would feel like someone had hit his knees from behind.

He put the lock of hair to his lips. A piece of Libby.

Then he stuffed it down the disposal and stood there for a long time listening to the motor grinding away.

Alex made a rare appearance at church on Sunday.

Helen had bumped her hand getting out of the car, and it was throbbing. She sat there feeling her own heartbeat, sitting shoulder to shoulder with her husband of nine years, struggling desperately to decide if she loved or hated him.

She hadn't slept for the past three days. Had barely eaten. Her whole body hurt.

If it hadn't been for the children, she would have left. Maybe forever. Maybe just long enough to sort out her feelings.

The children were the reason they were here this morning. Beth was singing in the children's choir.

Helen wished she could close her eyes and nod off like the man in the pew in front of her. Just a few minutes of peace. A few minutes of not thinking.

She stared down at her wedding ring. All she'd ever wanted

was to be Alex's wife. The day he asked her to marry him was the happiest day of her life.

When in all that tumultuous period of falling in love, with all that glorious, soul-searing sex at every opportunity, had Alex taken Libby to the cabin? Were the last nine years built on a lie? And did that matter? She and Alex had made a family together. A nice family. He was a good father. If she hadn't found that picture, she would probably have lived out her years never knowing her husband had an affair with her best friend, without ever wondering if she was his second choice.

They couldn't go on like this. At her request, Alex was sleeping in the guest room, which upset Beth. Helen explained that Daddy kept bumping Mommie's sore hand in his sleep. But Beth looked at them with wary, fearful eyes. Mommies and daddies were supposed to talk. Even argue. Not carefully avoid being in the same room together.

This morning Beth had crawled into bed with Helen. "Daddy says you're mad at him for something bad he did a long time ago," Beth said, snuggling close.

"Yes. Something like that. When did he tell you this?"

"Just now. Ben and Buster are sleeping with him. Are you going to stay mad at him?"

"I don't know, sugar. My feelings are hurt. Sometimes it takes a while to get over it."

"But if it happened a long time ago, should your feelings still get hurt? Daddy's been good for a long time."

"Maybe not," Helen had said, stroking her daughter's thin, delicate back. Beth's body had changed so. No baby plumpness. Skinny arms and legs. Her fine hair tickled Helen's nose. Ben had gotten the good hair. And an easygoing disposition. Beth worried about things—houses that needed paint, what you stood on in heaven, why God let babies die. And now, she was worried because her parents weren't sleeping together when they always had—every night of her life.

"Will you still let Daddy come to church this morning and see me sing?" Beth had asked.

She looked like an angel in her choir robe. She was standing in the front row with the other children who knew all the words. The whole congregation was one big smile. Helen desperately wanted to share the moment with her husband, to reach for his hand. *Precious little Beth.* But they sat there, carefully not touching, eyes forward.

They drove over to Berthoud after church for an old-fashioned fried-chicken dinner at the Wayside Inn. The kids were unusually quiet. No one ate much. The waitress kept asking if everything was all right.

Alex didn't drive straight home but stopped near Chautauqua Park, at a sloping lot overlooking the city of Boulder below with a fine view of the south arm of the Flatirons.

The lot was his surprise.

"I can just see it," he said. "A real Colorado house with a rough exterior and lots of light. A great view from every window. A veranda all around. And a big basement with a playroom and a woodworking shop."

"When did you buy it?" Helen asked.

Alex paused. Helen knew he wanted to lie, to say he'd had it for weeks, for months, that it had nothing to do with a long-ago photograph of Libby.

"I've had my eye on it for some time," he said. "I want it for us, honey."

She understood. No matter what happened before, she was his wife and he wanted a life with her.

But now ugly doubts clouded her vision of the past. She resurrected scenes from their married life, scenes in which Libby was a player. Alex had always been aware of her. But then, they all were.

Why had Libby come back to Denver?

Had Alex been a faithful husband?

Helen might never know.

No matter how she tried to tell herself that present-day reality was more important that past transgressions, Helen could not forget the look on Libby's face in that picture. It was the expression of a woman sure of herself. Teasing. *I can have whatever I want.*

Braced against the wind on the sloping lot, making one leg shorter than the other, she and Alex stood facing each other. Farther up the hill, Beth and Ben were hunkered down examining a rotting rabbit carcass.

It was cold. She held up her bandaged hand to help relieve the throbbing.

"Well?" Alex asked eagerly, poking his hands in his pockets, the wind blowing his hair over his forehead.

"It makes me think of that Jeep. You should have talked to me about the lot before you bought it."

"Look, if you don't like it, if you don't want a new house, I'll return this, too."

Helen looked at her husband. "Did you want to marry her?"

"No. I never wanted to marry anyone but you."

"Did you have sex with her after we were married?"

"No. Only before."

Helen knew that was the best she could hope for. Whether the words were true or not, he felt obliged to say them.

"Do you know what happened to her?"

He shook his head.

She wanted to ask him to swear on something sacred. On the lives of their children. But she didn't want to tempt fate.

She loved her big old house near the campus. She didn't want a modern house in an upscale neighborhood. But a new leaf was in order. Could they start anew on this expensive scrap of rocky land?

"We have to wait," she said.

"For what?"

"To see if I can stand for you to touch me. Right now, I'm not sure."

Eight

Libby had been a cheat. Helen felt a desperate need to let Jen and Bonnie know this. She even practiced telling them, making up imaginary conversations. They never really knew Libby at all. Helen could see that now. Always so secretive. Always wanting to know their every thought but never sharing hers.

But Helen couldn't bear to have her friends know the humiliating truth about her husband.

Of all three men, Alex had seemed like the prize catch. He was more handsome than Ted and would earn more than Lenny. Alex was outgoing, generous, dedicated to medicine—women's medicine and bringing babies into the world. Men and women alike admired and respected Alex.

Now, Helen could shatter the images of her perfect husband and of their dearest friend with one sordid revelation.

But she didn't want to see the horror and pity in their faces, hear it in their voices.

If they knew, they would avoid Alex and, with him, his wronged wife. Her tarnished marriage would make them forever guarded with her, their conversations careful. Their chaste marriages would separate them from her. *Poor Helen,* they would think.

No, she'd never tell.

Jen commented from time to time that Helen was quieter than she used to be. "I don't like these silences," she said. "We used to talk nonstop."

"We used to have more energy," Helen countered. "Motherhood makes me tired."

Bonnie noticed Helen's reluctance to talk about Libby.

"It gets boring after a while," Helen insisted. "We've already all but beatified her. What more do you want?"

When the three couples got together, Lenny would rub the knots in Helen's shoulders and tell her to loosen up.

With Ted, it was "lighten up." He kept refilling her glass, telling her she was only going to live once so she might as well enjoy it.

For the most part, the dynamics of their friendship continued unchanged. The women telephoned and lunched. After a couple of years of being too busy for each other, the men were fishing together again, spending months in advance planning each trip. And the three couples were once again getting together every month or so for dinner and poker. Or bridge. Alex never criticized her playing anymore. Or anything else.

But Jen and Bonnie worried about Helen. At times, she just wasn't herself. "Do you think she and Alex are having problems?" Bonnie asked Jen over cocktails.

They'd been shopping. Bonnie was in demand as an ERA advocate, and Jen insisted that she upgrade her wardrobe. Look better for her speaking engagements. Avoid unisex. Be more like Gloria Steinem.

"Problems? Like what?" Jen asked, her tone wary. A troubled marriage usually meant one thing.

"I'm not sure. Alex has always been kind of impatient with her," Bonnie said. "He'd never seen a dust kitty until he married Helen."

"And now he wants to build a fancy house," Jen said. "Maybe that's it. Helen doesn't want a new house. You know how attached she is to that old barn."

They agreed. It must be the new house.

Still, Jen thought. Alex was so good-looking. And women tend to get a little foolish over their OBs. Alex would be an easy man to get foolish over.

With the help of a CU professor of architecture, a house began to take shape on paper. While Alex had latched onto the house project like a drowning man to a floating log, Helen never formally agreed to building a new home. To Alex, the house stood for the future, for a continued marriage, for a happy family, for his success in providing for that family.

And the fact that he wanted those things so desperately had reached in and begun the meltdown in Helen's heart. (Or was it that, no matter how much she tried to project a future without Alex, she failed?) She had done the very thing Bonnie preached against. She had been absorbed by a man. Her only identity came as the wife of Dr. Alexander Radcliff and the mother of his children.

Finally, she agonized her way to a conclusion. The knowledge of her husband's affair with her dearest friend made her hate him, but it did not diminish her need of him in her life. She kept remembering that long-ago fall day she opened her apartment door and saw him standing there for the first time. At that precise moment—or so it seemed now in the remembering—she had taken her heart out and given it to him. And she was not capable of reclaiming it.

And little by little, the house that began to take form on the steep, rocky hillside assumed for her the same symbolic significance it held for Alex.

Every night before dinner, they'd drive out to the building site with the kids and Buster to check on what had been done that day. After dinner she and Alex would spread out plans and samples of carpet, tile, paneling, paint, and wood finishes on the kitchen table. Frequently, they argued.

The house Alex envisioned was too pretentious for Helen's taste. Alex accused her of wanting a big kitchen surrounded by bedrooms.

"You always said you'd use that wedding china and crystal if we had a formal dining room," he reminded her.

"That was just an excuse. I'm not a formal person. I don't want the trappings to be more important than the food."

So they compromised. The house they were building would have large living and dining rooms for entertaining. *And* a huge kitchen/family room. The state-of-the-art kitchen would be big enough to fit both leaves in the big round table and have yards of counter space and a built-in bookcase for her cookbooks. She pored through home magazines searching for innovations to include in her wonderful kitchen.

Often, they would continue talking in bed after the lights were out, speculating about all the ways their life would be better in the new house. More privacy. Grilling steaks on the deck. A Christmas tree tall enough to touch the living room's cathedral ceiling. Dinner parties in the spacious dining room. And family celebrations, which Alex assumed would also be in the dining room but Helen knew would be around the kitchen table. Touching that turned into fondling, and that led to love-making. They both took a long time to come. Too long. Too forced. Hard work. Sweating bodies. Pounding hearts. Ragged breathing. And no lovely sense of peacefulness afterward.

Did he ever think of Libby when he made love?

Alex still wouldn't talk about her. He insisted that he would have no part in Helen ruining their lives over something that happened so long ago. He made it seem like Helen's fault.

After she found the picture, it was almost three months before they made love, and then only because Helen could no longer stand the tension. Her indecision became a decision. Doing nothing meant that their life together would continue. And continuing meant they had to come to terms. Sex was the beginning.

Now, when the others brought up Libby's name, Helen couldn't look at Alex. Still. He'd refill his drink, go to the bathroom. She felt cold and strange. *Libby and Alex.*

She had loved them both so much. She wasn't sure about her love for Alex, but her love for Libby had died when she saw that picture. A cold hand had grabbed her heart and squeezed it away.

She hoped Libby was dead. That's how she thought of her —dead and buried deep in the ground in a dark, airless casket, her head on a satin pillow, her face still beautiful.

Sometimes Helen thought about paying Alex back, about balancing the scale. She thought about it a lot after a carpenter named Hawkins was hired by the contractor to work on the house.

Hawkins was a weathered, sinewy man with intensely blue

eyes. He wore scuffed boots and a black cowboy hat pushed back on his head. Whenever Helen arrived in her station wagon, she looked first to see if he was there, even before checking to see what progress had been made on the house since her last visit. If he was there, she felt self-conscious.

She put on makeup before she made her visits to the construction site. Sometimes she changed her clothes.

She started bringing treats to the workmen. Cookies, homemade doughnuts, jugs of coffee or lemonade. Hawkins always thanked her, the only words they exchanged.

When she visited the site with Alex, she felt even more self-conscious, not holding her husband's hand or arm as they climbed about the emerging house.

Jen and Bonnie noticed the carpenter on their first visit to the building site. They giggled all through happy hour about "Helen's carpenter." "He looks like the Marlboro Man," Bonnie said. "Surely he's not real."

"He flusters you, doesn't he?" Jen asked Helen.

Helen blushed. "Yeah, I guess."

Bonnie stared at her. "But you wouldn't . . ."

"Of course, I wouldn't!" Helen snapped back.

"Sometimes a woman wonders, though," Jen mused. "But if our husbands ever screwed around on us, we'd have a hard time mustering up righteous indignation if we'd done more than wonder. Right? I'll tell you one thing, though. If Ted Echols ever did screw around on me, I'd find myself a man like that carpenter to pay back the son of a bitch."

"Why that kind of man?" Helen asked.

"Because it'd just be for lust," Jen said with a shrug, as though such a truth were self-evident. "I wouldn't be screwing my marriage, just some male who drifted by. Then I could deal with Ted on a more even footing."

"Deal with him how? Would you take him back?" Bonnie wanted to know.

"It depends on who he was fooling around with," Jen explained. "If he was bonking a bimbo, yeah, I'd probably take him back. If he was doing it with a real person, I don't think I could."

Helen felt knots in her stomach. Libby had been real. But Jen didn't know what she was talking about. She'd never been there.

Once, when Hawkins was sweating, shirtless, Helen could see muscles in his back lengthening and contracting as he unloaded lumber from a truck. She'd be feeling those muscles while he humped away on her. Hard fucking. That took her breath away. Nothing tender. Just one time, to even the score.

Then one night, when Alex was making love to her, Helen realized that in her mind, she was making love to a carpenter named Hawkins.

And the next night.

Suddenly she was perpetually horny. She even masturbated during the day—something she hadn't done in years.

And Hawkins knew. His blue, blue eyes said he could look through her clothes and seen her open and lusting. His gaze rattled her, made her trip on boards, made her skin feel hot.

"You always lived in Colorado?" Hawkins asked her one afternoon as he took a swig of the lemonade she'd brought.

"Yes. I grew up in Denver," she said. "What about you?"

"North. Home's near Walhalla, up by the Canada line."

"You have family there?"

"Wife. Two kids. I come here for the work. In Colorado, rich people build homes like this one with lots of wood that take a long time to build."

"Will you work on another house around here when you finish this one?" she asked.

"No, ma'am. I'll winter up home. I'll be heading out as soon as I get all the cabinets built."

Helen wondered what Hawkins's wife was like. If they had good sex. Hawkins wouldn't hurry in bed. She bet he'd take great pleasure in driving a woman crazy.

Ben and Beth were spending the weekend with their grandparents in Aspen. Helen cooked a special dinner just for Alex. Veal paprika. Sweet potato soufflé. Steamed zucchini. Brandied plums. Chocolate chiffon pie. She tried a little raspberry liqueur in the pie. And sherry in the soufflé—with freshly ground nutmeg. She'd been experimenting a lot with soufflés lately. And cheesecakes. She loved combining flavors, coming up with something different, having people's faces light up when they took the first bite.

He complimented the meal; they talked about the house, about Ben's new preschool. Beth's upcoming birthday. They decided to have the pie and coffee after a movie. *M*A*S*H* was playing, which turned out to be a bad choice. All that infidelity made any discussion afterward impossible. They drove home in silence.

"Was it only lust with you and Libby?" Helen demanded in bed as Alex took her in his arms.

He rolled away from her. "Christ, Helen, we agreed that we weren't going to talk about her."

"*You* agreed. I just want a simple yes or no. Was it only lust?"

"There is no simple answer. You know that."

"Then lie to me. Say, 'Yes, I only wanted to fuck her. It had nothing to do with love.'"

"If I said it, you wouldn't believe me."

"What if I had sex with a man? Just sex. No love. Do you think it would make me feel better?"

"That carpenter you so carefully avoid when I'm around?" Alex asked.

Helen was shocked.

"Please, don't. I couldn't bear it," Alex whispered in the darkness.

One evening, just at dusk, Hawkins was there alone, burning scrap lumber. Alex had a delivery and Helen and the children had come on without him. Buster, too.

The rooms had walls now, and the windows had been installed. A big house that the architect called Colorado contemporary. Three levels. Lots of glass and rough wood. Alex's verandas on three sides with a huge deck in back.

The fire felt good. Already fall was in the air. She wondered if they'd have Christmas in the new house as the contractor had promised. Alex and the kids had already decided where they would put the tree. They'd have enough room for both sets of grandparents.

The children threw pieces of wood in the fire, then raced off with Buster to check on the progress of their bedrooms.

Helen remained, toasting her hands together over the flames.

"I was hoping you'd come," Hawkins said, throwing a shovelful of debris into the blaze. "You haven't missed a day yet."

"We were waiting for my husband to come home. He was delayed."

"You're a fine-looking woman," Hawkins said, leaning on the shovel. "That doctor husband of yours ever tell you that?"

"Yes. Sometimes. Do you tell your wife you like the way she looks?"

"All the time."

"The kitchen cabinets are beautiful. The architect says you're quite a craftsman."

He smiled. The detailing on the cabinets had been his idea. His teeth were white against deeply tanned skin. Heavy black stubble covered his chin, the kind of whiskers that destroyed a woman's face.

The fire cracked loudly, like it was fueled with small firecrackers. Inside the house, Ben was calling out to his sister. "Beth, where are you? I don't want you to scare me."

"I think about you in the night," Hawkins said softly.

In the night. At the Aurora Motel, where she had seen his blue truck with the dented fender and the North Dakota license plate. "And I you," she admitted.

"Nice things?" he asked, moving closer. He smelled of wood smoke and sweat.

She nodded.

He touched her arm. "Sunday afternoon," he said. "You want to meet me someplace, or come down to the motel?"

Helen backed away.

"What's the matter?" he asked. "Isn't that what this is all about?"

Suddenly, she was having a hard time breathing. "No. I'm sorry. I guess it isn't. I can't. I really can't." She backed away another step, stumbling.

Ben was running down the driveway screaming, followed by a barking Buster.

Helen knelt and opened her arms to him.

"Beth beez bad to me again," he wailed.

"You go on to the party without me," Alex's voice said over the phone.

"Oh, honey, are you sure?" Helen asked. "The last time we went out with the Hoovers, you had to leave in the middle of the meal. Maybe you can finish up in time to meet us afterward for a drink."

"I've got big problems. The Epperson woman is going bad." His voice wasn't right.

"The nurse from ER? Surely she's not still in labor."

"No. I sectioned her. The baby's dead, and she's dying."

Dying. Helen had to pause a minute to digest the word. OB patients didn't die. "Oh, Alex, no," she said. "How come? What's the matter?"

"An infection. Staph probably. Killed the baby, and now it's gone to her kidneys. She's not putting out any urine."

"But the kidneys can start up again," Helen said hopefully.

"Not this time."

Helen was stunned. Sometimes babies died or were born dead. And GYN patients sometimes died—older women usually—with cancer. But physicians didn't lose their obstetrical patients. Maybe it happened in big cities when the police brought a pregnant addict in off the street, already in labor, malnourished, infected with venereal disease and all kinds of other health problems. But not in Boulder with its middle-class patients, who had prenatal care and loving families.

A nurse, too. Barbara Epperson. A small, pretty redhead. About thirty. Helen had met her when Ben had cut his chin and had to have stitches. The nurse had gushed. Dr. Radcliff was *her* doctor. He'd delivered her little girl. And now she was expecting again. Helen had talked to her again the night before last when she called to report her water had broken. Two weeks early. She was crying, on the verge of hysteria. Helen thought that strange from a nurse. Delivering two weeks early was hardly a crisis. And she wasn't even in labor yet.

119

The doorbell rang. The Hoovers.

Bill Hoover was a general surgeon. He and Alex referred cases back and forth and sometimes assisted each other in the operating room. A colleague. But Helen knew she couldn't bring herself to explain that Alex was losing an OB.

If Barbara Epperson died, the whole medical community would know soon enough. The whole town. What would happen to Alex?

"Helen, dear, you're white as a sheet. Are you ill?" Lois Hoover asked the minute Helen opened the door.

"No. Well, maybe a little. Alex is tied up at the hospital. Could we take a rain check?"

"Oh, God. It's not his patient that's gone bad?" Bill groaned, slapping his forehead.

Helen nodded dumbly.

"An ER nurse," Bill explained to his wife. "I heard them talking in ER while I was examining Lottie's boy, but I didn't realize she was Alex's. Renal shutdown after delivery. Dead baby. A real mess."

The Hoovers looked at Helen like mourners at a funeral offering condolences to the bereaved. She accepted their pats, their assurances that "it happened sometimes" and they'd plan another evening soon. She was relieved to shut the door behind them.

Helen sent the baby-sitter home, put on her robe, and settled down in bed with her children and a stiff bourbon. She read Ben and Beth to sleep. *Babar. The 500 Hats of Bartholomew Cubbins.* A chapter out of *Winnie-the-Pooh.*

The Babar book was falling apart. It had been Helen's when she was little. "Helen Jane Donaldson" was carefully printed in the front in large capital letters. Her parents used to read it to her. No, actually, her mother used to read it to her. Her father was generally at the hospital or making house calls. When she had her father's attention, they played cards. Gin rummy. God, how she had loved that.

After the children were asleep, she called her father.

"Gee, honey, that's a tough one for Alex. But it happens sometimes. Even dentists occasionally have a patient die in the chair. Every condition, every procedure, every pill, is not without a degree of risk. And no one ever said pregnancy was safe."

"But I've never known anyone who died of it," Helen insisted.

"That's because the people you know have excellent medical care, deliver in modern hospitals with safe blood supplies, and have fine physicians like Alex. But even so, that's no guarantee. I'd say the odds were nine in ten that Alex would lose at least one OB patient during his career."

"Did you?"

"Sure. Back in the 'old days' it wasn't quite so rare. I lost three. Actually, I hated deliveries. They were the first thing I gave up, if you remember. Figured with the combined life expectancy of the mother and the infant, I had well over a hundred years of human life in my hands. That's a lot of responsibility. And the little varmints insisted on getting born in the middle of the night. It was making an old man out of me, and I wanted to spend more time with you and your mother. Remember, we celebrated the last baby by taking that trip to Williamsburg."

"Yes, I remember. Daddy, what should I do?" Helen asked.

"Just give him a little extra loving. Your mother was good at that. Tell Alex to call me if he'd like to talk to an old doc who's been there."

Helen turned out the light and listened to her children breathing. Inhaled their smell. Touched their silky hair.

A *little extra loving.*

If only her marriage were that simple.

Alex sat by the bed of his unconscious patient and stared at the face of disaster. A pretty face. Wonderful skin. Beautiful red hair. A perky nose. Only thirty-two years old.

She hadn't been pretty yesterday. Kept screaming that she was going to die. Hysterical even before her labor began.

He'd had a full office and left the obstetrical nurses to deal with Barbara Epperson. There was no indication of anything wrong. Good fetal heart tones. The mother had normal vital signs. When her labor didn't start spontaneously, he had it induced.

When her labor began, a nurse called to report the patient was combative. Alex ordered more hypos.

The next phone call informed him that the patient had spiked a low-grade fever. Alex ordered IV fluids.

Then the head nurse called. Fetal distress. Alex ordered a surgical crew and flew out the door, leaving all three examining rooms and his waiting room full.

He'd heard her as soon as he walked into the labor and delivery wing. A real screamer.

Her fever was higher. The baby's heart rate was dropping rapidly.

Alex worked fast and with great precision. In a matter of minutes, he had sectioned the woman and delivered a baby boy. The amniotic fluid was green and filled with pus. The waiting pediatrician began working on the infant. Alex learned later that the baby had moved but had never taken a breath. The infection had killed him and would soon kill his mother.

A normal vagina was the harbinger of enough bacteria to

kill should those bacteria enter the bloodstream. And there was always more danger of infection after the amniotic sac ruptured. The rule of thumb allowed a physician to wait twenty-four hours for labor to begin spontaneously. And that was just about when Barbara Epperson's labor was induced. Maybe an hour or two more. By then, the infection must have already taken hold.

She should have been put on antibiotics the minute her fever began. He should have gotten her delivered sooner.

But he hadn't realized he had a disaster in the making. Dehydrated patients often spike a fever.

Strange how Barbara Epperson kept insisting she was going to die. Alex wanted to blame the whole thing on a self-fulfilling prophecy, but knew that wasn't going to fly in court.

And there *would* be a lawsuit. Malpractice or not, any time there was a bad outcome in an OB case, the physician got sued.

Alex needed to go face the family in the waiting room. The young father with pinched lips—already he knew, had read the signs. He'd lost his baby, and now his wife was going to die. The prayerful mother who kept insisting God would look after her Barbara. The alcoholic father with his red nose who kept telling the medical staff that money was no object. His little girl was to have the best.

Somehow, Alex got through the next two days. He went home only to shave and shower. Helen would try to get him to eat something. She didn't try to talk to him.

He waited with Barbara Epperson until the end, pronounced her dead, offered his condolences to the weeping family. The young husband shook off Alex's hand on his shoulder. Alex wondered if he had already talked to a lawyer.

When he opened the door of his house, Helen was coming down the hall. She didn't say a word as she took him in her arms.

Now, he could cry. For Barbara Epperson. Her angry husband. Her puzzled parents. Her little girl. Her dead baby boy. Himself. His marriage. His sins.

He had never needed anything more in his life than he needed his wife's arms, her soothing voice.

Bonnie's phone call was the first. "How did you hear so fast?" Alex asked.

"Her husband called it in. I just wanted to warn you. You'll be asked for a statement."

Every Denver television station called. Several radio stations. Half a dozen newspaper reporters. Helen took the calls. *Dr. Radcliff would not be making a statement.*

The story was page one in the *Post*. DEATHS OF MOTHER AND INFANT UNDER INVESTIGATION. The story read like an indictment.

When Alex arrived at the office the next morning, his staff was hysterical. Patients were calling—canceling appointments, asking for their medical records to be sent elsewhere.

"But you're the best doctor in town," Annie said, tears rolling down her cheeks. "It wasn't your fault."

But Alex wondered. Maybe his crime had been arrogance. *Nothing like that would ever happen to him.* Maybe believing in his own infallibility had made him less cautious.

When he walked down the corridors of the hospital, nurses stopped talking at their stations and quickly turned their attention to patient charts.

One by one, most of the other physicians stopped him in the halls or sat with him in the cafeteria to offer condolences. Alex represented every physician's worst nightmare. They would not be casting stones.

Alex's malpractice insurance carrier decided to settle out of court for one million dollars, the first million-dollar obstetrical malpractice settlement in the state. The story of the settlement was well covered in both the Boulder and Denver newspapers and by the three Denver television stations. A settlement was considered tantamount to a confession of guilt.

His insurance rates soared. He lost twelve of his OB patients. And a large number of GYNs did not call to make appointments for their yearly examination and Pap smear.

How in the hell was he going to pay for that half-built house out on the hill? Educate his children?

Should they move away? Start over?

But then Mildred Hollingsworth, the head OB nurse at the Boulder hospital, sent a letter to the editor of the Boulder newspaper. "The only doctors who don't lose patients are ones who don't treat sick people," she wrote. "Alexander Radcliff is a competent, compassionate doctor. He delivered my first grandbaby, and if I have any say, he'll deliver all the rest."

The letter was followed by a statement of support signed by every OB nurse on the hospital staff.

Mildred's letter turned the tide. Alex didn't know how to thank her. A new car? A trip to Europe? A diamond ring?

She hugged him and told him to go tend to his mothers.

Alex felt older. Fallible. The practice of medicine would never be the same for him.

And his marriage?

He wasn't sure.

Was their careful marriage her fault for not letting the past die—or his for fucking up that past?

He told Helen constantly that he loved her. He was wearing out the words.

Nine

Helen refilled the wineglasses and settled back onto the over-sized burgundy-colored sofa in her new living room with the huge stone fireplace and expanse of pale beige carpet.

She felt a bit high—not from the wine but from being with her friends. And on her own turf. Usually Helen went to Denver. When Jen and Bonnie came to Boulder, it was with their husbands—to attend a CU football or basketball game, with Helen feeding them before and after.

Their evening together had been filled with good talk. Watergate. *The Godfather.* Tired marriages. Jen and Bonnie were staying over—a first in all the years since college.

"I wish we could do this more often," Helen said, taking a sip of wine.

Bonnie nodded as she lit a cigarette. "Yeah. It's like old times, being back on the campus, eating at The Sink. Did you see those guys at the next table looking at us? We weren't old enough to be visiting parents. We weren't seedy enough for faculty. And we looked like we could afford better."

"Oh, but no one does greasy hamburgers better than The Sink," Helen said. "I take the kids down there sometimes. They like Sink fries better than McDonald's. But we don't tell Alex. He's on a crusade about fat. He wants me to change the way I cook. Nothing fried. No butter. No egg yolks. No whole milk. No cheese. Have you ever tried to *bake* fat-free?"

"Tonight's been great," Jen said, "but I kind of dread tomorrow. We haven't seen most of the DG sisters since Libby disappeared."

Helen understood.

Tomorrow was a reunion of their Delta Gamma pledge class. The fifteenth anniversary of their initiation into the DG sisterhood. Nineteen fifty-eight—the second semester of their freshman year. Jen was the reunion organizer. And doubtless, all the sisters would want to talk about Libby. Speculate. Ask dozens of questions of Libby's three best friends.

"You used to talk about writing a book about Libby," Jen said to Bonnie. "Think you ever will?"

"Books need endings," Bonnie said.

After hamburgers at The Sink, the three of them had walked to campus to attend an ERA rally. Congress had finally passed the amendment. And Colorado would be one of the first states to ratify. The state legislature had already made abortion legal—six years ago. Colorado was where affluent women from surrounding states came for a safe abortion. Other female citizens of those states still had theirs on kitchen tables.

Legal or not, Alex wouldn't do abortions. He referred patients who requested one to a clinic in Denver, but he did not perform the procedure himself. Most physicians with a thriving middle-class practice did not. "Abortionist" was still an ugly, back-street word.

The rally was in the field house. Alex had come. He'd said he might, but Helen was pleased to the point of tears when she saw him waiting out front for them. Which was silly. Alex was more of a feminist than she was. He admired women like Bonnie. When his medical group had an opening for an internist, Alex insisted that they choose a woman.

Alex wasn't the only male in attendance. A sprinkling of men—mostly professorial types—was scattered throughout the audience of females—students, faculty, and townspeople. Hand-painted banners hung from the balcony. DON'T IRON WHILE THE STRIKE IS HOT. REPENT MALE CHAUVINISTS, YOUR WORLD IS COMING TO AN END. OUR MOTHER, WHO ART IN HEAVEN.

The meeting had a pep-rally atmosphere as speaker after speaker explained why the ERA was needed. They were preaching to the choir, Helen thought. The people here were already believers.

Wearing a smart red suit, Bonnie had taken the podium to urge middle-class women to get involved in the movement. "You students need to talk to your mothers and aunts. Without the middle class, the ERA will fail. Middle-class women think they don't need help. They feel safe in their suburban homes with their well-clothed, well-fed children. But no woman who depends on a man for support is out of harm's way. We want women from all walks of life, from all races, from all religious persuasions to support this battle because it is morally just. All human beings deserve the dignity of equal rights. And isn't it exciting to live in a time when this will come to pass? Won't it be grand to tell our daughters and granddaughters, 'I was there. I helped make the ERA happen!' "

They had all stood and cheered. Clapped until their hands hurt. Alex even whistled.

The ERA seemed so simple and just. But middle-class support or not, the amendment faced an uphill battle, Helen thought as she propped her feet in their worn scuffs on her new glass-topped coffee table. Glass tables, she was discovering, showed every speck of dust.

Jen, with her feet curled under her, was smoking a rare cigarette—one of Bonnie's. Jen had changed from a pretty girl to a lovely woman. People still told her she looked like Grace Kelly, but Helen thought she was more beautiful. Her jaw was softer, her mouth fuller.

Jen was steering the conversation back to a topic begun over dinner. Tired marriages. She was a great believer in the power of sexy lingerie to revive sagging libidos. "Of course, there's the matter of stretch marks. But they've faded, and I don't parade around in a spotlight."

"Christ, Jen, that's so demeaning," Bonnie said. Bonnie's dark brown hair was still long and straight—like in college. She frowned too much. The vertical creases between her eyes were getting deeper.

"Then what do you suggest?" Jen asked.

Bonnie shrugged. "God, I wish I knew," she said, and emptied her wineglass. "Good sex is scary. It creates great expectations. And who can shoot par every time out?"

"We fall asleep in front of the television," Helen confessed. "Here Alex and I are, living in this fabulous house, sleeping in a bedroom glamorous enough for a movie star, with the kids' rooms so far away we need an intercom to hear them at night. We have a wet bar, built-in stereo, a glorious view, and yet life

is pretty much like it was when we lived in the old house—
except now I feel guiltier about smudges on the walls and dust
under the furniture."

Getting settled in the house had been exhausting. And once
their possessions had been weeded out, transported, and either
arranged or put away, it was time to tackle the arid, rocky hillside
that was now their yard.

Months passed before they could just sit through the evening. And inactivity hit them like Valium. After the dinner
dishes were done and the children tucked into bed, if Alex
wasn't off delivering a baby, they would nod off by the end of
the news whether they were watching on the big set in the
family room with a bowl of popcorn between them or on the
smaller one in their bedroom propped up in their new king-
sized bed.

Helen thought about sex during the day; at night she was
usually grateful to avoid it.

"Lenny and I usually save special-occasion sex for hotels,"
Bonnie said. "Then we don't have to try as hard at home. I took
him to the Brown Palace on his birthday."

After a brandy to cap off the evening, Helen hugged Jen
and Bonnie good night, then went to check on her children.
She removed some of the stuffed animals from Ben's overpop-
ulated bed. Beth, who worried about monsters, had the lamp
on by her bed and the light on in the closet. Helen left the one
on in the closet and started down the length of the house to
her sleeping husband in their secluded bedroom.

The moonlight shining through the skylights bathed the
interior of the house a surrealistic blue. It looked more like a
movie set than a home. Helen imagined the camera lens scan-
ning the rooms until the victim's body was located in the middle
of a huge bloodstain on the pale, plush carpet by the L-shaped
divan. Even the body would look blue.

Holding her arms out for balance, she tried to walk in a straight line down the hallway. She couldn't. It made her giggle.

She tiptoed as best she could across the bedroom. Alex had graciously excused himself when they got home and left the three women to their visiting. The lamp was still on. He was asleep, a medical journal opened across his chest. His eyes opened when she took away the journal. "Hi. Have a good visit?" he asked.

"Yeah. Thanks for coming to the rally. Bonnie really appreciated it. So did I."

She kissed him and turned out the light. When she came out of the bathroom, he was curled on his side, breathing deeply.

Alex twitched a bit and muttering something into his pillow. He did that sometimes. Just sounds, nothing comprehensible. She used to pay no attention. Now she listened.

She felt restless. Too full of booze and talk. She curled her body against her husband's back and said words that normally came from him. "You asleep?"

"Hmmm? Yeah. Asleep. What's the matter?"

"I want you to be unasleep."

Out of a pledge class of twenty-seven, nineteen women came to the reunion, seven from out of state. Of the missing women, Jen had lost track of three. Two others lived abroad. And two had other commitments—which, according to Jen, meant their husbands wouldn't let them come. The final missing member was Libby.

The reunion began with a brunch at the union followed by an afternoon bridge tournament. And in the evening, they had dinner with the actives at the Delta Gamma house. After dinner, actives and alumnae joined voices in the songs of their sisterhood. Helen still remembered all the words.

As predicted, conversation throughout the day included a lot of Libby talk. Libby, who had been so sweet, so crazy, so beautiful. And such talent! Everyone had expected great things of her.

They relived that last recital. How could anything have been more romantic? Was Zubov still with the university? "When Libby was in the class, he hardly knew the rest of us were there," said Marion Dungess Carter, who was now a professor of dance herself at the University of Oklahoma. "Such an intense man. I've always wondered if he didn't kill her in a jealous rage."

After dinner, the group adjourned to Helen's house for cheesecake and coffee to be followed in the evening by what Bonnie called "a little serious drinking." Jen had promised Helen's cheesecakes in the reunion invitations—and sent a clipping from the Boulder newspaper featuring Helen's recipe for praline crunch cheesecake and announcing that three of her cheesecakes would be among the items to be auctioned off at an upcoming benefit for the library.

Alex and the children arrived home from their movie and came in to say hello. Alex took the women on a tour of the house and stayed on to visit for a while. He got rave reviews after he had excused himself. If a handsome, charming husband guaranteed happiness, Helen should be delirious.

"God, Helen, this is fabulous," Gretchen Fairbanks Hightower said as she took a bite of cheesecake. The group's only widow, she had lost her husband in Vietnam. "What kind of cheesecake is it?" she asked.

"White chocolate macadamia nut," Helen answered. "The other one is apricot almond."

"She not only makes them from scratch," Jen bragged, "but she invents the recipes."

Everyone had to try both flavors. And insisted that Helen could sell the cheesecakes and make a fortune.

"Now, back to Libby," said Milly Richardson Freck, putting down her empty plate. Her husband was an assistant football coach at Notre Dame. "Is anyone still looking for her?"

"I was always a little bit afraid of her," admitted June Billings St. John, who had come all the way from Los Angeles for the reunion.

"Afraid of Libby!" Jen said. "Why in the world?"

"Afraid she wouldn't like me, I guess," June said with a shrug.

But several women insisted that Libby was one of those people who liked everyone. A darling girl.

"The cheesecakes are really fabulous," Gloria Addison Risenhover told Helen as she helped carry dishes to the kitchen. "But I never thought your claim to fame would be found in a kitchen."

"Neither did I," Helen admitted.

Gloria had been the pledge class president. She now lived in Omaha and presided over a house with six children. Other than Bonnie and Jen, Gloria was one of the few DG sisters Helen had stayed in touch with—but only through Christmas cards and birth announcements.

"Of course, Libby was going to be the famous one," Gloria said. "She never did like me, you know."

"Why do you say that?" Helen asked as she placed plates in the dishwasher.

"Because you and I spent too much time together. After we decided to room together our junior year, Libby told me it would be better if I lived at home that semester. I told her to bug off, and the next day every sweater in my bureau had been slashed with a razor blade. I'll never forget opening that drawer. It still makes my blood run cold to think about it."

Helen almost dropped a plate. She turned to stare at Gloria. "But you don't know that Libby did that."

"Yes, I do. You and I had become good friends. That wasn't allowed. I moved home. June wasn't the only one afraid of her."

Helen sank onto a bar stool. "I always wondered what happened. We had even bought those matching bedspreads."

For a dozen years, Helen's best friends had been only Jen, Bonnie, and Libby. Other friends existed only on the periphery of their circle of four. And Helen had wanted to expand her horizons. She wanted to know other people as well. She started spending time with Gloria, who was also majoring in English. They studied together a lot. And on nights when Helen wanted to stay out past closing, she spent the night with Gloria in her home near the campus.

Gloria wanted to live in the DG house her junior year. When she asked Helen to room with her the first semester, Helen had accepted, feeling both pleased and guilty. She was doing something without Libby's blessing.

"I was always a little surprised that she let you get married," Gloria was saying. "I thought sure she'd find some way to sabotage your engagement. She didn't want anyone else to get too close."

Helen carried the coffee pot into the living room for refills. The room was full of conversation and laughter. How strange to be with these women after so many years. Helen had first known them as young women barely out of girlhood. Now they were mature women in their mid-thirties with thickening waists and settling faces.

Bonnie was sitting on the floor with three other women, reliving the night of their initiation into the Delta Gamma sisterhood. A slumber party had been planned in Gloria's basement rec room. Libby had insisted they do something memorable in honor of the occasion—like stealing the bell from the roof of the Old Mission Café.

Under Libby's direction, they had gathered up ladders and tools, commandeered vehicles, established lookouts. Ice coated the tile roof. Helen had never been so scared, the wind whipping against her back as she pried the bolted mounts out of the plywood. The bell was plywood, too. Not real at all. Which was just as well. A real bell would have weighed hundreds of pounds.

Later, in Gloria's basement, they had danced around their trophy bell, pouring beer on each other, laughing so hard their sides hurt. Libby was proclaimed the Mission Belle. After a time, she had clapped her hands, calling a halt to the hysteria, and made each of them in turn touch the bell and, with eyes closed, solemnly repeat the words, "I can do anything."

Even now, as much as Helen wanted to convince herself otherwise, she had adored Libby. Libby had enriched their lives and made them feel special, and the three friends had all loved her the best. But maybe even back then she had known that Libby was a bit mad.

Sabotage. Was that what was going on when Libby went with Alex to the cabin? Did she want the man himself or only to lure him away from Helen?

But why Alex and not Lenny and Ted?

At the podium, the president of the American Medical Association was overspeaking himself on what was obviously his favorite topic—keeping the government out of medicine.

Helen scooted her chair closer to Alex's and started rubbing her knee against his thigh.

He glanced at her and grinned.

They were sitting with four other doctor-wife couples at a round table in a sea of round tables for the Saturday-night banquet of the convention of the National Association of Obstetricians and Gynecologists being held at Kansas City's Crown

Center Hotel. One of the doctors was dozing, his wife studying her fingernails. The others seemed to be listening. As was the dozing doctor's young redheaded wife. A second wife. Or third. If her age didn't give her away, her jewelry would. First wives never merited such treasures. Helen wasn't paying attention to the speech. She'd heard it all before. She was thinking about later.

For three years now, Helen had declined offers to accompany Alex to out-of-town medical conventions. Hotel sex had always been more kinky. And now, after three years of careful sex, Helen needed more.

Last night, after all the wine and brandy, had been nice. Alex held her for a long time before and after. As she drifted off to sleep, she realized she hadn't thought of Libby—not even once. In fact, she hadn't thought of her for days, maybe weeks. She curled her body against her husband's back and inhaled the smell of his skin, absorbed his warmth. They were alive. And Libby was dead. She must be. Soon, it would be seven years since she'd disappeared.

Today, Helen had felt incredibly good. High. Like she'd won a race or climbed a mountain. And daring enough to go lingerie shopping this afternoon while Alex attended a seminar on "The Latest Trends in Infertility." In fact, the wives' printed schedule had "Free time for shopping" listed after the luncheon fashion show, and a packet of discount coupons from stores in the adjoining mall had been included in the welcoming packet.

Did Jen really wear this stuff, Helen wondered as she examined an amazing collection of boudoir lingerie.

She debated about the color. Pink or blue were for babies. White lace somehow seemed naughtier than black. She had used her coupon. Fifteen percent off.

She rubbed at Alex again, then took his hand, pulled it under the tablecloth and placed it on her thigh. He took a few seconds to comprehend, then glanced at her again and slid his hand under her skirt only to discover that she was wearing stockings and a garter belt. His eyebrows shot up.

Helen felt excited and silly.

He stroked the bare flesh above her right stocking, then moved his hand upward. Helen uncrossed her legs.

That was when he realized she wasn't wearing any panties.

"Christ," Alex whispered. The gray-haired doctor on Helen's right looked over at him.

Helen reached across to feel her husband's crotch, which was bulging. She wanted to laugh out loud.

Alex shifted his body so he was facing her and switched hands for better access.

Helen opened her legs. She was so wet she wondered if there would be a wet spot on the back of her skirt when she got up.

His finger slid in and out.

Alex was groaning. Softly. But the gray-haired doctor turned to stare.

Alex pushed his chair back and smiled apologetically at the those around the table. Holding his tux jacket closed in front, Alex pulled Helen's chair back with his spare hand.

She straightened her skirt before getting up. And followed him out of the room.

In the hallway, they burst out laughing. "I can't believe you did that," he said, struggling to catch his breath.

In the elevator, she unzipped him.

He pulled up her skirt and thrust his hand between her legs.

Once in the room, she pulled off her sequined sweater, revealing a lacy push-up bra with straps that dug in her shoulders but made her breasts look like Ann-Margret's. Alex pulled the half-cups back so her nipples popped out and bent over to nibble them. Helen pushed him away so she could step out of her skirt.

And there she was like something straight out of *Playboy*. Sort of. She was fleshy. Not enough waist. But the front view wasn't too bad if she stood up straight and held in her stomach. She looked in the mirror to see what Alex was seeing. A bit baroque, but definitely sexy. Someone else. Not Helen at all.

She pushed him down on the edge of the bed, kicked off her shoes and straddled his lap.

The image in the mirror was incredible. A man in a tux. A woman in her lacy white underthings. She wrapped her legs around him and rode him.

They came like thunder. Laughing. Gasping for breath. He rolled them back on the bed and hovered over her. Kissing her. Fondling her pushed-up breasts. Tugging gently at her hardened nipples with his teeth. Reaching between her legs to delight in how much wetness was there.

They took a shower together, then made love again, lingering this time, kissing endlessly. Helen was inside her own skin now, reaching out to him, begging him. She did love him. She said it over and over.

When finally they fell back on their pillows, Helen studied her husband's face in profile, watched him relax, his jaw slacken. Such a beautiful man. A shiver went through her. She loved him, and her love made her vulnerable.

She woke in the night chilled and reached for her nightgown. Alex's side of the bed was empty.

He was standing by the window, staring out at the city, holding the white lace garter belt, one of the stockings still attached.

She should have bought black, Helen realized with a pang. White was for Libby.

"She dressed up for you like that, didn't she?" Helen asked.

Alex jumped. Then groaned. "Don't, Helen. We were really good tonight. Can't we just leave it at that?"

"I don't know." She was shivering as she struggled into her nightgown.

He came to the bed and gathered her in his arms. "You've got to believe, my darling, that whatever happened in the past, whatever doubts I may once have had, that you're the woman I love, the woman I want to be married to, the woman I want to be happy with. Please, Helen, let's be happy. Misery isn't our style." He kissed her forehead, tenderly. Then her eyes, her nose, her chin.

"Will you tell me about her, explain what happened? It makes me crazy not to know. For three years, I've struggled with this. If I just knew, I could quit speculating and come to terms with it."

"No. I'm not going to put pictures in your head. It was sick, Helen. I wanted it to be over before it was."

"Do you know where she is?"

"You asked me that before. No, I don't know, and I don't care. I just hope she stays gone forever. She was poison."

$\mathcal{T} e n$

Evelyn Ballard looked much the same. A small, pretty woman with graying hair, a quiet smile, and wise eyes. The difference between her age and her husband's seemed to have increased. Fred Ballard was stooped and frail, fleshless skin hanging on bones, a man at the end of his time leaning heavily on his cane.

Bonnie tried to calculate how long it had been since she had last seen Libby's parents. At the fortieth anniversary party Jen had held for her parents, she decided. Five years back— after Bonnie had written the story marking the fifth anniversary of Libby's disappearance. And now, it was ten years. Hard to believe.

Bonnie had pulled the article out of her file and realized the only thing that had changed since she'd written it was the number of years Libby had been missing. Not one clue, not one shred of information had surfaced in all that time. Even Libby's friends didn't speculate much anymore. She was just gone. No understandable reason why.

Half-heartedly, Bonnie pointed out the anniversary to her editor. Did he want a story?

At first, Ralph said no. Then he'd decided a series on mysterious disappearances might be a good idea.

Jen's mother loved to redecorate. Helen's and Bonnie's mothers would occasionally rearrange the furniture. But except for worn carpet and faded upholstery, the front room at the Ballards' was exactly the same as it had been when they'd raced by it on their way upstairs to Libby's room or to the family room to say hello to Carl. The mantel clock still didn't work. A collection of delicate porcelain birds still occupied a round table by the window. The portrait of Libby on *pointe* still dominated the room. Carl still smiled out of a frame on the coffee table. The room smelled of furniture oil, and the lace curtains were freshly starched.

A television set had been left on in the back of the house. Soap opera music.

Bonnie had to stare a minute at Libby's picture. Her pose was so pure of line, her expression serene. Bonnie tried to recall freckles or moles on that flawless skin but could not.

"We're so pleased you called," Evelyn said, indicating Bonnie was to sit in the wingback chair. She and her husband took their seats across from her on the sofa. "We see that nice husband of yours on the television almost every night, and Jen tells us you're working on a book."

Bonnie felt a stab of guilt. *Jen stayed in touch.* "Jen *thinks* I should write a book," she explained. "If I get enough material, maybe I will someday. But for now, it's just a series for the newspaper on famous disappearances in the state."

"Yes, I saw the story in last Sunday's paper on that Italian family from Grand Junction. My goodness, you even called up their relatives in Rome and Canada. I showed it to Fred. I said, 'Just look what our Bonnie has written.' "

Fred Ballard cleared his throat with a wet, hacking sound, then fished in his sweater pocket for a rumpled handkerchief. Once found, he spat into it and returned it to his pocket. "So, you're here to talk about Libby, I suppose," he said.

"Yes. I wondered if anything else has occurred to you? Any new thoughts on what may have happened to her?"

"I told you five years ago," Fred said in his grating, old man's voice. "I think someone kidnapped her and killed her. Her car was never found. Someone drove off with her in it."

"You don't think she might have just run away?"

"She didn't take anything with her," Fred said. "Not her clothes. Her grandmother's jewelry. Her record collection. Her address book. Nothing. And she didn't have any money. She hadn't made a payment on that building for months. She owed people all over town."

"Maybe she wanted to leave the past behind and start over," Bonnie prodded.

"Maybe," Fred allowed in a tone that said he really didn't want to talk about it.

"Where are her things now?" Bonnie persisted. Twice before, when she'd been writing about Libby's disappearance, she'd asked to look through Libby's possessions and been refused. The police had already done that, Fred Ballard had informed her, and the private detective they'd hired.

"Eventually, we gave most of it to the Salvation Army," Evelyn explained, "after we gave up hope of her ever coming back."

"What about little things? Photographs, letters, yearbooks —stuff like that?"

Fred Ballard shook his head. "Why are you dragging all this up again?" he asked.

"Mostly because my editor assigned the series. But I think about Libby a lot. I'd liked to know what happened to her because I care about her. She was one of my best friends. If someone killed her, I'd like to see them brought to justice. If she's dead, she ought to be buried next to her brother."

"She didn't care about her brother," Fred said. "Didn't shed a tear when he died."

Bonnie stared at the old man. He didn't love Libby any more than she'd loved him. "Well, I'd still like to see her things," Bonnie persisted. "It might help me write the story."

"There's no need for you to write anything more about my daughter," Fred said. "It's all been said."

Evelyn walked with Bonnie out to her car. At the curb, she gave Bonnie a hug. "I'm sorry, dear. Fred's not himself, you know. And he still grieves for Carl. After all this time. Almost thirteen years now."

"But he doesn't grieve for Libby?"

"I like to think that he does. We don't talk about Libby much. But he looks at her picture some when he thinks I'm not watching."

"If she's dead, wouldn't *you* like to have her buried with Carl?"

"I'm not sure it really matters," Evelyn said, shading her eyes against the sunlight. "But I do think about it. She had a hard time when she was growing up. Fred and I spent all our time keeping Carl alive just a little bit longer. Fred doesn't think about Libby's side. Just because she wasn't sick didn't mean she didn't need her mother and father."

"He's very ill, isn't he?" Bonnie asked.

"Yes, the cancer's in his bones now. But even when he's

gone, Bonnie, there's nothing for you to see. Just a few recital programs, photographs, newspaper clippings. The rest of it, I got rid of. Her clothes, her shoes, her hairbrush, her cosmetics. I didn't want to open those boxes anymore or even think about them up there in the attic. The clothes even smelled like her." Evelyn had tears in her eyes. Her brown eyes had faded. Once, they had been as dark as Libby's.

"But will you let me look at the things you did save? It will make the story more poignant—a box of old dance programs —all that's left of a young dancer who aspired to greatness."

"But what you really want is clues. You want to solve the mystery," Evelyn said.

"Don't you want that, too?"

"Yes and no. I'm almost afraid to know."

After his dad had developed crippling arthritis, Alex's parents used their two-story cabin on the side of Carter Mountain less and less. With their blessing, Helen redecorated, modernizing the kitchen and bathroom, buying country quilts and rag rugs, making it hers. Even when the children were babies, she liked to go there if for no other reason than to sit on the broad front porch in the evening, to enjoy the view and smells and sounds of the mountains.

After she found the picture, Helen wondered if she'd ever go back to the cabin again. She didn't want to look at that front step and see Libby sitting there. She didn't want to lie in bed and wonder if Alex had made love to Libby there.

And they had had a house to build. Helen didn't have time for porch sitting.

The Echolses borrowed the cabin some. Alex's nurse and her family used it from time to time.

Beth often asked when they were going back. Helen found she missed the cabin, too. The mountains were calming. At the cabin, she forgot to worry about the holes Buster dug in their and the neighbors' yards, about the extra pounds on her hips, about the leaky basement. So after more than a year's hiatus, she had started going back to the cabin. That first time, she fried some chicken, bought two new mysteries, and packed the car. Buster recognized the signs and jumped in the station wagon at the first opportunity and waited patiently until their departure.

Alex came, too. That surprised Helen. She wasn't sure she wanted him to.

The first night, she and Alex got into bed without a word and rolled away from each other. After a time, Helen said in the darkness, "I can't sleep here," and went up to the loft and crawled into bed with Beth.

She couldn't sleep in Beth's bed, either.

She took her sleeping child in her arms, felt her breath against her neck. If only the love between a man and woman could be as strong and simple as mother love. As absolute.

In the night, she went back downstairs and put her arms around her husband. Alex was awake instantly. Maybe he hadn't been asleep. "I need you so," he whispered.

They kissed as though they were trying to devour each other. Hard kisses. She grasped at his shoulders, digging in her nails, wanting to inflict pain, love and hate at war inside her.

She started to come as soon as he entered her. Not a gradual building to shared climax. Just immediate hard waves of raw sensation.

The clinging afterward was better. Tender. He stroked her hair, kissed her eyes, her neck, her tears. But they said nothing. And in the silence, they retreated into their separateness, Libby back between them. Still, another obstacle had been overcome. They'd had sex at the cabin. And Helen knew they would come here again, which was good for their family even if she never could completely reclaim this place as her own.

As the children grew older, Helen hiked with them in the mountains, teaching them names of birds and wildflowers, helping them find wild berries and sassafras root. The cabin was a perfect place for young imaginations to flourish. They'd dig caves, pan for gold, stalk Russian spies and marauding Indians in the groves and ravines, always with Buster tagging along. In the evenings, they'd build a fire in the yard or in the big stone fireplace and roast wieners and marshmallows. There was no phone or television to intrude on the tranquillity.

Alex came with them if he could, but if he was off delivering babies, Helen and the children would still go. Sometimes they left on the spur of the moment. Other times, Helen would plan for days, making casseroles and pies, inviting Jen and her kids, or Ben and Beth would bring friends from school. Occasionally Bonnie would drive up for a night.

Helen would take Ben's Cub Scout den to the cabin for cookouts and nature walks. Beth celebrated her tenth birthday there with a slumber party.

When it was time to decide about the 1978 anniversary party, Alex suggested a big party at the Brown Palace for a horde of mutual friends. He and Ted could take care of some professional obligations while they were at it. Everyone would get a kick out of meeting Lenny in person. Maybe they could invite some of the CU football coaches. But it was Jen's year to plan the party, and she held out for the Radcliffs' cabin. "A whole glorious weekend of adult conversation, card playin' and drinkin' too much," she insisted. "We might even take a few hikes and pick enough berries for Helen to make a pie."

They converged on the cabin Friday afternoon, except for Bonnie, who left a message for Lenny at the station to say she would be late and for him to go on without her.

They settled in, making up the beds, putting up the badminton net, putting away food, making preparations for dinner, opening the first beers.

Ted and Alex took a football out in the sloping yard. Jen and Helen had slipped on jackets against the evening chill and went to wait for Bonnie in the rockers on the front porch. Such a peaceful evening, Helen thought. The night sounds just beginning. No breeze. The stars popping out here and there. The shadowed mountains all around them.

"Hey, Len, I'm hungry," Jen called out. "Where is that wife of yours?"

"Beats me," Lenny called back. "The message I got was that she had a hot story and would get here as soon as she could."

Jen settled back and began rocking gently. "God, it's nice here. Wasn't this a great idea I had?"

"A great idea," Helen agreed, her feet propped up on the porch railing.

Jen finished her beer and went inside for another.

"I wish Bonnie would hurry up," Helen fretted when Jen returned. "That road's difficult after dark."

"And you are bursting with something you want to tell us."

"Is it that obvious?"

"Only to certain people. What gives? You get to tell it twice this way. You're not pregnant or having an affair or anything stupid like that?"

Helen smiled. "Depends on what you call stupid. You know the cheesecakes I've been making for the Aspen Inn. Well, they want to serve them in their other restaurants—two in Denver, one in Colorado Springs, as well as the one in Aspen. And a couple of other restaurants have contacted me."

Jen stopped rocking and scooted her chair around so she was facing Helen. "You're really excited, aren't you?"

Helen nodded. "I'm a *businesswoman*. I've been making eleven dollars forty-two cents' profit on each cake, but I told the Aspen Inn guy I'm raising my prices, and he didn't bat an eye. I'm going to hire someone part-time to help me."

"Why, honey? Alex must be making an arm and leg with his practice. It's not like you need the money? What in the world made you start such a venture?"

"Because I need to do something," Helen said, resenting the need to explain. She should have waited for Bonnie. Bonnie would understand. "Because it's time. Because I'm damned good at it," she added. "Because people will pay me. I keep thinking about that woman who made the chocolate chip cookies and has gone public with her company. Being Alex's wife isn't enough. He's special because he's a doctor. I want to be feel special, too."

"I hate to tell you this," Jen said as she resumed her rocking, "but baking cheesecakes isn't going to get you those kind of strokes."

"Maybe not," Helen admitted. "But it's the only something I could come up with that I really wanted to do and feel confident about. I don't want to teach. I'm not executive material. I'm a homebody and a good cook."

"What does Alex say?"

"Not much."

"It sounds like so much work. You sure you wouldn't settle for bringing Junior League to Boulder?"

"I'll leave that high honor to someone else," Helen snapped.

"Hey, I've hurt your feelings, haven't I?" Jen asked, putting her hand on Helen's arm.

"No. I'm sure most people would agree with you. It's silly for me to knock myself out when my husband the doctor can make more in fifteen minutes than I can in a whole day, maybe a whole week. And Alex has always wanted me out of the kitchen. He would prefer a more sophisticated wife, not Betty Crocker. He wants a . . ."

Lenny was yelling at them. Helen stopped to listen. "She's coming," he called out. "I hear the Bronco on the hill."

Bonnie honked several times as she pulled up between Helen's and Jen's station wagons. Bonnie leaped to the ground. She ducked under the badminton net and ran across the yard to the house.

"They found her car," she was calling out. "They found Libby's car!"

Helen sat up straight and grabbed Jen's hand. "Oh, my God!" she said.

"Christ!" Jen said. "I don't believe it."

The men were racing toward the porch.

Bonnie collapsed on the bottom step, the others clustered around her, expressions stunned.

Helen looked at her husband, but he avoided her eyes. Her heart was pounding. *Libby's car.*

"Where?" Jen asked.

"In New Mexico. At the bottom of a pond. No sign of human remains. Jesus. After all these years."

"New Mexico?" Jen asked. "Why would her car be in New Mexico?"

Bonnie shrugged. "How would I know? Jesus, what a day. I'm starving and need a drink. Jesus, do I need a drink! And a hug from my husband."

It took Lenny a minute to react, but he sat beside her and put his arms around her. "Who found it?" he asked.

Helen handed Bonnie the open beer can she was holding

and stuffed her hands in the pockets of her jacket. They were shaking. All of her was shaking. *What did it mean?*

They all watched Bonnie drink, as though there was a clue in the way she downed her beer. Any makeup she'd had on this morning had long since vanished. Her hair was windblown, her blouse wrinkled. But there was excitement in the way she moved, sparkle in her eyes.

"An earthen dam crumbled on an abandoned farm pond miles out from Raton," she said in a rush. "Someone saw the top of the car and reported it to the sheriff. They pulled it out this morning and identified it as Libby's Thunderbird. Nothing in the car, but they're going to dig in the sediment for remains, clues, etc. I went by to see her parents. The police had already called."

"Oh, my," Jen moaned. "Are they okay?"

"Yeah. At least Mrs. Ballard seemed to be. Mr. Ballard wasn't too coherent. Evelyn said that finding the car doesn't help a bit. She still doesn't know where Libby is. She said the police asked her if she had any idea why Libby might have driven her car to New Mexico. She didn't."

"Were clues of any sort found in the car?" Helen asked.

Bonnie shook her head no. "Not that anyone has reported. I'm going down there and see for myself. The paper wouldn't dare assign anyone else to this story. I want to solve this thing. I want wire service. I want to stop thinking about it. Jesus. It's been twelve years."

"Why New Mexico?" Jen asked again. "I'd always wondered if maybe she didn't go back to New York and change her name."

"Why would she change her name?" Ted asked.

"So we couldn't find her," Jen answered.

"Let's cook the steaks," Alex said, still not looking at Helen. "I'll start the charcoal."

"Great idea," Bonnie said. "I didn't have time for lunch, and this beer is going straight to my head. Can you guys believe it? A *clue*, after all this time."

"The last time we saw her was at an anniversary party, and here we are again," Jen said. "Pretty strange."

After dinner, the women retired to the porch, while the men cleaned up the kitchen and Lenny made the usual brandy alexanders—a tradition. Like the anniversary party itself.

The night sounds were soothing. The air was full of forest smells—pine and fermenting earth. The nighttime sky wasn't as spectacular as it used to be—Denver's brown cloud was creeping up the Front Range.

Helen was quiet while Jen and Bonnie went over that night twelve years before. She wanted to put her hands over her ears. Libby's dress. Libby's tears. An image of her husband's face as he took Libby's pulse.

"I've always felt guilty," Jen admitted. "It is so stupid. We couldn't go on being her little playmates forever. God, I remember when I told her I was engaged. She was so sweet, but I knew how disappointed she was. I felt like I had broken her heart."

Jen stood and leaned over the porch railing, staring out into the darkness. "Where in the hell is she?"

Lenny served the drinks and raised his glass in a toast. "To number seventeen. And friendship. Marriage. And most of all to my darling Bonnie."

Seventeen. Soon it would be twenty and more. The years hurrying by.

The drink was smooth with cream and strong with good brandy. Helen sipped it gratefully. She wished Alex would sit beside her. Touch her hand. What was he thinking now? Did he feel as strange as she did?

"I want Jen and Helen to drive down to New Mexico with me," Bonnie announced.

"I don't think that's necessary," Alex said from the shadows.

"I wasn't asking your permission," Bonnie said dryly. "Maybe they can help me figure this thing out. I need them to come."

Jen touched Helen's hand. "What do you think, honey?" she asked.

"Sure," Helen said. "Why not?" But she wondered if they weren't looking for the key to unlock Pandora's box.

At last, she could stand it no more. She went to her husband and slipped her arm around his waist. He pressed his lips against her brow.

Eleven

It was almost dark when they pulled into the Raton, New Mexico, Holiday Inn. The motel marquee said, "Welcome, Racing Fans." The desk clerk offered them free racing forms.

Six hours of smoke from Bonnie's cigarettes had given Helen a headache, which repeated aspirin didn't help. Or maybe it wasn't the smoke at all. Helen felt uneasy. Confused. Why was she doing this? Why did she need to go stare at a dead car? Wasn't Libby already enough of a wedge in her marriage?

Last night, Helen told Alex that Mrs. Benson was coming in to look after the children. "So you're really going?" he asked from the kitchen table. The children were already in bed. Helen was heating his dinner. Alex had just delivered his fourth baby of the week. This evening's family got a boy after four girls.

He had grinned as he told her how thrilled they were. Now, he was frowning.

She nodded. Yes, she was really going. She was tempted to put the blame on Bonnie. *Bonnie wants me to go. Bonnie insisted.*

"I want to go," she said.

"And just what do you hope to accomplish?" Alex asked, opening a can of beer and pushing aside the newspaper.

Usually, on his late nights, after he had finished any comments he had about his day, he would only half listen to Helen as she chattered about this and that while he drank his evening beer and looked through the evening paper.

But tonight, she had his full attention. "Obviously, we hope to get a lead on Libby," she said, putting a loaf of her homemade sourdough bread in front of him. And a jar of preserves made with wild crab apples she'd found near the cabin.

"And just why do you three women think you can do what the police haven't been able to do?" he challenged.

"Because we care," she said. "Because we knew her better than anyone else. Because maybe I can stop thinking about her so much if I know what happened."

"In other words, you want to prove to yourself that I had nothing to do with her disappearance." His voice was too soft. Too controlled.

Helen reached in the cupboard for a plate. "Maybe."

"I suppose that every time I leave town, you wonder if I've gone to see her."

"It has crossed my mind."

Alex swore and threw the can of beer against the pantry door.

Helen jumped.

Beer splattered everywhere.

She couldn't look at his face.

The oven timer buzzed, but Helen ignored it. She went off to bed, leaving Alex to deal with his dinner and the mess.

The motel dining room was full, with many people studying racing forms over their meals. After dinner, the three women went to the bar for a nightcap.

A man wearing cowboys boots and a Stetson asked Jen to dance. They did a smooth two-step to "Tulsa Time," and Jen came back to the table flushed and pleased.

But she smiled and shook her head no the second time he asked her.

Helen understood. Jen didn't want to start something. One dance was all the man would get. Jen didn't play games.

"You think Ted is faithful to you?" Helen asked.

"Yes," Jen said, gesturing to the waitress for another glass of wine. "I'd know if he wasn't. Besides he's getting so fat, who'd have him but me?"

Bonnie admitted she worried about Lenny sometimes. He was gone from home so much. All his fans weren't male. "What about you, honey?" Jen asked Helen. "You don't think Alex has ever been unfaithful, do you?"

"I don't think any woman ever knows for sure."

The next morning, a boyish deputy sheriff named Carson took them to a salvage yard to see the car.

It was still bright red. The windows were broken out, but it looked surprisingly intact after twelve years under water.

They stood there, staring at it. Libby's jaunty little Thunderbird. With the hard-topped roof that came off. Her parents had bought it for her graduation from CU. "To soothe their guilt," Libby claimed. She'd driven the car to New York. And back.

Helen had driven the car to Libby's apartment that last night. Helen had still loved Libby then, been concerned about her. Now, she hated her. Hated this car. Hated pretending she still loved her. Maybe she wouldn't do that anymore—pretend.

"I wish it could talk," Bonnie said.

"I can see her still, driving ninety miles an hour, daring God and Highway Patrol to make her slow down," Jen said.

Deputy Carson explained that the car was starting to rust out, but when they pulled it out of the water, there hadn't been a spot of rust. "And the tires were still inflated," he added, kicking a tire with a booted toe to prove his point.

He explained how the silt that filled the inside of the car had been carefully sifted but revealed nothing. The upholstery had completely rotted away, revealing the car's metal skeleton.

"We figure someone rolled the car down the incline and into the pond," he said. "When we pulled it out of the water last Friday, the windows popped out from the pressure of the water inside. But they had been rolled up. Unless the windows are down, you can't open the doors of a submerged car 'cause of the pressure. No one was in that car when it hit the water. We bulldozed the bottom of the pond just to cover all bases, though—like someone going in after it and not making it out again."

"Why would anyone get rid of a perfectly good car like that?" Helen asked. "I can understand getting rid of a body in a car, but to get rid of just a car doesn't make sense."

"Maybe the body's someplace else, and the car was incriminating evidence," the deputy speculated. "Or maybe the lady didn't want to be traced."

Other than a spare tire and a rusting jack, the only thing in the trunk was a rotted mass of wool that could have been a blanket.

"No suitcase or purse?" Bonnie asked.

Carson shook his head.

"What about the glove compartment?"

"A hairbrush and a metal nail file. Paper doesn't last long in water."

"That's it?" Bonnie asked.

" 'Fraid so."

"What happens to the car?" Helen asked.

"The woman's father said to sell it for salvage when we're done with it," the deputy said.

"Has a picture of Elizabeth Ballard been circulated to see if anyone remembers her?" Helen asked.

"Yeah. The Boulder PD wired one to the local newspaper. It appeared night before last with the story about finding the car. But no one's called in. The newspaper says they'll use it one more time. Pretty woman, your Elizabeth. When I talked to her father on the phone, he sounded like he didn't want to be bothered. But you ladies must have liked her a lot to come all this way."

"She was like our sister," Bonnie said. Jen nodded her agreement. Helen looked away.

They waited while Bonnie took a number of photographs, including a couple with Deputy Carson standing beside the car.

He took them to his office, where they sipped tepid, oily coffee while he drew a map, showing them how to get to the place the car had been found.

The twelve miles seemed more like twenty on the rough roads. The pond was on the edge of a mountain meadow that was enclosed by a crumbling rail fence. Across the meadow were the ruins of a long-abandoned farm house along with a collapsed barn and several outbuildings.

It would have been easy to roll the car down the short, steep slope into the pond. They could see where the center of the earthen dam had given way, allowing enough water to escape so that the top of the little car was revealed.

The pond was completely empty now. According to Deputy Carson, all that was found in the mud at the bottom were animal bones. A forensic anthropologist at the state crime bureau had examined them to make sure.

The three women stood on the rim of the empty pond and stared down at the muddy bottom. "I shouldn't have dragged you guys down here," Bonnie admitted. "I don't know what I thought I'd find. Evidence or something. Libby living as a hermit or the head of a new religious order. *Something.*"

Jen linked arms with Bonnie. "I wanted to come. I was curious as hell. More so now than before. Why here? What possible reason is there for her car to be in a pond twelve miles west of Raton, New Mexico?"

They walked over to the farm house. The roof was gone. A rusty pump stood sentry by the back door. An even rustier pot-bellied stove sat in what had once been a kitchen. Pieces of linoleum still clung to the floor. A family had lived here, trying to carve out a living on this rocky scrape of land. Raised children. Been happy and sad. Now they were gone.

"God, how depressing," Jen said.

"We're all just passing through," Helen said.

"I'm glad I've got you guys as traveling companions," Bonnie said.

The three women hugged, in the kitchen of the lonely, roofless farm house. Helen found she had tears in her eyes.

They peered under the collapsed roof of the barn and into a chicken coop and adjoining shed. No skeletal remains. No suitcase or purse. Helen found a large Mason jar. "You don't see the two-quart ones much anymore," she explained. "I could use it to store pasta."

But she really didn't want it in her kitchen. She put the jar on the back step for someone else to find.

Helen took a turn at the wheel of the Ranger as they headed back through Raton and up I-25, the Front Range on their left, the endless flat plain of eastern Colorado on their right. Normally, Helen would have taken great pleasure in the melancholy beauty of this great empty land. Today, she was too preoccupied.

Libby was back among them. And Helen was too tired and confused to face her alone. "Alex had an affair with her," she said, keeping her gaze on the lonely highway.

She sensed Jen stiffening beside her, Bonnie leaning forward from the backseat. "What are you saying?" Jen demanded, her tone almost hostile.

"Alex and Libby."

"Christ, Helen! Are you sure?" Bonnie demanded.

"Yeah. I'm sure."

"*Alex and Libby,*" Jen said in disbelief. "No way. How can you possibly know a thing like that?"

"He admitted it after I found a picture he'd taken of her in front of the cabin. It was with his Vietnam stuff. I knew what it meant as soon as I saw it. The day I cut my hand." Helen opened her hand and stared at the scar across it, remembering that awful day.

"Libby never went to the cabin with any of us," Helen continued, "so it had been just the two of them there. And the way she looked in that picture. *Seductive.* I'd never seen Libby like that. She was being that way for Alex, posing for him. All those months I was crazy with missing him in Vietnam and praying for him, and he was looking at *her* picture. I didn't think I'd ever be able to go to the cabin again. But I did."

"The bastard," Jen said, reaching over to squeeze Helen's arm. "And *Libby!* Our little vestal virgin. God, we didn't know her at all. And you, Helen—how did you stand it?"

"Don't make me cry, Jen. I'm driving."

"I always thought she didn't care about sex," Bonnie said. "And *Alex!* He'd be the last one I'd think would do a thing like that."

"Thanks a lot," Jen said.

"You know what I mean," Bonnie said. "Alex was always more proper. Lenny and Ted were always teasing her. Telling her she needed to get laid. Trying to find out if she ever screwed Zubov."

"Lenny and Ted didn't have anything to hide," Helen said.

"What did Alex say when you told him about the picture?" Jen asked.

"For me to let the past die. That he loved me and wanted to stay married to me. He said it happened before we were married. And so, that's what I've been trying to do—get on with things. But it's hard."

"And now with all this car business, the past comes roaring back," Bonnie said. "I thought you and Alex seemed awfully quiet the other night."

Helen nodded, hands firmly on the wheel. Concentrating on the road to keep back the tears.

"Why did you wait so long to tell us?" Jen asked.

Helen waited until a truck passed before answering. "Because I was humiliated," she said. "Because you guys wouldn't feel the same about my husband, and I was afraid it would change our friendship. And I had to sort it all out, figure out what I wanted to do. My oldest friend and my husband—I was never so hurt in my life. Just because it happened years ago didn't make it any easier. But somehow, I blame her more than him. Isn't that strange? How could any man resist her? *The snow princess.* Was it Ted or Lenny who called her that? She seemed so unattainable."

"At least it was before you were married," Jen said.

"But do you know that for sure?" Bonnie asked.

"No, I don't," Helen admitted. "Not really. We didn't see her for years. But he had that picture with him in Vietnam. I know he did. Then when he came back home, she did too. I can accept him having a fling with her before we were married. I'm not sure I could accept it if he had started up with her again when we all came back to Denver. But I think of how it must have been for them. Every time they looked at each other, they must have thought about *their* secret. Maybe whatever it was that made them want to sneak off and screw before Alex and I got married didn't go away when he said, 'I do.' "

"Do you think they were in love?" Bonnie asked.

"I don't know about Alex," Helen admitted. "And I wonder now if Libby ever loved anyone. Even us."

"Maybe it's out of line to ask, but—" Bonnie paused. "Does Alex know what happened to her?"

"He said he doesn't. He said the last time he saw her was when he took her home from the anniversary party."

"And you believe him?" Bonnie asked, reaching between the seats for the cigarette lighter.

"Yeah, until I have some reason not to. Obviously, he didn't run off with her. But maybe he has her secreted away in a mountain love nest. Maybe the guys don't go fishing at all." Helen laughed. "Wouldn't that be a kill? Maybe they buy all that fish at the market."

"That's not funny," Jen said, her voice hard.

They stopped for a sandwich and gas in Pueblo. Jen took a turn at the wheel, and Helen crawled in the backseat.

"For the first time in a dozen years, I'm not sure I want to know what happened to her," Bonnie said, lighting another cigarette. "Her mother said she was afraid to know."

"I want to know," Helen said. "I'm tired of thinking about it, tired of living under her shadow."

"I think Evelyn Ballard knows something," Bonnie said. "But Mr. Ballard didn't want any more sleuthing."

"He's dying," Jen said.

"I know," Bonnie said. "He was in the hospital for almost a month. They had just come home when I called about the car. Evelyn said he wants to die at home."

Jen asked Bonnie for one of her cigarettes. She inhaled deeply then choked a bit, clutching at the steering wheel to steady herself. "Sometimes I wonder if all of our husbands weren't in love with her," she said a sigh. "I used to get jealous when Ted danced with her. And all three of them liked to watch her. Of course, the three of us did, too. Libby was fascinating. Addicting, almost. The way she moved. The way she held her head. The line of her neck. You know—Ted called me Libby once when we were making love. He swore he didn't—that I imagined or misunderstood—but I don't think so."

"Jesus. And you just let it go?" Bonnie asked.

"Of course, I did. Do you think Lenny's never thought about another woman when he makes love to you? Hell, I've fanta-sized about other men when Ted and I made love."

"Yeah, about Alex," Helen accused from her corner in the backseat.

"And you've never had an unpure thought, I suppose," Jen said dryly, with a challenging glance over her shoulder.

Another silence filled the car.

"I wasn't sure that's what he said," Jen said finally. "Maybe he didn't say 'Libby, baby.' Maybe he said 'Love you, baby.' "

"What are we going to do now?" Helen asked.

"Stay friends," Jen answered at once.

"And find out what happened to her," Bonnie added.

"Yes. That's what we should do," Helen agreed. "But it scares me to death."

"You still love Alex in spite of everything, don't you?" Jen asked.

"I love him, and I love our family. But it's been a rough three years. I can't get Libby out of my head. I call the hospital sometimes just to make sure that's really where Alex has gone. I look through his billfold while he's in the shower. I've even searched his medical office. I don't even know what I'm looking for. Libby's secret phone number? Some other woman's phone number? Another photograph? But I don't really want to find anything. I want to believe that she was just an escapade. If it was some other woman, I might be able to believe that. But Libby? Libby was different. Libby needed to own people."

Twelve

"I think we should spend the night in Colorado Springs instead of driving on in tonight," Jen said.

"Yeah," Bonnie agreed. "Helen needs a little decompression time before she surfaces."

Helen started to protest. Alex was expecting her tonight.

But then, what difference did it make? He was already mad at her. "I have to make sure Mrs. Benson can stay over," she said. "There has to be someone in the house in case Alex gets called to the hospital."

They used a pay phone at a service station. Mrs. Benson agreed to stay. Jen left a message with Mandy. Bonnie left a message at the station for Lenny.

Jen drove on into Colorado Springs, taking the first exit,

pulling into the first motel. She insisted Helen take a long bath while she and Bonnie found something for dinner. Helen was stretched out on the bed in her robe when they returned with Chinese food and a six-pack.

"I don't want you to tell your husbands about Alex and Libby," Helen said, accepting a beer from Bonnie. "And I don't want Alex to know that I told you. Let's keep everything as normal as possible for now, okay? Everyone friends."

While they ate, they started planning. Bonnie fished her reporter's notebook out of her purse and kept notes as they reconstructed times, dates, circumstances, trying to jar each other's memories.

These strategy sessions continued in the weeks that followed, with telephone calls, meetings at the midway Howard Johnson's, or Helen driving down to Denver.

They made lists of every man Libby had dated since high school. Of friends and acquaintances. Of her dance students and their parents. Of peripheral people—dentists, doctors, bankers, insurance agents, mechanics, repairmen. Of the trips she had taken. Of anyone who might be classified as an enemy. And then they listed questions.

Was she in love with anyone?

Was anyone in love with her?

What was she wearing that last night?

They kept going over the last night they saw her, writing down every bit of conversation they could remember, what they ate, what everyone wore, anything to trigger memories.

Libby had acted so strangely. Maybe she was suffering from some sort of emotional breakdown. Maybe she went out again after Alex took her home. Maybe someone saw her. But after so many years, how could they pick up the trail?

Helen asked Alex what Libby's pulse had been that night.

"God, you women have gone crazy," he responded.

"Why? Because I want to know if her pulse was elevated."

"Of course, it was elevated. She had been dancing around the room."

"Then if you knew it would be, why did you bother to take it?" she had asked.

Had Libby been murdered? Bonnie started another list. *Murder suspects.*

"Should we put Zubov on it?" Bonnie asked.

"He was out of town," Helen reminded her.

"He could have hired someone to kill her," Jen said.

"Not his style," Helen insisted. "If he wanted her dead, he'd have done it himself."

"Did the police ever verify that he really was out of town?" Bonnie asked.

"I suppose we have to check him out," Helen said. "But put him down at the bottom of list."

"Then who goes at the top?" Bonnie wanted to know. "And in between?"

"What about those strange men she was always taking up with?" Jen suggested. "God, I used to wonder where she found them all. Maybe one of them got mad when they figured out she was only playing a game."

"Yeah. I think she still went to roadhouses," Bonnie said. "Remember that place up by Boulder she used to drag us to? She could have picked up some total stranger who did her in —like that book you were talking about, Jen. *Looking for Mr. Goodbar.*"

"If we believed Mr. Goodbar killed her, we wouldn't be going to all this trouble," Helen said. "We'd never find a total stranger after all these years."

"Okay, then," Bonnie said. "Who do we list as suspects?"

"Her father maybe," Helen offered.

"*Helen,*" Jen chided.

"Why not?" Helen asked. "They couldn't stand each other. Mr. Ballard sure isn't interested in anyone snooping around."

"Fred Ballard did not kill his own daughter," Jen said indignantly.

Bonnie wrote "Mr. Goodbar," "F. Ballard," and "Zubov" near the bottom of an otherwise empty page.

Bonnie went to see the Denver police detective who had investigated Libby's disappearance. Bill Weatherford liked Bonnie and had given her information for stories in the past. They always flirted a bit before getting down to business—this time, Bonnie asked him to reopen the case.

No plans for that, he informed her. But he was willing to tell her what he knew. Yes, Libby had been broke. The bank had already started foreclosure on the Broadway property. She had lots of creditors.

"Do you think any of them were mad enough to kill her?" Bonnie asked.

"Killing a person doesn't get your money back," he said, leaning back in his chair, folding his hands behind his head.

"What about the dance professor? He was involved with her."

"Yeah. Zubov. We checked him out. He really was out of state when she disappeared. In New York. And don't forget, there's no evidence that anyone killed her. Or even that she's dead. There was no blood, no body, no known motive, nothing."

Jen talked to Libby's dentist and her banker. Helen visited the Ballard family doctor.

They fanned out in Libby's old neighborhood, asking questions. But no one remembered Elizabeth Ballard's School of Dance. The building itself now housed a law firm.

They visited the contractor who had turned the dance school into an office building. Was there anything strange about the building? "You mean did I find a body in the walls?" he had asked with a chuckle.

Fred Ballard died in August. Evelyn decided on a graveside service. Jen's and Bonnie's parents came together from the old neighborhood. A few other neighbors were there.

The canopy flapped in the hot, dry wind. Evelyn was seated by herself on a row of folding chairs. Her sister was in the hospital and couldn't make the journey from Florida. Fred's brother and cousin were too elderly to travel from Indiana. Bonnie, Jen, and Helen stood behind Evelyn, the rest of the mourners clustered behind them in the square of shade. The same minister who'd conducted Carl's service kept his remarks brief. *A man who lived for his family. Beloved father and husband.*

The mourners waited quietly to pay their respects. Evelyn thanked them one by one for coming. Yes, she'd let them know if there was anything they could do.

Bonnie had wondered what would comprise a discreet period of time before she could talk to Evelyn Ballard again about Libby's disappearance. Ask to see her things. But Evelyn surprised her. "Why don't you girls come by next week," she said, hugging each of them.

"The minister didn't say anything about folks dropping by after the service. You're not going home to an empty house, are you?" Jen asked.

"Yes, I am, dear. I've had enough company the last couple of days. I told the church ladies to save their casseroles. I'll be fine."

They met at Jen's house the following Saturday and drove to their old neighborhood, to Libby's house.

Libby the ballerina still presided over the living room. Carl still smiled out of a frame on the coffee table.

Evelyn looked pale and tired. "You need to take care of yourself," Jen told her. "Just because you're alone now doesn't mean you shouldn't cook real meals. And go out sometimes. Did Mother call? She and Daddy and I want you to go to the symphony with us the rest of the season. I've decided to let Ted off the hook. He sleeps through most of the concerts anyway."

Evelyn smiled. "Yes, she called. We'll see. Now, how can I help you girls?" she asked.

"We went to New Mexico last June, Evelyn," Jen began, "after Libby's car was found. Somehow seeing that little red car made not knowing what happened to her all the more unacceptable. You know how much we loved her. All three of us thought of her as our best friend."

"You girls knew a different Libby than I did," Evelyn interrupted. "In this house, she wasn't very happy. Libby thought her father and I loved her brother more than we loved her. So, she found herself another family to love—you three girls. She assumed you felt the same about her until you all fell in love and got married. She didn't take that well. She thought you at least owed her a few years of chasing dreams."

"We did love her like family," Bonnie said. "But people grow up and go their own way. That's how life is."

"I couldn't believe it when Fred wanted to get her a car for graduation," Evelyn continued, refilling their cups with tea from a china pot. "He even let her pick it out. We were already in debt, but I think it was his way of saying he was sorry. But a car is not the same as love. I must admit, however, that I breathed a sigh of relief when she drove away in it to New York. With her gone, I didn't have to feel guilty all the time."

"You told me to come back when Mr. Ballard died," Bonnie

reminded Evelyn. "What can you tell me that will help us find out what happened to Libby?"

Evelyn patted Bonnie's hand. "Yes, dear. I haven't forgotten why you're here. But I'm getting old and need to ramble. I thought that after Carl finally died, Fred and I would find some peace and have a chance to rebuild our life. But Libby came back to Denver and upset it again. We tried to reconcile things with her, but she had a score to settle. Carl had gotten all our love and attention. Libby was left to fend for herself. I was always cooking Carl's favorite dishes. I don't even remember what Libby's were. If Carl wanted a book or game, he got it. If Libby wanted something, she was reminded of Carl's medical bills." Evelyn sighed a bit, fluttered her hands. "Jen dear, would you hand me that decanter? I like to take a little sherry in my afternoon tea."

Evelyn poured sherry into her half-empty cup, took several sips, then leaned her head back against the high chair back before resuming. Bonnie was sitting on the edge of her seat, hardly daring to breathe, certain that Evelyn had secrets to tell.

"When she disappeared," Evelyn continued, "we didn't know what happened to her, but we knew she wasn't coming back. We knew she was dead. And it broke my heart. Both of my children gone. I'd always thought that after Carl died, Fred and I could do better with Libby, make it up to her somehow. And now, we were never to have the chance. But at least life would be easier with her gone. Then Fred got stomach cancer. He had surgery and chemotherapy and more surgery and more chemotherapy. Now he's gone, too. It's only me. I had been looking forward to quiet years on my own with my television programs and my garden. A cat for my lap. My sister kept saying I should come live with her in Florida after Fred passed on, but I didn't want to do that, not for a few years anyway. But now, I find that I'm not very well, and I have this need to get things in order. Maybe this family of mine that was so unsuccessful in life can at least get tidied up in death. Remember, Bonnie, when you said that Libby should be buried among her own? Well, you were right. If you find her, will you put her beside her mother? I did love her. But I was always disappointing her. She wanted perfect love, and I didn't have it to give to her."

Bonnie swallowed hard. *Evelyn—alone and dying.* Jen was sniffling. Helen was reaching in her purse for a Kleenex.

"Oh, dear," Evelyn said. "Now, I've made you girls cry. Please don't. The doctor says I should manage just fine for quite a while. Maybe even a couple of years. I won't get a cat but maybe a bird. Birds don't get so attached. And I can plant a few flowers and some tomatoes this summer. I'll have radiation as long as it helps, but I don't want to live on and on like Carl and Fred. I think it's really better to know ahead of time. I can get the house cleaned out. Write letters to old friends. Say some thank-yous. I won't need to write to you three now, will I? I have you right here to say thank you for being my Libby's friends. And you will bury her properly if she's ever found, won't you?"

They nodded. Jen blew her nose. Bonnie cleared her throat and asked, "How can you be so certain that Libby's dead?"

"Well, I could understand her leaving behind possessions, but there was money, too. We didn't find it until we cleared out her apartment and were storing some of her things here in this house. She had it locked in an old cedar chest up in the attic—under all her old costumes. In a shoe box. Almost seventy-five thousand dollars. In large bills. Some of them brand-new. She would have taken it along."

Helen gasped. Bonnie's and Jen's eyes met. *Money.* Bonnie could feel her pulse quicken.

"We waited six months—in case she came back," Evelyn

continued. "Then Fred said we were entitled to the money. He had cosigned the note for the down payment on Libby's building. Almost twenty thousand dollars we were going to have to pay the bank. And we still had so many debts left over from Carl. A second mortgage on the house. I didn't feel right about it. The money had to belong to someone. But Fred said if someone had a rightful claim to it, they'd inquire about it. We never told the police. Never paid any taxes on it. I used to worry we'd go to jail if anyone found out."

"Do you have any idea where the money came from?" Bonnie asked.

"Fred said it wasn't honest money, that she'd either stolen it or was blackmailing someone. But I kept trying to come up with a good reason. Maybe she'd won a contest. Or found it someplace. Or was keeping it for someone. But no one gives away a lot of money without publicity. And no one seemed to be missing seventy-five thousand dollars. I even wondered if someone she'd known in New York left it to her. Then Fred decided she was blackmailing someone. And maybe that person got rid of her to keep her quiet."

"Then why didn't you tell the police?" Jen asked. "The money could have been a valuable clue. Surely finding out what happened to your daughter was more important than paying your bills."

"Fred didn't want the world to know what an evil person she was. He said whatever happened to her was her own doing."

"And you?" Helen asked. "What did you think?"

"That the truth would hurt people."

"Why did you think that? Was there anything with the money?" Bonnie asked. "Letters? A diary?"

"No," Evelyn answered firmly. "We didn't find anything like that." She took another sip of her sherry-laden cup. "She wasn't a bad girl, you know. Not a bad girl at all. And such a dancer! She should have stayed in New York. Some dancing for her was better than none at all. But she was angry. Angry at dancing. Angry at the world. Angry at her parents." Tears were rolling down her crinkled cheeks, leaving a trail in her powdery rouge.

"And angry at us," Helen said.

Evelyn nodded. "Yes, she blamed you girls. The dream had been for the four of you. It didn't work with just her. Nobody knew or cared who she was."

Evelyn showed them the bureau drawer where she kept Libby's mementos and left them to their looking.

Bonnie and Helen pulled out the drawer and set it on the floor. The three of them knelt around it and began searching through Libby's past. Yearbooks. Recital programs. Certificates. Shoes boxes of photographs and newspaper clippings.

Tucked in the pages of a CU yearbook, Helen found Libby's copy of the picture taken at The Sink their last night as undergraduates. Their faces had been carefully cut out and white paper taped behind the holes. Libby was sitting in the booth with three faceless companions.

"Jesus," Bonnie said, staring at the mutilated photograph.

"She must have hated us," Jen said. "Were we that awful to her? Poor Libby. Poor mixed-up Libby."

"Poor mixed-up Libby was a monster," Helen said, reaching for the photograph. "And I know what you're thinking. But Alex couldn't have given her that money," she said as she methodically tore the photograph into tiny pieces. "We didn't have any. The month she disappeared, we had to borrow the rent from my parents."

Thirteen

"Why are you ladies taking up this quest now?" Mikael Zubov asked Helen and Bonnie from behind his desk.

He had remembered them. He asked about Jen—with the beautiful blond hair.

Such a tidy desk, Helen thought, remembering other professional offices with clutter everywhere. But dance professors didn't given written tests or write scholarly papers.

Now past sixty, Zubov still maintained his lean dancer's body. And he was still sleekly handsome, like an aging Rudolph Valentino.

Bonnie was answering him. "Recently, we've learned some things about Libby that we didn't know before. We know someone took her car to Raton and got rid of it." Zubov nodded. He knew about that. He would have read it in the newspaper. "We know that she had a great deal of money hidden away," Bonnie continued. "And we know that she wasn't above betraying her friends. We hoped you might be able to help figure out some more things about her."

"I told the police everything twelve years ago," he explained, coolly, toying with a silver letter opener.

"Yes, but maybe you remembered something over the years that might shed some new light on Libby's disappearance," Helen said. "Maybe you knew things about her you didn't realize until much later or didn't seem important enough for you to tell the police."

Zubov put down the letter opener and moved his chair back an inch or two. He's going to get up and show us to the door, Helen thought.

But he relaxed and fixed his gaze between the two women. "Yes. Hindsight often cures blind spots. I realize now that I never should have been her teacher. Great teachers maintain a distance from their students. They maintain authority. Discipline. With Libby, I found that impossible."

"What do you think happened to her," Bonnie asked. She took a package of cigarettes out of her purse and put them back when she realized there was no ashtray.

"I think she is dead, but it is just a feeling. Looking back, I wonder if she wasn't destined to die young. Life had to be on her terms or not at all. I can't imagine her as anyone's mother or wife," he said, leaning his head against the high back of the chair.

Helen remembered all the rumors about Zubov that had floated about the campus—hints of a tragic life, a young wife killed in the war, children he couldn't find after the war, a dramatic defection to the West. But no one knew anything for sure. When Bonnie had tried to interview him for the student newspaper, he had responded, "I'm a dancer. That's all you need to know."

"I think those of us who were involved with Libby need a way to close the door," Helen explained. "I think that's what our little investigation is all about. We want to be done with her. Not knowing what happened keeps her alive."

"And you are ready for her to die," he said, nodding. "Yes, I can understand that. But isn't Mrs. Brewster trying to keep her alive on the pages of her newspaper by making a legend out of her?"

"She's already a legend," Bonnie said. "What I want is the truth. There's been enough speculation."

"I suppose," he said. "I have decided to leave Colorado after the fall term. So I guess it doesn't matter what I tell you."

He paused, and they waited. Helen leaned forward in her chair. Bonnie looked like she was holding her breath.

"I miss my native tongue," he continued. "Since I can never go back to my native land, I will live among my fellow Russians in New York and drink good vodka and never witness another amateur ballet as long as I live."

He paused again. "You will be disappointed. There is not much I can tell you. She let me do things for her. Let me teach her what I could. Let me escort her around when she needed someone who looked well in evening attire. Let me help her start her school. The police asked endless questions. One detective accused me of 'knowing something.' But I did not."

"When was the last time you saw her?" Bonnie said.

"A few days before she disappeared. She drove up here. A turnabout. Normally, one went to Libby. She was very troubled. And ill, I think. Not herself at all."

"What did she want?" Bonnie prodded. She had taken out
a cigarette anyway and was holding it unlit between two fingers.

"I'm not sure exactly. She hated her life. And she could not
figure out how to make things different, but I had heard all that
before. I asked her to marry me—that, too, was nothing new.
The asking had become a habit. And she always said no, that
she would never marry. But the next day she called to say she
was actually considering it. The strangest thing, though, all at
once I realized I did not want her—at least not anymore. She
had exhausted me—I had no more energy to give her. I told
her this and hung up the phone. I didn't even cry. I taught my
afternoon class and had dinner with friends, then packed for a
trip I was taking to New York. I felt normal. Relieved even.
When I returned from my trip, I learned that Libby had vanished. I often wondered what would have happened if I had
rushed down to Denver and claimed her. Maybe her talk of
marriage had been her way of asking for help. Maybe she would
still be with us if I had responded. But I for one am glad she
is not."

The room was very quiet.

Bonnie cleared her throat. "Did you ever give her any
money?" she asked.

"Yes. I 'loaned' her money from time to time. I knew she
would never repay it, but we always called it a loan. She
shouldn't have bought that building. Dance schools are started
over hardware stores, not in elegant old buildings that suck
away any profit."

"A lot of money?" Bonnie asked.

"What do you consider a lot of money?" he asked.

"Seventy-five thousand dollars."

Zubov laughed. "On a professor's salary?"

"Were you in love with her?" Helen asked.

"I thought I was," he admitted. "But she was not a nice person. She used people."

Zubov sat for a long time after his visitors departed, staring at the place on his wall where the famous poster of Libby used to hang. The football player lifting her over his head. He used to stare at the man's huge hands on Libby's tiny waist. Mikael's own hands were slender—almost like a woman's. Which did Libby prefer?

His walls were empty now, all the memorabilia removed, his life in Colorado soon to be over. He had come here expecting to be uplifted by the mountains. Instead, he found them humbling.

And he had grown weary of the unrelenting stream of young dancers who came to him wanting more than he could give. Every semester, he felt older than the one before. Every batch of new faces was younger than the one before. It was time to go.

He crossed the hall to the empty practice room and went to the barre for a series of shallow *pliés*, dipping and rising, dipping and rising, until his aging knees called a halt.

The practice room was the only place where Libby would make love to him—late at night, with improvised choreography to recorded rhapsodies, mirrors all around. She loved the images in the mirrors of their naked dancers' bodies engaging in every possible sexual act. He never was sure what she thought about the lovemaking itself.

He followed the *pliés* with a few half-hearted *battements*. He had warded off old age longer than most, but now the battle was over. Even Libby would no longer be young. She would be like her friends. Helen and Bonnie. He remembered them as pretty coeds with flowing hair, sweet smiles, and sorority pins on their sweaters. Now they were mature women, attractive enough but the freshness gone.

Libby must be dead. He could not imagine her growing old.

Once she had lit a dozen candles, their light reflecting and re-reflecting in these mirrored walls. Libby said the candles were an exorcism. Zubov knew who she meant. His dead wife. Hedda. Libby wanted to erase Hedda from his mind.

Unquestionably, Libby had more talent than any student he had ever taught, but he could have made her better, made her tougher, more prepared to deal with what lay ahead. Other students he pushed to anger, pushed to the point where they did well just to show him that he was wrong with his taunts. That they did have talent. That they would sacrifice a normal life for the sake of their art. That they would drive themselves to the limit and beyond. He never made Libby do it over and over and over to the point that hate glimmered in her eyes. Not when what he wanted to see was love. He was obsessed with her and therefore doomed her to failure.

He felt guilt about that but nothing more. He didn't need those two silly women playing amateur detective to exorcise Libby. Age had done it for him. In his old age, he wanted only to surround himself with the sweet memories of his youth. Libby had come in middle life, when men are foolish and vain.

Hedda came back to him now in his sleep with their two daughters. Baby Tova in her arms. Dear Natasia smiling at her mother's side.

He knew that in death it would be Hedda's face that he saw, her hand that he reached for.

Damn, Helen thought. Mrs. Benson's car was gone from the driveway. That meant Alex was home, his BMW parked in the garage. Helen left her station wagon out. She would need to make a run to the grocery yet this evening for orange juice and bread. And toilet paper. Laundry soap.

Tomorrow, she simply had to take time to stock up. And bake six cheesecakes. Pay bills. Call about dental appointments for the children.

Ben and Alex were sitting at the kitchen bar eating pizza out of a box.

"Smells good," Helen said cheerily. "Where's Beth?"

"At Charlene's house," Alex said without looking at her. "Charlene's mother was cooking a real meal. Meat loaf and scalloped potatoes. Charlene's mother took Beth to her piano lesson."

"Oh, my gosh! I forgot about her lesson." Helen flushed with embarrassment. It wasn't the first time she'd forgotten.

Alex waited until Ben had gone to watch television before he began, his hands folded in front of him.

"You've been to Denver again, I take it?"

"Just for a couple of hours. I talked to a couple of her former dance students. I can't expect Bonnie and Jen to do it all."

"And what earthshaking discovery did the three aging Nancy Drews find out today? That Libby had her tooth filled on a rainy Tuesday? Or that she bought a new set of tires at the Goodyear store? That she stubbed her toe on the fourth of May? And while you're off playing detective, the children spend more time with Mrs. Benson than they do with their mother. The lawn is drying up. The laundry piles up. Our daughter has to beg rides from neighbors. This family is surviving on pizza and Kraft macaroni and cheese. And I see a stack of unfilled orders for cheesecakes on the spindle."

"First, you didn't want me to start a business," Helen reminded him, "and now you're criticizing me because I haven't been working at it."

Alex sucked in his breath. "If you will remember, I have always encouraged you to do something in addition to keeping house and raising children. I would have preferred some endeavor other than baking cheesecakes, but if that's what you really want, it's fine with me. And I think you know that, Helen. Right now, you're doing a half-assed job taking care of this family *and,* I'd be willing to wager, you haven't been delivering half of the cheesecakes you've promised."

Helen stared at the window over the sink, her own tense face reflected back at her. An angry husband behind her.

"When is it going to stop?" he demanded.

"When we find her," Helen said. She picked up a Brillo pad and began scrubbing the coffee gunk that had accumulated on the inside of the coffee pot.

"And suppose you never do. Will this investigation continue from the old folks' home?"

"Maybe."

He knocked over a bar stool getting up. "Come on, Ben," he called. "We're going to water the lawn."

"But it's getting dark."

"The grass doesn't care."

Helen wearily picked up the stool, sat on it, reached for a slice of cold pizza and picked up the phone.

"Did the mechanic remember her?" she asked as soon as Jen answered.

"Of course. She and the car both were pretty memorable. He said she was bad about having it serviced."

"That's all?"

"Yeah. You still coming for the day on Saturday?"

"No, I need to shore up the home front. But I'll make my list of calls. You talk to Bonnie?"

"Her friend at the police department checked the records.

The police had never been called to Libby's address. No break-ins or prowlers. No disturbing the peace."

"Jen?"

"Yeah?"

"Are we crazy?"

"Probably. But even if we never find out a thing, I love being with you guys. I'm having a glorious time."

"Yeah, but I'm having a hard time putting the rest of my life on hold."

There was no need for Helen to call Bonnie, but she did to hear her repeat what Jen had just told her.

Then she dragged her weary body to a nearby 7-Eleven. Tomorrow, she'd hit the supermarket and buy a station-wagon-full. And cook ahead, make a couple of casseroles and a pot of beans while she baked cheesecakes. The whole day in the kitchen. If she had time, she'd make a double batch of cheese-cakes. She could make calls while she cooked.

When she got out of the shower, Alex was reading in bed. Wearing his new reading glasses. She still wasn't used to them. "You're right," she said. "Everything is half-assed right now. I don't want to stop looking for her, Alex. I need to do this."

Alex took off his glasses and closed his eyes for a long minute. Helen touched his face.

"Okay," he said, kissing her fingertips. "But don't let your cheesecake business go down the tubes, honey. I know you can make something out of it. Everyone says so. You're already famous for them in Boulder."

"And that doesn't bother you anymore?"

"It never did *bother* me, Helen. I just wasn't sure the cheese-cakes were right for you. Now, I'm sure. But businesses don't run themselves. You need to keep at it. And hire some help. Which reminds me, Annie's niece is looking for a part-time job. I told her to call you."

"Being a boss scares me," Helen admitted. "Bosses have to be organized. Maybe it's not just this investigation that keeps me out of the kitchen. Maybe I'm not cut out to be a businesswoman."

She put her arms around him and laid her face against his chest. While she listened to the steady beat of his heart, he stroked her hair. She felt his lips against her brow.

She did love him. At moments like this, that seemed like enough.

The first weekend of trout season, the men went fishing and the women and children went to the cabin.

Having Bonnie along was a special treat for the children because after dinner she always told ghost stories from her seemingly endless repertory. Helen remembered some of them from grade school when Bonnie had entertained at slumber parties. Helen and Jen rocked on the sidelines, sipping their wine, enjoying the sight of their four beautiful children sitting on the floor in front of Bonnie, their captivated faces glowing in the firelight.

After the children were tucked in for the night, Helen locked up, Bonnie put more wood on the fire, and Jen brought the wine bottle from the kitchen. Time for the adults. And another ghost story. Their own private ghost story.

Bonnie looked at her watch. "The guys are sitting around the campfire right about now, drinking one last beer and talking about how nuts we are."

"Yeah," Jen agreed. "Ted says we're wasting our time. The trail is too cold."

"Alex wants his shirts picked up at the cleaners and bills paid on schedule," Helen said, seating herself in the big wooden rocker by the fireplace. "And I've discovered that the way to make him appreciate my brilliance in the kitchen is to stay out of it."

"Why *was* she so acting so strangely that last night?" Bonnie said, reaching for her package of cigarettes.

"Like we've already said, her life was falling apart," Helen said with a shrug, wishing they had a new scenario for critique. But they kept coming back to the last night—Bonnie called it "The Last Supper." There had to be some secret they were overlooking. And so they played it over and over again, mentally circling around the players, examining the action from every angle.

"I wonder why didn't she pay her mortgage when she had all that money?" Bonnie asked. "Maybe she was going around the bend."

"Yeah. Somehow, she even *looked* different," Jen said, wrinkling her brow as she struggled to remember.

"She looked different because she had on an inch of lipstick," Helen recalled.

"She was on the edge that night," Bonnie insisted. "I'll never forget her dancing around in that white dress, holding—"

"Wait!" Jen interrupted, sitting up very straight, putting a hand to her breast. She stared blindly at the fire, her gaze fixed back in time. "Her boobs! Jesus Christ, her boobs!"

"What about them?" Bonnie asked.

"That last night. She wasn't wearing a bra," Jen said.

"Yeah," Helen agreed. "You could see her nipples. So what?"

Jen was excited. She got up and started pacing. "She was bigger. Even her nipples were bigger."

Bonnie shook her head. "I don't think so. She was small, like always."

"She may have seemed small to you guys, but I would have

died to have as much as Libby did," Jen said, running her hands over her almost-nonexistent bosom. "While I was pregnant and nursing was the first time I'd ever been bigger than she was. But that night, Libby and I were the same size. I swear we were. I remember sitting there nursing Mandy and thinking that very thought. Libby hadn't danced in so long, I wondered if she had gained weight."

"What are you suggesting?" Helen demanded, already knowing the answer.

"She could have been pregnant," Jen said.

"I don't think so," Bonnie said. "If Libby was screwing some guy, she would have used birth control. Motherhood wasn't her style."

"Not necessarily," Jen insisted. "People slip up. Or maybe she wanted a baby. You know how she loved Beth and Mandy."

"No, she didn't," Bonnie said. "She just pretended like she did. But if she was pregnant, what would that tell us?"

Helen felt ill. What indeed?

"Maybe she went off to have a baby on her own. Just up and left. Started over," Jen said, resuming her position on the sofa and reaching for her glass.

"Wouldn't she have taken that money to start over with?" Bonnie demanded. "Especially if she had a kid. And what about her clothes, her furniture, her dishes, her record collection? She walked out of there with what she could carry in an overnight bag."

"Maybe she was just getting fat," Helen offered. "That's what you thought at the time, Jen. And anyway, it's impossible to diagnose pregnancy after more than a dozen years just on the basis of a seemingly enlarged bosom."

"She was so weepy," Bonnie recalled, warming up to the notion. "Not herself at all."

"I don't think weepiness is a symptom of pregnancy," Helen insisted.

"It could be if you don't want to be pregnant," Bonnie said. "Remember, she tried to get Zubov to marry her. He admitted that was really unlike her. She had never wanted to get married before."

"I think he would have married her if she was pregnant with his child," Jen speculated. "Those Old World types don't fool around when it comes to honor."

"And surely she would have told him she was pregnant with his child if she was trying to get him to marry her," Bonnie said. "If it was his child."

"Maybe when Zubov refused to marry her, she went to New Mexico for an abortion," Jen said. "Except she could have gotten one here."

"Not legally," Bonnie reminded her. "They weren't legal in Colorado until sixty-seven. They weren't legal in New Mexico either. And that wouldn't explain why her car ended up in a farm pond."

"Of course, we don't know Libby went to New Mexico," Jen said, "Someone else could have driven her car there."

"But why?" Bonnie demanded, hands clutched together. "Why? Why? Why?"

Helen rocked slowly back and forth. Jen was probably right about Libby being pregnant. Another piece of the puzzle was slipping into place. If they kept up, they might accidentally find them all.

But isn't that what they wanted?

"Are we sure the guys went fishing that morning after the party?" Bonnie asked.

"They left together and came back together," Jen said. "Jesus, Bonnie, what the hell are you saying?"

"If one of them was with her, would the other two guys cover for him?" Bonnie asked.

"You mean, would Ted and Lenny cover for Alex?" Helen interjected, her tone flat.

"Not necessarily," Jen said. "You don't know that Alex was still involved with her. Maybe she had taken up with someone else—someone we don't know."

"If she was pregnant," Bonnie speculated, "and the father was a respectable married man, maybe she *was* threatening him—demanding that he marry her. Or maybe she was blackmailing him. God knows, she needed money. We've sure as hell established that."

"All that money," Jen said, excited. "Maybe it really was blackmail money. Evelyn said that's what her husband thought."

"Naw," Bonnie said. "If you're going to kill someone for blackmailing you, you don't give them money first."

"Maybe the person who gave her the money trusted her to keep quiet," Jen said, reaching for the wine bottle.

Helen felt cold in spite of the fire. She hugged her arms to her chest and stared at the flames.

Suddenly the investigation was no longer any fun.

Fourteen

Helen went again to the home of Dr. Rex Donley, the Ballard family physician, now retired.

"Nope, Libby Ballard never came to me pregnant," he insisted. He was in his garage, polishing his restored emerald green 1936 Parkard Custom Town Car.

"But would you tell me if she was?" Helen persisted.

"I might not tell if she was, but I don't mind telling that I have no knowledge of a pregnancy," he said, lovingly buffing an already glistening fender.

"But don't you need to check your records?" Helen asked.

He shook his head no. "Not for Libby Ballard. I'd remember."

On a whim, Jen called on the GP in Golden, where Libby

had taken her to be fitted with her a diaphragm. Their junior year in high school. *Imagine!* Sixteen years old and screwing almost nightly. She'd send Mandy to a girls' school with very high fences if she ever got involved like that.

Dr. Lillian Stafford was retired, her medical records stored in her garage. "What made you think of me?" the woman wanted to know as she searched through the drawers in a row of file cabinets.

"It was a long shot," Jen explained. "Libby made an appointment with you years ago—when we were in high school —for me to be fitted with a diaphragm."

Dr. Stafford nodded. "The word got around. I fitted lots of high school girls—all of whom claimed they were eighteen. I figured if they were asking for birth control, they needed it. Yes, here it is. Elizabeth Ballard. So, she did come to see me," the woman said as she opened the yellowing folder and examined the two pieces of paper inside. "I remember reading about the young woman who disappeared. Years ago. The dancer. But I saw so many young girls back then. I didn't realize she was one of them. Only once, I see. May 22, 1966. She never came back."

"And?" Jen asked. "Was she pregnant?"

"I really can't betray that kind of confidence."

"But it could be an important piece of evidence."

"Why are you and your friends investigating instead of the police?"

"The police have had twelve and a half years. And they can't get inside her head like we can. She was our best friend."

Dr. Stafford cocked her head to one side and regarded Jen. "And if she was pregnant?"

"It could be a motive."

"For murder?"

"Maybe. Or running away. Look, what if I have her mother call you?" Jen asked hopefully. "Would you tell her?"

The tiny woman hesitated. "No, I don't think so. Twelve and a half years. That's a long time to not know what happened to someone. Excuse me a minute, dear. I think I hear my telephone."

Jen didn't hear a telephone. It took her a minute to realize the doctor had left Libby's folder on top of the dusty file cabinet. Jen slipped out its two pages and put them in her purse.

Helen, with her secondhand medical knowledge, helped Jen decipher the file. Libby had indeed been pregnant. Gravida two. Her second pregnancy. The patient had reported being pregnant once before in 1957 and been aborted at approximately ten weeks. No complications. Libby's chart indicated prescriptions had been written for prenatal vitamins and antinausea suppositories. The patient was to return in one month.

Jen and Helen stared at each other. Libby's second pregnancy! An abortion in 1957. Their freshman year at CU.

"Jesus. I would have sworn she'd never even touched herself in 1957," Helen said. "Our virginal little Libby."

"The way she got after us about letting boys do it, you would have thought she was some sort of saint," Jen said, staring at the incriminating pages.

On her own, Helen went to see Evelyn Ballard, who looked frail and tired. There were boxes scattered about the hall and dining room. She was giving up her house, she explained. Two neighbors were helping her pack up—shipping most of her things off to Goodwill. No, she wasn't going to Florida. Her sister had a new gentleman friend. Evelyn didn't want to be in the way. She'd found a nursing home here in Denver with a nice garden. Of course, there was no hurry—the doctor said she would see another spring. But she wanted to get her life in order while she still could.

190

"Did you know that Libby was having an affair with someone?" Helen asked.

"I suspected."

"Did you know she was pregnant?"

"No, but I'd wondered. She'd be sick one day and starved
the next. I was like that when I was pregnant. And her breasts
were fuller. She had such small breasts, like my sister. But I
wasn't sure. She wasn't dancing much. That could have made a
difference."

"Could she have been blackmailing someone?"

Evelyn sighed. "Fred always said she was. Where else would
she have gotten all that money?"

"Do you have any idea who she was involved with?" Helen
asked.

"She saw that dance professor some. The only people she
ever talked about were you girls and your families. But sometimes she was gone, and I didn't know where. Not that I kept
track of her. But I was trying there at the end to do better with
her. She seldom came home, but I called her every day or two.
And I'd drop by with something I'd cooked. She seemed to like
for me to do that. I had a key. If she wasn't there, I'd leave it
in the refrigerator. And she borrowed money sometimes. That's
what she called it. 'Borrowing.' But she never paid it back. I
guess she didn't get all that money until the end. Seventy-five
thousand dollars. So much money."

Evelyn paused and took a couple of deep breaths.

"Are you all right?" Helen asked.

"Just a little light-headed," she said.

Helen got her a glass of water. There were more boxes in
the kitchen.

"Maybe she found a man to make her pregnant," Evelyn
continued, after a few sips of water. "You know, just any man.
She talked about doing that once. Said she'd like to have a little

191

girl to raise 'right.' I would have liked that. A grandbaby. Boy or girl. And I wouldn't have cared if she was married or not. Her father would have, though."

"Libby was pregnant," Helen said. The words she'd been trying to say for days slipped out suddenly in the middle of the late news.

As soon as the words were spoken, Helen was sorry. Fearful. She didn't want to have this conversation.

But she had to tell Alex. He would have found out eventually. And then her *not* telling him would have seemed ominous.

Using the remote, he muted the sound. His movements seemed staged as he carefully leaned back in his chair and picked up his coffee cup. "Now, how could you possibly know a thing like that?"

"I saw her medical chart. 'Gravida two.' She had an abortion in college," she said, shivering. She pulled the afghan over her legs.

Alex was frowning. "Her medical chart? What are you talking about?"

"Libby went to a GP in Golden. The woman is retired now. Jen stole Libby's file out of her garage. Her due date was December eleventh. Did you know?"

"Of course I didn't know. And do you think her being pregnant is important?" he asked. "Did it have something to do with her disappearance?"

"I don't know. Did you guess?"

"That she was pregnant? How could I without examining her or running a test?"

"What did she say to you when you took her back to the apartment?"

He sighed. They had the topic all discussed before. "That her life was shit," he said. "So, what do you ladies do now?"

"Keep searching," Helen said. "It is possible to find out things. We have a real sense for that now. If you open enough closet doors, you'll find the skeleton."

Alex stared at her, his eyes sad. "You're letting this become an unhealthy obsession," he said, and picked up the remote.

"You just wrote a story about the Ballard disappearance," Ralph Clark said from behind his cluttered desk. "You can write another one on the twenty-fifth anniversary of her disappearance—or when someone digs up her bones."

"But there's been some progress made on her case," Bonnie argued, using one of several empty diet Dr Pepper cans scattered about the desk as an ashtray. "And you never did run that picture of her car. You're always bitching at us to 'get the picture,' and then you don't use them half the time. You could run the picture of the car and one of Libby along with the story, and maybe someone would remember something—you know, connect that pretty young woman with that sporty little car. There couldn't have been more than a handful of red fifty-nine Thunderbirds driving around in nineteen sixty-six."

"Hell, I don't remember what kind of car *I* was driving in nineteen sixty-six," Ralph said, peering at her over the top of his reading glasses. "I'm not running a picture of a car that was pulled out of a pond three months ago. Now, just what progress are you talking about? Did a neighbor remember seeing someone carrying a very large trunk out of her apartment? Has Ballard been spotted in Nome, Alaska?"

Bonnie hesitated. She couldn't reveal the seventy-five thousand dollars—not while Evelyn Ballard was still alive. No estate or income taxes had been paid on the money. And, according to Ted, there was no statute of limitations on back taxes if there was intent to defraud—like intentionally not reporting found money.

And if she told Ralph that Libby had had an affair with the husband of one of her best friends, and with her dance professor, Ralph would want to know if either man was connected to her disappearance. And Bonnie didn't know that.

"She was pregnant," Bonnie said.

"And that's why she disappeared?" Ralph asked, his chair creaking as he shifted his considerable girth.

"I don't know. But it could be related."

He made a face. "Don't be late for the governor's press conference."

"Will you give me page one when I find her bones?" Bonnie said.

"If war isn't declared the same day. Ask Lamm if he's going to run for president."

Bonnie stood. "I'm going to find those bones, Ralph. I'll probably get a Pulitzer Prize for my investigative journalism."

"And when you do, I'll run naked through the news room. Look, kiddo, I got you the statehouse beat just like you always wanted. Now, go make me happy about it. And take a photographer. The nukes may picket the capitol."

The nukes were out in force. Lamm said he had no plans to run. He declared war on the brown cloud of pollution that now hung over the Denver area more days than not. Bonnie turned in the story, raced home to change clothes, and drove too fast to Louisville, where Lenny was speaking at a fund-raising benefit for the high school athletic program.

Lenny was in great demand as a speaker. He tried to attend when Bonnie spoke on the ERA, and he liked to have her accompany him on his speaking engagements. She went when she could. If the master of ceremonies didn't mention that she worked for the *Post* when he introduced those at the head table, Lenny would when he got up to speak.

Lenny warmed up his audience with stock stories about his playing days at Greeley High School and the University of Colorado. Bonnie had heard them before, had helped him organize most of them. And she had helped him write the more serious remarks that would follow. "Something really special, about how it feels to be with guys on a team and really care about them," he'd said last night, pacing back and forth in Bonnie's office at home, with frequent stops to look over her shoulder as she typed. "About how that part is more important than winning or being famous. And that I wasn't much of a player, but I learned a lot about life, and I loved playing and being with those guys."

He was doing a good job delivering the speech. He always did. He practiced beforehand and could give a prepared speech with only glances at the script. He knew when to pause, when to chuckle, when to soften his voice almost to a whisper. He was doing that now. Finished with the lighthearted stuff, his tone became reverent. There wasn't a sound in the room, and all faces were turned toward him.

"There's a short story you kids will probably run into in your freshman English class at college," he said. "It's called 'The Eighty-Yard Run' and tells about how us older guys all need to look back on that one perfect moment when we were the hero, when we made our own kind of eighty-yard run.

"But I never was a hero. Not really. I made a few good catches. Scored a few touchdowns. But nothing spectacular. I was never first-string. Nothing I did ever went down in the record books. No pro scouts looked twice at me. I barely made the season highlight films the coaches showed to recruits.

"For me, the eighty-yard run was in being there. In playing the game. In making memories and buddies for a lifetime. I get tears in my eyes just thinking about it, and I wouldn't trade my years as a high school and college athlete for anything. I learned that sometimes you get good calls and sometimes you get bad ones—just like the other team. I learned to play the best I could and never to make excuses for not playing better. I learned to celebrate victories with humility and to hold my head up after defeat."

Lenny was more than the city's top sportscaster. He was the sort of television personality that people called out to on the street. They came over to his table in restaurants, sent him birthday presents, critiqued his haircut and clothes. Colorado born and bred, he was one of their own, and they loved him. The fact that he had been a player but not a star made him even more beloved. He was in demand for telethons, banquets, benefit golf tournaments, charity fun runs.

And his series last year on unsung Colorado sports heroes had won him a regional Emmy. Bonnie had suggested the series after his story on the one-handed high school basketball player from Shelton got so much attention. She had done some of the research. Helped him with the script.

The Emmy brought a rash of job offers. Portland. Albuquerque. Indianapolis. But he'd turned them down. Colorado was their home, he'd say firmly. He couldn't imagine life without CU football, without skiing the Rockies or fishing mountain streams, without their families and friends.

But now the NBC affiliate in New York City wanted him. Bonnie had heard about it secondhand from the station receptionist.

"I haven't said anything to you yet because I didn't know what to tell you," he explained when she confronted him. "I know I've always said we'd never leave Colorado. And those other jobs I was offered weren't all that much better than what I have now. But *New York*. It could be a stepping-stone to a network job, and they're offering a hell of a lot more than I make here."

"What did you tell them?" Bonnie asked, fearfully, her heart pounding.

"I told them I'd have to talk to you."

Yes, Bonnie thought. A talk during which she was supposed to tell him whatever he did was okay with her. *Whither thou goest . . .*

"Maybe getting away from Colorado would be good for us," he said.

"In what way?" she asked.

"It'd be you and me against the world. Starting over. New faces. New challenges. Excitement. Not the same old stuff."

"Except that we both like the same old faces and the same old stuff."

Lenny had not assumed it was his decision to make. Bonnie did take comfort in that.

New York. Where Libby had wanted them all to go. The irony of it made Bonnie dizzy. And she felt ill just thinking about what lay ahead. She could be the dutiful wife and agree to whatever was best for her husband's career. Or she could refuse to leave Colorado.

She lost either way.

Would he go without her? Maybe that was why she was so involved in his career. If he depended on her enough, he would never leave her.

How had it come to pass that the dedicated feminist was put in such a position? Whose career was more important anyway?

He made more money, but she'd achieved a lot. Legislators and print journalists considered her a tough professional. And even her more senior colleagues at the *Post* were starting to assume that someday she'd take over Ralph's desk when he retired.

Unless she gave it all up to follow her husband to New York.

And leave Denver. The mountains. Her aging parents. Her friends.

And what about finding Libby? Maybe Jen and Helen would quit if she left.

God, she would hate to give up the hunt. Hate to back off from the intensity, the sharing. They hadn't been this close since college. Bonnie loved it.

If she moved to New York, the three of them would become long-distance friends like those years after graduation.

She didn't want that. Bonnie had made lots of friends over the years—through school, work, her husband's job, the women's movement. But for her, the word "friend" meant only two people. Helen and Jen. They knew her better than anyone else, even her own husband.

Except that Bonnie was afraid sometimes. She felt like the three of them were standing with their toes on the edge of a large, dark abyss. And Libby was down there waiting.

Lenny claimed they'd had no right to look at Libby's medical records. "An invasion of privacy," he called it. "Dead or alive, she still has the right to keep her secrets. Why can't you women leave poor Libby alone?" he'd demanded, storming from the room.

When Lenny finished his speech, Bonnie rose with the rest of the crowd to give him a standing ovation. He looked at her and grinned.

Later, in his arms, their bodies still moist from loving, Bonnie told him she didn't think she could be happy in New York. She'd try if that was what he really wanted. She just wanted him to be sure it wasn't something he'd regret.

"I remember when New York was the ultimate dream," he reminded her as he stroked her back. "Bonnie Miller, internationally renowned journalist. The Pulitzer Prize. Talk-show guest. A movie of your life. It's not too late, you know. We could both climb to the top in markets that really matter."

"All that New York stuff was Libby talking. All I want out of life is some professional respect and a good marriage."

"And can't you have those in New York? Come on, Bonnie, I'm being handed the chance of a lifetime. You don't want to go because of all this Libby business. And that's one of the reasons I think we should go." He rolled away from her, his head on his own pillow.

"Why? So we never have to find out what happened to her? Alex has all but ordered Helen to cut it out. Ted pouts when Jen isn't there to watch him watch television. He's put on ten more pounds just to punish her. And sneaks out in the garage to smoke. When he has his heart attack, it will be all her fault. What is it with you guys?"

"We like our wives around. Is that so bad?"

"Were you ever in love with her?" Bonnie asked from her side of the bed.

"Jesus, Bonnie," he said, rolling on his side to face her. "You know better than that."

"No, I don't. She was captivating. Different. Surely you noticed."

"Yeah, I noticed. But she was also a spoiled brat. She couldn't hold a candle to you, babe."

"You mean she couldn't write your speeches for you."

Bonnie regretted the words as soon as they were spoken. She didn't write his speeches; she *typed* them.

She wasn't the feminist she pretended to be. The thought of facing the world without her man at her side made cold fingers of dread grab at her insides. Lenny's fans weren't all men. Women far more attractive than she was looked at him with fawning eyes. Flawed as he was, Lenny was still her anchor, still her darlin' boy. With Lenny in her life and in her bed, she felt strong. Oddly enough, she was able to deal with men as equals because she was married and wanted nothing from them except respect and acceptance.

"Are you sure I have to eat oatmeal for breakfast?" Ted asked. "Whatever happened to Sunday morning waffles?"

Jen leaned over and patted his large, round belly. "This is what happened," she said. "Eat your oatmeal, now, like a good boy, and enjoy the peace and quiet."

Mandy and Scott were with Ted's parents in Winter Park for the first skiing of the season. And last night, Jen had prepared dinner for two, lit candles, put a Barry Manilow album on the stereo, opened a bottle of twelve-dollar wine and not mentioned Libby all evening. After dinner, they had made love in front of the fireplace. Just like in the movies.

Good loving. In spite of his tummy. The kind of loving that made tears come to her eyes.

Jen poured herself a second cup of coffee and scanned the front page of the newspaper. Carter and Sadat at Camp David. More snow was predicted. She looked out the window at the backyard under its pristine white blanket.

"Who do you think made her pregnant?" she asked.

"God Almighty," Ted groaned.

"Are you swearing or suggesting an immaculate conception?" she chirped.

"Is *she* all you ever think about?"

"Of course not. But I'm asking your opinion. Who do you think?"

"The dance professor, maybe," Ted said, adding another package of sweetener to his cereal. "Or some truck driver. Hell, I don't know."

"I used to wonder about you and her. You were always dancing with her."

"Libby was the best dance partner in the history of the world. You know that," he said, taking a bite of oatmeal.

"Yeah, but I was jealous sometimes."

"And I get jealous when you flirt with Alex."

"I just flirt. You know that."

"Yeah, I know that," Ted admitted. "I don't screw around on you, either."

"I know you don't now. But sometimes I wonder about back then. With Libby."

Ted grimaced and reached for the sports section of the newspaper.

"Well, did you?"

"Hell, Jen. Of course not. We were all just good friends."

"But would you tell me if you had?"

"Probably not. Would you tell me if you'd screwed Alex?"

"Of course not. But I haven't."

As always, Jen whisked the empty bowl away the instant the last bite of oatmeal was in Ted's mouth.

He watched her carry it to the sink, rinse it and put it in the dishwasher. She had already put the pan in the dishwasher.

Already wiped off the counter twice. Already called Winter Park to check on the kids. Already tidied up the family room from their romp last night.

Sometimes Ted couldn't stand his wife.

"You guys can't imagine how hard it is to be married to someone who's perfect," Ted would complain to Lenny and Alex on their fishing trips. "Hell, I've been living with the woman for almost eighteen years, and I never once heard her fart."

If he remembered to hang up a towel, she'd straightened it. If he set the table, she rearranged the silverware. And God forbid that he put the scissors back in the wrong drawer. In their household, everything had a place.

Jen never lost anything. She had a file cabinet in the laundry room for newspaper clippings, receipts, coupons, appliance guarantees, tax records, medical and dental records. She had a file on gifts she had given for various gift-giving occasions so she wouldn't duplicate them.

She even had a file on Libby. Ted had looked at it. Old photographs. Newspaper clippings. Notes about the "investigation" and lists of unanswered questions.

For months now, ever since her car had been found, the quest for Libby was all Jen talked about. He wanted to tell her to drop it. But knowing Jen, that would probably only make her more determined to keep it up. And surely she'd get bored with it eventually.

Sometimes he felt jealous of her friendship with Helen and Bonnie. Sometimes he wished she didn't have a life outside this house.

When she returned for his empty cup, he pulled her down on his lap and nuzzled her neck.

"Last night was nice," she said, nibbling his ear.

"How about an encore?" he suggested. "To make up for the oatmeal."

She laughed as he placed her hand on his already hard crotch.

Ted had been second string as a football player, barely made it through law school, struggled mightily to pass the bar, and had never broken ninety on the golf course. He made lots of money only because he was a partner in his father's law firm, where he earned his way doing the bread-and-butter stuff— divorces, wills, civil suits. He wasn't brilliant enough for criminal law. He wasn't meticulous enough for tax or corporate work.

The most remarkable thing about Ted Echols was his wife. Jen was his center. Every evening, Ted looked forward to walking in the back door and knowing she would be there, even planned on the way home the things he would tell her. A case that was particularly interesting. Office gossip. She fussed over him—like she did the kids, asking about his day, giving him something hot or cold to drink depending on the season. She always asked questions about his cases and listened to his answers.

He hated the evenings she wasn't there.

He wondered if Jen was lying when she said she had never screwed around. She was still a damned good-looking woman.

And he had lied to her.

Ted talked it over with his father. Jen had always wanted the house. Her favorite in the whole world, she had said for years whenever they drove by the Southern colonial-style mansion only a block from the Denver Country Club. And now it was for sale.

Jen was happiest when she was redecorating, Ted explained to Judson Echols. A twelve-room house with a large yard would keep her busy for years. She could turn it into a real showcase.

"Or she could get some kind a job," Ted offered as an alternative. "With the kids getting older, Jen has too much time on her hands. She's already been president of Junior League and everything else she belongs to."

"No. You don't want her working," Judson said firmly. "Women get too independent when they start earning their own money."

Ted wondered what his father could know about independent women. Ted's mother had never worked a day in her life.

"Well, the house was just a thought," he said. "I know we can't afford a house like that."

Judson puffed on his pipe. A huge man, well over three hundred pounds. Ted knew if it weren't for Jen, he'd end up looking just like his father. "No, you're right, son," Judson said. "I never did like that Brewster woman. Jen should be spending more time with her own kind of people. We'll see what we can work out."

"Oh, Jen honey, this is a house fit for a queen," Grace Venable said as she took in the spacious entry hall with its gracefully curving staircase and French doors leading out to a broad veranda. "Just look at the parquet in these floors. And the woodwork. This house is a work of art. Your dad and I are so thrilled for you."

Their footsteps echoed as they inspected the empty living room and the library beyond with their marble fireplaces and arched windows. Grace, tanned and slim, was wearing tennis attire for her four o'clock doubles match. After a fifteen-year hiatus—what Jen thought of as the Miltown Era—her mother had emerged from her tranquilizer haze and rediscovered tennis—with a vengeance.

"We haven't bought the house yet," Jen reminded her. She turned on the lights in the dining room to show off the spectacular crystal chandelier—imported from Belgium, according to the realtor. "It's a great house," Jen said almost sadly, "but I really don't see how we can afford it."

"Now, Jen, you let Ted worry about the money. That's a man's job."

"Oh, Mom, that's nonsense. Ted's my husband, not my daddy. After all, we're talking about my future, too. And the kids'. Mandy wants to go to Stanford or Berkeley. Scott is not going to have a growing spurt and play football at CU like his dad keeps dreaming about. He thinks he'd like to study art back east someplace. And I want the kids to study abroad for a year. I was always sorry I didn't do that."

"Your daddy and I think Mandy and Scott should go to CU like their parents did," Grace said, frowning at the flocked wallpaper in the dining room. "And you did just fine without studying abroad."

"Mandy needs to go someplace where a girl doesn't have to be cute—where girls can be serious students," Jen insisted.

"Serious students seldom get the best husbands," Grace warned. Jen was showing her the breakfast room with greenhouse window.

"I always used to worry about Helen, not finding Alex until the last moment," Grace added. "Boys aren't attracted to girls like that. Helen was lucky."

"Mom, Alex was attracted to Helen *because* she's smart," Jen snapped.

"Maybe. If Mandy goes away to college, all that will be accomplished is she won't marry a Colorado boy and your father and I will never get to see our grandchildren," Grace said as they walked through the drab, outdated kitchen that would have to be completely redone. The bathrooms, too. "If you could just slim Mandy down a little, she'll do just fine at CU," Grace insisted.

"Meaning find herself her husband?"

"Well, that's what her mother did. What would you have the girl do, Jen? Be a spinster?"

"No, of course not. I just don't think it has to be one or the other. Not anymore."

Grace pursed her lips, which meant she didn't agree but didn't want to talk about it any more.

Grace stood at the bottom of the broad, curving staircase. "Can't you just see Mandy in a bridal gown coming down those stairs on her daddy's arm?"

Sometimes Jen thought of the Miltown Era as the good old days. With an irritated sigh, she followed her mother up the stairs, which would indeed be a great staircase for a bride to come down. And Jen wanted her daughter to have a beautiful wedding, a beautiful dress, a day to remember for the rest of her life. But Jen was more concerned with what came after her daughter's wedding than the day itself.

Mandy wouldn't want to live in a house like this. Or be in Junior League.

Mandy was an excellent student. She loved science and math. And Jen was fiercely proud of her.

The house was wonderful. No doubt about it. Jen had already been through it half a dozen times, mentally changing wallpaper, refinishing floors, adding carpets, arranging furniture.

She couldn't sleep at night for thinking about the house. Wondering what it would do to her life. Moving. Redecorating. Not having time for other things.

A house like that mandated a certain life-style, and Jen wasn't as concerned about her positioning on the Denver social ladder as she used to be. She hadn't gone to a meeting since June. Hadn't entertained other than relatives or close friends. Even her tennis game had suffered.

But they were getting close. Jen was sure of it. One of these days, she and Helen and Bonnie were going to find out what happened to Libby. And when they did, maybe they would drift apart. Maybe then she would need a new house to fill her life.

Fifteen

Helen climbed down from the step stool and accepted the can of beer Lenny had brought her. Miller's. Bonnie wouldn't let them drink Coors. Adolf Coors was against the ERA.

She stepped back to inspect the framed color photographs of cheesecakes she'd just hung. Jen had suggested them and helped stage the pictures for the photographer. For someone who'd had reservations about Helen as a businesswoman, Jen didn't hesitate to roll up her sleeves and pitch in.

Helen took a draw of the beer, then asked Lenny about his interview.

"It was great. How can I go wrong with an All-Big-Eight forward who wants to be a concert pianist? He even played a sonata on camera. A black kid who grew up poor. His mother played at church and gave him his first lessons on the church piano. The spot's a shoo-in for network."

"I like the way they introduce you now, 'Lenny Brewster, Colorado's Number One Sportscaster.' And it's the truth. Alex and I are so proud of you. I know it's selfish, but I'm so glad you guys didn't move away."

"Me, too. Most of the time."

"But you still think about it some?"

"I guess I'll always wonder if I could have been big time. But when we got up there and started looking at where we'd have to live and what kind of life we'd have, I realized I'm pretty much a down-home boy who prefers fishing to commuting. And Bonnie didn't belong up there either. Colorado is her beat. It wouldn't be fair to make her start all over with a new state and new politics."

Lenny was leaning against the counter, looking like a beer commercial. The all-American guy. Sandy hair. Athletic build. Endearing smile. A Peter Pan of a man, the realm of sports his Never Never Land. "The place is really lookin' good," he said, surveying the freshly painted walls and the freshly varnished floors. "I remember when we used to come here between classes. Great old building. Alex said you got it for a steal."

"I suppose." Helen looked around, too, at the building that had once housed the Campus Bakery. "I still have to pinch myself over all this. Alex is certainly full of surprises."

Helen hadn't planned to move her cheesecake operation from her own kitchen, at least not for now. That seemed too bold a step. Hiring Annie's niece part-time forced Helen to be organized. But if she was going to have any volume at all, she needed commercial ovens and more freezer space. And she missed having her kitchen to herself, she'd admitted to Alex.

One evening a month ago, on Valentine's Day, Alex showed

up with a realtor, a contract, and a dozen roses. Apparently he had driven by the empty building and just knew it was what she needed for her business.

And it was a nice old building with a high pressed-tin ceiling and wooden floor—like something out of a turn-of-the-century movie. For as long as Helen remembered, CU students had come here between classes for doughnuts and a carton of milk from the refrigerated case that still stood in the corner.

Alex had it all planned. Her staff would be students working part-time. That way she wouldn't have to worry about benefits or unemployment compensation. She could sell over the counter as well as to restaurants. Turn the front part into a snack shop. If she was going to run a business, she might as well do it right.

"You've been Dr. Radcliff's wife for all these years," he told her. "Now I'm ready to be Helen Radcliff's husband."

Helen had been touched. And Alex's enthusiasm had been seductive. A bigger operation. More help. She could work fewer hours for bigger results.

Helen explained all this to Lenny as she showed him around. There was even a small room in the back she could use as an office. "That's the part that intimidates me. The stuff you're supposed to do in an office."

"I hear you. Anything that involves deciphering small print, I hand over to Bonnie."

"The grand opening is Saturday," Helen told him as he put on his overcoat. "You and Bonnie have to come. The sign is being put up this afternoon. 'Helen's Heavenly Cheesecakes.'"

"We wouldn't miss it," he said with a good-bye hug and kiss. "Bonnie and I both think you'll be a big success, Helen. All the best restaurants will be serving your cheesecakes before long."

He paused at the door. "I almost forgot. The station is talking about launching a local cooking and restaurant show next fall. I'm going to suggest you as the hostess."

"Me? I couldn't do that, Lenny."

"Why not?"

"Cook on camera? Come on. You've seen my kitchen. I'm not smooth and organized."

"Neither is Julia Child," he said with wave.

Sample cheesecakes in miniature foil cups were Jen's idea. She found the foil cups and colored cellophane paper to wrap them in. She had business cards and a price list printed. Jen, Mandy, and Beth personally delivered the samples to every restaurant of note in the Denver/Boulder area.

"You and yours have cheesecakes for life," Helen told Jen. "You know that, don't you? Why don't you at least let me put you on the payroll? It would be a pittance, but that way you could at least deduct your gas and meals away from home."

Jen waved away her suggestion. "Not right now. I just want the business to be what you want it to be. And besides, it's the only way I ever get to see you. Do you really want to be *this* busy, Helen?"

Within weeks of moving to the new location, Helen hired two more part-time employees. And closed the snack shop portion of the business, which she could immediately see was a mistake. Helen and her help didn't have time to make the snacks and wait on the customers. Before long, she would need to enlarge the kitchen. She and the girls were bumping into each other. They didn't have enough storage. Enough counter space.

Bonnie wrote a wonderful article for the *Post*. "Boulder Woman Turning Cheesecakes Into Gold." The accompanying picture showed Helen presenting a cheesecake to the governor's wife. The article ran in the women's section. Which irritated Bonnie. She had written it as business news.

In May, Lenny announced that the station was ready to shoot a demo. The cooking and restaurant show was a definite maybe for fall. Probably for a Sunday morning slot—in place of the usual church service.

At first, Helen declined. But her family and friends ganged up on her. At least, she should give it a try. If the trial run was a disaster, she could forget about the whole thing. If it went well, *then* she could consider what she wanted to do.

Alex wanted her to buy a new outfit and have her makeup professionally done. She didn't do either.

And she didn't supply the requested script to the director. How was she supposed to know what she was going to say before she said it?

She did buy a bib apron to tie over her shirt and sweater, but at the last minute she reverted to the usual oversized dish towel tied about her middle.

Helen knew she was going to bomb, so she really didn't feel all that nervous. She shouldn't have let Lenny talk her into this camera test, but since she had, she would do it her way and go home.

She checked her ingredients against her recipes once again and nodded at the director. He gave the go-ahead signal.

Helen smiled. "Hello, there. Welcome to 'The Food Show.' I'm Helen Radcliff, and I love to cook.

"Mealtimes are the events around which we build our days and lives. Meals are often the only time the whole family is together. We do our celebrating at mealtime. And nothing makes a meal more special than capping it off with a homemade dessert.

"Today, I'm going to show you how to make three desserts. For my mother's bread pudding recipe, you use stale bread and that old box of raisins in the back of the pantry that has turned into a raisin brick. The second dessert is crumble torte, which looks spectacular for a party and is really quite easy. And in honor of my doctor husband who thinks fat is a four-letter word, I'm going to show you a simple, delicious pear cake that doesn't call for a single ounce of shortening or oil!

"So, get your pencils and paper. Kick off your shoes. And let's cook."

Her timing wasn't bad for a beginner. She wasn't afraid to look right into the camera. Her ingredients were premeasured and set out in the right order. She had the finished products prebaked and standing by to pull out at the proper moment. She didn't panic when she spilled flour. Or when she couldn't find her wooden spoon. And she never stopped talking.

"My Aunt Lura had a pear tree," she said as she dumped chopped ripe pears into a mixing bowl, "and there was a war on. Half the time she couldn't get Crisco or butter. If she didn't have sugar, she used honey or corn syrup or molasses. This pear cake is good any way you make it. But don't try to make it with any other fruit. It'll taste like leather."

Alex, Beth, and Ben watched from the shadows in the back of the studio. Alex got tears in his eyes. "Isn't she something?" he whispered to his daughter and son.

Helen took a sip of her wine, then closed her eyes to relish the moment—the taste and aroma of the wine, the warmth of the fire toasting her face, the smell of hickory smoke and the pungent green smell of the freshly watered cedars that grew along one side of the deck, the high-pitched cicada chorus in the darkness beyond the circle of firelight, the contented feeling that came from the company of her friends.

June evenings would be too cool for sitting on the deck except for the warmth radiating from the fire pit. When Alex insisted on including the pit in their house plans, Helen considered it an unnecessary expense. Stupid even. Polynesians had fire pits. People in Colorado used charcoal grills. But she had been forced to admit that the pit was a great idea. They used it for family cookouts with the kids and social evenings with friends. Sometimes, when the kids weren't around, they even used it to make evenings more romantic.

Tonight, six old friends had gathered for their annual anniversary party. Jen provided the salad, Lenny a squash casserole, and Helen chocolate mousse. The men were in the kitchen talking baseball and assembling the shish kabobs that would soon be laid on a grate over the fire.

The anniversary party. Number eighteen. Somehow, the marriages and the friendships had endured.

Jen wanted a cruise for number twenty. A photographic safari to Kenya for number twenty-five.

Time was going by too fast. Amazingly, Beth and Mandy were teenagers. Sometimes when Helen looked in the mirror, she saw her own mother.

In the softening glow of the fire, Jen looked as young as ever. Her hair was long again, twisted in an elegant French knot. Lovely—more so now than in her youth.

Bonnie was thinner, her remarkable bosom a little less ample. She had celebrated her fortieth birthday by cutting her hair and was now sporting a chic, ultra-short cut.

"It's been quite a year, hasn't it?" Bonnie observed. "We turned forty and we didn't find Libby. Jen didn't buy her dream home. Lenny and I didn't move to New York. And Helen's cooking her way to fame and fortune, leaving Jen and me to carry on the quest. At least one of our husbands was successful with his diversionary tactics."

"What are you talking about?" Helen asked.

Jen was leaning against the deck railing, a wineglass in her hand. "Yeah," she interjected with a knowing nod. "I kept wondering if our investigation had something to do with Ted wanting to install me in a house we couldn't afford."

Bonnie nodded. "Lenny wanted to drag me off to New York. Ted tried to buy a mansion for Jen to redecorate. And Alex bought Helen a business—and got her a job on television."

"Now wait a minute," Helen said. "Alex didn't get me that job."

Bonnie shook her head. "I heard Lenny talking to Alex about it. On the telephone—after you did that sample show last month. He said Alex had had a good idea. Everyone at the station thought Helen was a natural and that the show would probably be scheduled."

"I'm sure you misunderstood," Helen said indignantly. "Alex wouldn't do anything underhanded like that."

"I don't know, honey. They all seemed damned determined to distract us from looking for her," Jen said. "And even though I didn't buy a house and Bonnie didn't move to New York, we sure haven't been doing as much together since you've been so busy."

Helen swung her feet off the chaise and sat up straight. "Did it ever occur to you that maybe Lenny just wanted to give New York a try?" she demanded. "And Ted wanted to buy his wife her dream house, and Alex wanted me to have a successful career?"

"And you're too busy for your own good," Jen insisted. "This is the first time the three of us have been together since the grand opening in March."

Helen's shoulders sagged a bit. "Yeah. Too busy. I'm never

at home. I have to schedule my kids. But that doesn't prove anything."

"If our husbands did scheme against us, who were they protecting?" Bonnie wondered. "And why?"

"What do pregnant girls have when they don't want a baby?" Jen asked, grabbing a chair and pulling it in close.

"An abortion," Bonnie answered, leaning forward, her eyes bright in the firelight. "But they were illegal in 1966. Libby would never have gone for one of those back-alley jobs on some woman's kitchen table."

"No. But she would go to a physician—an OB/GYN resident," Jen said, not looking at Helen, her tone apologetic.

"No, damn it!" Helen exploded. "I know you both have been dying to suggest that ever since we started on this thing. But Alex doesn't do abortions. He never has."

"But why?" Jen asked. "He's always claimed to be pro-choice."

"He just doesn't," Helen said, feeling the heat of anger course through her body. "And I wouldn't want him to. Physicians who do abortions have picket lines in front of their offices, and their families get hassled."

"We're not talking about a legal abortion in an office, Helen," Bonnie said evenly.

"An abortion still doesn't explain where she is," Helen insisted.

"Maybe he made a deal with her?" Jen said. "He gets rid of the baby if she goes away and leaves him alone."

"Jesus, you two!" Helen said, standing abruptly. "Alex wouldn't have risked his entire future and his family's well-being by performing an illegal medical procedure. And what about all that money? *He* didn't have family money to help him pay off a blackmailing bitch."

"What are you suggesting, Helen? That she screwed Ted, too?" Jen asked hotly.

"Why not?" Helen demanded. "And don't tell me you haven't considered the possibility. I remember how you used to watch them on the dance floor. Cozy, weren't they?"

The arrival of the ready-for-the-fire shish kabobs abruptly ended the conversation. The three men didn't seem to notice the silence around them.

The skish kabobs were cooked to perfection, but Helen was too upset to eat more than a few bites. Alex asked if she was feeling all right. "I'm just not hungry," she told him.

In spite of a threatening headache, she kept drinking. She felt as though she were separated from the others by a pane of glass—near them but not with them.

Strange to think that men might share secrets like women. Helen watched the three men as they laughed, joked, even roughhoused a bit. *Were the Pirates going to win another series?* Lenny didn't think they could get past Philadelphia. She had never thought of the husbands as having more in common than a mutual love of sports and the out-of-doors. Ted and Alex enjoyed having television sportscaster Lenny Brewster as their best buddy.

Tomorrow the men were going fishing for four days, and the three women were going to the cabin. Just the women. Both Beth and Mandy had left for their very first summer jobs as junior counselors at the YMCA camp near Winter Park. Ben and Scott had been farmed out to friends. Helen had looked forward to four days of nonstop visiting. Now, she wasn't even sure if she still wanted to go.

Maybe she'd call it off. Blame it on a migraine.

Libby. Damn her to hell.

What had passed between her husband and Libby must have

been damned potent. Why else did he refuse to talk about her? *Still.* The truth couldn't possibly be worse than not knowing.

Poison. He had said that once about Libby. But he had experienced a passion with her that apparently made his relationship with his wife pale in comparison. That was the legacy Libby left her—a legacy that Helen now lived with every day of her life.

Last summer, Helen thought they had been close to discovering the truth. She had wanted that.

Now, all she wanted was for it to stop. If she had the power to erase all memory of Libby from their minds, she would pull the lever without hesitation.

The men were collecting the dishes, carrying them to the kitchen. Lenny was ready to make after-dinner drinks.

Bonnie came over and sat beside her. Helen stiffened as Bonnie's arm went around her.

"You have to know, honey. Not knowing is eating you alive."

"That's easy for you to say," Helen said, crying. "It's not your husband who was involved with her."

Jen came and knelt at Helen's feet. "You're right," she said. "You give the word, and we'll never mention Libby's name again." She looked to Bonnie for confirmation.

Bonnie hesitated, then nodded. "If that's what you want. Never again. Maybe our husbands were right in trying to squelch the whole business. Maybe there should be a statute of limitations on skeletons in the closet."

Somehow, Helen felt better.

In the night, beside her husband of eighteen years, she made her decision.

They weren't policemen looking for an arrest. All the three of them wanted was the truth. And no matter how damning that truth might be, it would bring a peace of sorts. Bonnie was right. Libby had become a worm that was eating her from the inside out.

The television job was not what it had seemed. *Alex had suggested it to Lenny.* How busy did he want her to be? Was he *that* frightened of her taking up the Libby quest once again?

Was that why he decided to be in favor of her cheesecake business?

But he seemed so sincerely proud of her. And maybe he'd suggested the television program to Lenny because he thought she'd be good at it.

Anyway, there was no going back. The contract was signed. Her children had announced it to the world. Her parents were coming up from Phoenix for the inaugural broadcast in September. The station was already running a promotional blurb about the show.

And she wanted it. At first, she hadn't cared much one way or the other. But as she watched the demo tape over and over, she came to like that woman on the screen. Helen Radcliff. An attractive forytish woman who was a damned good cook. The show would make her *someone.* And Helen was determined to succeed.

Sixteen

And so, they began again. Getting organized. Bonnie taking notes and making lists.

But the excitement of last summer was missing. Helen felt silly making her calls. And she really didn't have the time. Only when she was with Jen and Bonnie did thoughts of Libby surface from the backwater of her memory.

Jen was busy, too. In August, her father had had a heart attack. And in September, Mandy had contracted a severe case of mononucleosis and was confined to bed for more than two months. For Jen's birthday, Helen and Lenny brought in dinner.

"Already forty-one," Jen lamented as she stared at her birthday cake. "Didn't I just turn forty 'bout a month ago? And I thought we'd all stay young forever."

It wasn't the end of youth that was so frightening, Helen decided as she watched Jen blow out forty-one candles. It was realizing that a finite number of good years remained. Helen felt an almost desperate need to make the most of those years.

Ted opened a bottle of champagne, and Helen joined the others in a birthday toast to their darling Jen. Helen raised her glass to health and happiness. To friendship. To life. She looked across the table to her husband, wanting to catch his eye, exchange a smile. But he was looking past her. At nothing. And an involuntary shiver went down Helen's spine.

Bonnie feigned disappointment over their lack of commitment to the renewed investigation. But she wasn't into it like before either, especially after she was named editor of the newspaper's annual progress edition, cutting into her evenings and weekends throughout the late summer and early fall.

In September, Helen's weekly television show aired. She was somewhat amazed at how little apprehension she felt. From the first broadcast, she didn't dress up for the cooking portion of her show, appearing instead in jeans and a shirt or sweater. After all, what person in their right mind would cook any other way?

The station wanted a fancier name for the show and accepted Helen's suggestion of "The Wooden Spoon." She was not super-organized with her presentations and usually made a mess in her television kitchen when she demonstrated her recipes. But she had a strong sense of her audience. She looked right at the camera and spoke to people as though they were visiting in her kitchen.

She explained how to spend the entire day making tomato sauce better than an Italian mama and how to get a reasonable substitute by doctoring up store-bought sauce.

She broke rules, mixing down-home cookin' with uptown gourmet. Combining different ethnic foods, she created the hollandaise burger, the Cajun hot dog, the Reuben pizza.

She did dress up in little black dresses with pearls at her throat for the restaurant segments, in which she would ask restaurateurs not only about their menus but also frank questions on how many customers a night walked out on their bills. And she interviewed the diners, too, about the service, if their steaks had arrived hot, if the salad was crisp, if the apple pie was as good as grandma's.

She cajoled caterers into giving prices on the air. "Now, how much exactly would a wedding reception for two hundred cost with this menu?" she would ask. "And does that price include the rental on plates, glasses, and silverware?"

And since no one ever told her she couldn't, during each program she always managed to mention Helen's Heavenly Cheesecakes, which were now available in several Denver-area supermarkets, as an excellent special-occasion dessert. She suggested throwing away the foil containers and garnishing the cheesecakes with fresh fruit so that guests would think they were homemade.

She had four part-time employees now at the bakery. Every month, there were more orders than the month before. Helen was always behind with her paperwork.

Her television show took a lot of time and thought. And the station liked her to make personal appearances at department stores and women's events.

People recognized her. *Helen, the cooking lady.* She even signed autographs! Alex often got introduced as Helen Radcliff's husband. She and Alex always got the best tables when they ate out. Proprietors and chefs hovered.

Her life was full and exciting—almost too much so. She

wasn't home enough. She wasn't spending enough time with her children. She never sat at her kitchen table with a cup of coffee and a book propped up in front of her. She couldn't continue being both the cheesecake queen and a television hostess forever. But for now, she allowed herself to take a great deal of pride in what she had accomplished.

In late November, Jen remembered the pianist. Joann Marshall was an old friend from East High who had played for Libby's dance classes. She was living in Germany with her army officer husband and had never answered the letter they'd sent during their first round of investigating.

Jen got Joann's number from her mother and called her.

Joann apologized about never writing. She'd meant to. Her mother had sent the newspaper article about Libby's car being found. But no, she really didn't know anything useful.

"Except I don't think you three realized how much she hated those children and that school," Joann said. "The last couple of months she didn't even try to be nice to the girls. A couple of the mothers complained. And she was in financial trouble. She hadn't paid me in weeks. I always thought she just walked out the door one day and kept on driving. But then, if that was the case, why would her car have ended up in a farm pond?"

It was after the first of the year that Bonnie thought of the cleaning woman. Dorthea. Evelyn Ballard supplied the woman's last name. Dorthea Mandez. Bonnie tracked her to the downtown library, where she worked as a custodian.

Libby had been a neat, clean person, Dorthea told Bonnie, and very particular about the laundry. She always paid in cash and bought little gifts for Dorthea's children. "Miss Ballard came to us one Christmas morning with presents for everyone," Dorthea recalled. "She was wearing a white coat with a fur collar. The children thought she looked like a princess."

After the Nebraska-Colorado basketball game in January, the three couples gathered at the Radcliffs' for a late supper. The men were in the kitchen rehashing the game. The women were warming themselves in front of the fireplace.

"I think I'll check on Libby's driving record," Bonnie announced. "She was always getting speeding tickets."

"I used to wonder if she didn't accidentally drive off a mountain road going ninety miles an hour," Jen said. "But now that we know that didn't happen, I don't see what good her driving record would be."

"It's in the category of one last thing," Bonnie said.

"Don't tell me you're ready to hang it up," Jen said.

"Maybe. After almost fourteen years, maybe it's time. Maybe someday, one of us will accidentally come across the last piece of the puzzle. But I think we've about exhausted our deductive powers."

Not really expecting much, Bonnie asked her detective friend at the police department if it was possible to check Libby's driving record for the period in 1966 right before she disappeared.

The next day, Bill Weatherford called Bonnie back. She was at her desk in the newsroom.

"Bingo," he said.

Bonnie swung her chair around to face the wall for a modicum of privacy. "You found out something?"

"Damned right. A sweetheart at the Highway Patrol checked it out for me. A speeding citation was issued to Libby Ballard at 2:45 P.M., June 17, 1966."

"Jesus. That's the day after the party."

"She was stopped going north on State Highway 72, a couple of miles off the I-70 junction. The highway patrolman clocked her at eighty-six miles per hour. Driving a fifty-nine red T-bird. The ticket was never paid."

Bonnie's hands were shaking as she returned the phone to its cradle. *North.* Not south toward New Mexico. On the road to Rollinsville.

She dialed Jen's number.

"Should I tell Helen?" she asked.

"We can't keep things from her," Jen said. "I don't think you have a choice."

"But would you want to know if it were Ted?" Bonnie asked.

"Maybe it was," Jen said.

Helen was at the television station taping her show. She felt strangely calm as she listened to Bonnie's news. *The cabin. Of course. Libby had been heading for the cabin.*

Maybe she had known it all along.

Helen returned to the set and finished the taping. The program was about soup. She'd already demonstrated a delicate lobster bisque garnished with caviar. Now she was working on a hearty vegetable beef. "Don't worry about recipes for soup. Be inventive," she said as she worked. "Save your stock when you stew chicken for a casserole. You can make stock by boiling bones—from baked poultry, roasts, steak. Or use tomato juice with a couple of cubes of bouillon. Then add any combination of vegetables to your stock. Include meat if you have it. I like to use at least one starchy ingredient, like rice, corn, beans, potatoes, or even pasta, so the broth will thicken. This is good food. It stretches your food dollar—I freeze every dab of leftovers to add to my next pot of soup. And making soup is an adventure. I'm never quite sure what I'll come up with."

The director gave her thumbs up. Helen left the mess and the soup for the crew and headed for the parking lot.

She sat in her car, trying to decide where to go. She did not want to see Alex. Not tonight.

Libby had not been one last fling for Alex before marriage. Five years into that marriage, he had still been involved with her. Had apparently gotten her pregnant. And was still sneaking off from his wife and two-month-old baby to meet her.

Helen decided on a hotel rather than Jen's or Bonnie's. She needed to think, not talk. And she didn't want to see their husbands, either. Ted and Lenny must have known. That long-ago fishing trip had been a cover so that Alex could be with Libby.

From the hotel room, she called home and explained to Beth that she was tired and since she had an early appointment in the morning, she'd decided to stay in Denver for the night. "Have your dad take you to the club for dinner."

"My mom's a famous cook, and we never get to eat her cooking," Beth complained.

"This weekend I'll cook up a storm. Promise."

"Stuffed pork chops, popovers, twice-baked potatoes, green bean casserole, Waldorf salad, and fresh coconut cake," Beth said without hesitation.

Helen laughed. "You can make the green beans. Ben can fix the potatoes. I'll do the rest."

"What about Dad?" Beth asked. "He needs to help, too."

Helen closed her eyes. *Her family. Her beautiful family.* Without Alex, what would they be?

"Mom? Are you there?"

"Yes, baby. I'm here. Is Ben around?"

"No, he's still at practice. Dad can chop up stuff for the salad and grate the coconut. Don't let him talk you into skinned chicken instead of pork chops."

Helen bought a bottle of Nytol in the hotel gift shop and took the recommended dose. But she couldn't sleep. If she closed her eyes, she saw them. *Alex and Libby*. Like two Greek gods. More beautiful than mere mortals.

Alex kneeling in front of her, his face buried against her lean belly. Alex sucking on the nipple of a small perfect breast.

Helen sat up in bed, hugging her pillow to her middle. "Where is she, Alex? You know, don't you? Damn you to hell for making me find out for myself."

In the morning, Helen drove to Oak Tree Manor out in Lakewood. She'd been there only once, when Evelyn Ballard first moved in.

Helen wondered for a moment if she was in the wrong room. The tiny, emaciated creature in a wheelchair couldn't be Evelyn Ballard. But then, she'd already lived longer than anyone expected.

"I see you on television," Evelyn said, smiling as she used the remote control to turn off "Hollywood Squares" and tilted her parchment cheek up for Helen to kiss. "Watching you makes me wish I could get back in the kitchen—or eat at some of those restaurants."

"I'm still trying out some of the recipes you sent. I plan to bake your aunt Mary's apple crisp on the air next month. I'll let you know when."

"That's nice, honey. Most of those recipes were ordinary. In my time, men mostly wanted meat and potatoes—with pie for dessert. But I had some nice quick bread recipes. Be sure

227

and try the zucchini-raisin-nut bread. That was Carl's favorite."

"I know Jen and her mother have been running your errands, but if there's ever anything I can do . . ."

Evelyn waved away her words. The sleeve of her robe fell away from her arm. Blue-veined skin on bones. "Just send me out some of the apple crisp."

Helen pulled her chair closer to the wheelchair. "We need to talk, Evelyn. You said you never found any letters when you went through Libby's things. But the way you said it made me think of how my mother used to make me go stand outside the back door before she'd tell somebody on the telephone that I wasn't home. You didn't find the letters among Libby's things, but there were letters, weren't there?"

"I can't talk about it, Helen."

"It's time."

"Why?"

"Because not knowing is ruining my life anyway."

"I promised myself I'd never tell," Evelyn said.

Helen waited.

"Libby gave me a metal box. Locked. She brought it to the house. On a Sunday morning. While Fred was at church. She wanted me to give the box to the police if anything happened to her. It was her insurance policy, she said. But she wouldn't tell me what she was insuring against."

Evelyn stopped, staring off into the past. Helen leaned forward and touched Evelyn's arm. "What was in the box?"

"I offered to move in with her. Or help her move home for a while. She wasn't herself. She insisted I just take the box and do as she said. But she came back a week later and said she'd changed her mind. She made me promise to burn what was inside if she died. The key was in her jewelry box. I asked her then if she was pregnant. She wouldn't answer me. Wouldn't tell me anything except she trusted me to do this."

"Did she seem afraid—like someone might hurt her?" Helen asked.

"No, not really. She seemed rather businesslike. Like she was trying to tidy up her life. But it was too late for that. The bank wanted possession of her building August first. They'd already served her with papers before she disappeared. When Fred and I brought her things home from her apartment and stored them up in our attic, we found all that money in the cedar chest we'd given her for high school graduation. A hope chest—but she never picked out a silver pattern, never embroidered any linen. It was up there with the stuff Libby hadn't taken to New York and never reclaimed. Fred said she must have been up to no good to have that money secreted away. Honest people put money in a bank. I told him that whatever she had done, we were partly to blame. We never gave her what she needed."

"The metal box," Helen reminded her.

"Yes, the box. It had letters in it."

"They were from my husband, weren't they?"

"Let it go, dear," Evelyn said. Her head bobbed up and down with an involuntary palsy, making her seem like she was perpetually agreeable. "Nothing can be accomplished except more pain. I don't care where Libby is buried. I don't even care where I'm buried. Not anymore. Dead is dead no matter where bones turn to dust."

Libby's portrait hung over Evelyn's bed. Carl's picture was on the bedside table. A wedding day picture of Evelyn and her husband was in a pewter frame on the dresser next to a crystal lamp that had once been in Libby's bedroom.

"Please," Helen said, taking Evelyn's bony hand.

"Why do you need to know after so many years? Libby should be a hazy memory to you girls. Your lives have been busy and full. I have to think about her because I'm her mother."

"But she haunts us," Helen explained. "I can't stop thinking about her until I find out what happened to her. What she was to my husband. I need to know if he's still my husband only because Libby died."

Evelyn looked up at the picture on the wall, thinking how Libby haunted her, too. Every day. She had chosen one child's welfare over another, and that was as great a crime as if she'd locked Libby out in the cold. She'd read all those articles that claimed genetics were more important than environment, and maybe in some children that was true. In strong children. But Libby was not strong. What had seemed like strength was only a facade. "Sometimes Libby did bad things," Evelyn said, "but she wasn't a bad person. Just fragile. She needed for everything to be just right, and if it wasn't, she got off center."

"Who were the letters from?" Helen asked.

Evelyn sighed again. She stared down at the ugly old hands in her lap. Every inch of her was ugly now. "She was using the men," her tired old voice tried to explain. "Libby didn't love them. She thought she was trying to get at you girls through them. You have to understand that. The men aren't completely to blame. You know how determined Libby was to get her way."

"What men do you mean?" Helen asked, frowning.

"There were letters from your husband and from Jen's and Bonnie's husbands, too. All three of them. Three stacks of letters tied with three ribbons. Red, white, and blue. The ribbon around your husband's letters was red."

"She was having affairs with all three of them?" Helen was shaking her head, disbelieving.

"I'm sorry, dear, but it's true."

"With Ted and Lenny, too?"

Evelyn nodded.

"Where are the letters now?" Helen asked.

"I burned them."

"What were the dates on them?"

"They'd all been written within the last year or so before Libby disappeared."

"You're sure about all this? Absolutely sure?" Helen's hands were tightly clutched in her lap.

Evelyn nodded, already feeling uneasy. She'd kept her mouth shut this long. Just a little longer, and no one would have ever known.

"Maybe I shouldn't have told you," she told Helen. "But I thought you might understand better if you knew about Jen's and Bonnie's husbands. There was this man in New York—you never knew that I went to see Libby up there, did you? There was this man in New York who paid her bills. A rather nice man—he's dead now. He told me that Libby didn't even like sex—she just used it to barter. Yet, only a few years after that, she was involved with *three* men. She was up to something. Scheming. Confused. Using your husbands for some crazy plan to get even with you three girls. Or get you back. I'm not sure which. She'd gotten so distant. So private. I never knew what she was thinking. I tried to get close to her. We were close for a little while in New York. I was always glad I went."

Helen was standing now, looking out the window, her shoulders and back tense. Evelyn knew that Helen would be wanting to leave now, needing time to be alone and digest what she had just learned. But Evelyn needed to keep her a little longer, to make sure Helen understood.

They went out into the spacious backyard with its spreading trees and neatly trimmed shrubs. The yard was the reason Evelyn had chosen this nursing home. If she was going to spend the rest of her days living in one room, she wanted to look out on something pretty. And in nice weather, she could take some sun in the yard and get away from the rest-home smells.

Evelyn found it amazing that people like her held on. She

had supposed that by the time she reached this point, she would have taken a bottle of sleeping pills or slit her wrists. She was terminally ill, and life hadn't been all that good. But she was not suffering greatly—at least not yet—and she had always enjoyed small pleasures. She had made rituals of coffee and the newspaper in the morning and a glass of wine with a good book in the evening. Even now, she found comfort in the routine of her life. Her television shows. Meals on time. Rice pudding every Wednesday evening. Pancakes on Sunday morning. A cup of tea at bedtime with one of the cream-filled chocolates Jen kept her supplied with. The hummingbirds that hovered in the evening about the feeder that Jen's boy had installed outside the window. And she was a coward. Sometimes she dreamed of a miracle cure. Whatever, Evelyn knew she would cling to life for as long as she could.

Helen pushed the wheelchair around the oval garden path. It was warm for May. Still, the blanket over her skinny old legs felt good, and Evelyn drew her coat closed in front. The garden was protected on the north and east by the long wings of the building. Shrubs partially hid the high fence on the other two sides.

Evelyn nodded at the old ladies in the lawn chairs as she rolled by. Only one old man was out. George. He used to teach history. George's mind came and went. Some days he was Abraham Lincoln. Other days he was heartbroken, grieving for his lost Beatrice.

Helen picked a sunny patch by the rose bushes, parking the wheelchair beside a concrete bench.

Helen was tense, seating herself just on the edge of the bench, waiting for an opening to leave. Evelyn could imagine the thoughts dashing through her mind. *All three men.* Her Alex hadn't been the only one who'd succumbed to Libby's demands. Did that make his sin any more acceptable?

232

Evelyn had no illusions. The men had been Libby's victims. To what end, she was unsure—except that Libby could not bear to see Jen and Helen and Bonnie content with their husbands and their lives. Their contentment had come at her expense.

Her poor Libby.

"Well, it's time I head back to Boulder," Helen said. "Thank you for telling me. I'll take you back to your room now."

Evelyn reached for Helen's hand. "Alex is a nice man," she said.

"Yeah. So nice he had an affair with his wife's best friend."

Evelyn winced at the bitterness in Helen's voice. "Did you think the world was going to be a perfect place with no hot coals to walk across?" she asked, hanging on to Helen's hand. "Dear ones die. Husbands stray. Dreams fade away. But there's also beauty along the way."

"So, what are you saying? That what Alex did was okay? That I should smell the roses and forget about it?" The sunshine highlighted the lines radiating from Helen's eyes. Would Libby have lines now? Her skin had been so perfect.

"No," Evelyn said. "You can't ever forget about it. But you can take things into consideration—like how much you have to lose."

"I wish you hadn't burned those letters. Now, I'll never know what was in his mind."

"Torment was in his mind," Evelyn said.

It took Helen until the following evening to work up her courage. To wait for just the right moment.

The children had gone to their rooms. Alex had gotten a beer for himself, poured a glass of wine for her. She hadn't asked for one. But she had been distant. Stayed carefully on her side of the bed last night. Avoided touching him.

He offered to build a fire on the deck, but she wasn't interested and went to take a bath, carrying the wineglass with her.

She took her nightgown with her into the bathroom. She couldn't possibly undress in front of him. Not tonight. Would she ever again?

When she came out of the bathroom, he was propped up in bed, arms folded across his chest, waiting for her to have it out with him for whatever it was that was bothering her. His skin was tan against the white of his T-shirt. His hair was beginning to gray—like hers. But his body was still lean, and the cragginess creeping into his face had thus far only enhanced his looks.

Helen looked better than she ever had looked in her life, but Alex was still better-looking. A head turner. A man that women acted silly over.

Helen wondered if she had been more beautiful, would her husband have been less easily seduced.

Helen seated herself cross-legged on the bed, facing him. "God knows where you got it, but I know you gave Libby money," she began. "I know she was screwing Lenny and Ted, too. I know that the three of you wrote her love letters."

He closed his eyes. "No, you don't know any of those things."

"Yes, I do. I don't have proof, Alex, but I know. What happened? Did you perform an abortion that went bad? Is she buried out back of the cabin?"

"Why couldn't you let it go, Helen? Does the life we've made mean so little to you?" He was crying, his nose starting to run. She handed him Kleenex from the box on her bedside table.

"Remember that song your mother used to sing to the children?" Helen asked. "About the wise man and the foolish man? The wise man built his house upon a rock, and it stood against the flood. But the foolish man built his house upon the sand. That's our house, Alex."

"And all these years since Libby haven't been enough to shore up the foundation?" he asked.

"Apparently not," she said.

And so, he told her. Everything. It was worse than she had ever imagined.

Alex's Story

Seventeen

He had first met Libby in a crowded, smoky roadhouse patronized by college students and truck drivers.

Helen's friends had gathered there to meet him.

He and Helen had been dating only three weeks but having sex since the second date and talking about the future since the third. Helen was the sort of girl one married. Alex knew that the first time he saw her. She was bright, pretty, kind. Sexy in a wholesome sort of way, with thick wavy brown hair that shone in the sunlight, a good figure, smooth skin, wide green eyes. And she didn't play games. She told him that she loved him before he said the words to her.

Libby Ballard was not that sort at all.

Libby was wearing tight faded jeans, well-worn cowboy boots, and a white V-neck sweater. A tiny gold cross on a delicate chain hung in the V. Her long hair hung like heavy black silk down her back.

"So, you're Alex, the man who's going to take my Helen away from me," she said as she shook his hand. Her hand was cool to the touch. Slim. Delicate. Like the rest of her.

"I wasn't aware that Helen belonged to you," Alex responded. But she was already looking past him.

Jen was blond and cover-girl pretty. Bonnie was heavy-breasted and had a wonderful laugh. Their boyfriends, both second-string players on the CU football team, were talkative and friendly—Helen had already told them that he was a football fan and loved to ski and fish. But Alex was so aware of Libby, he had a hard time tuning into the sports chatter.

She was with a history professor—B. Jacobson Newcomber, Ph.D. That was the way she introduced him, with a heavy emphasis on the "B," as though she was making fun. The professor kept looking over his shoulder. Alex decided he was self-conscious about being seen in public with a female student. Probably he had had something more private in mind when he asked Libby out. She seemed to enjoy his discomfort and called him "professor," making the people at the tables on either side of them turn and stare.

Professor Newcomber kept suggesting they leave, but Libby put him off. "I want to dance, dance, dance," she said, arching her back and lifting her wonderful hair from her neck.

Alex wondered if the gesture was for his benefit. Her neck was long and very white.

Apparently the professor didn't dance—at least not the sort of uninhibited gyrations that were taking place on the tiny, packed dance floor. Other men asked Libby to dance while the professor tried desperately to look like he was having a good time watching her get into the music with tough-looking men who danced without removing their cowboy hats or billed caps.

Alex watched her, too. The music was hot, and Libby could move her body like no other. He felt himself getting hard just watching.

Several times during the evening, Libby caught Alex staring at her. She would stare back. Eyes wide. Daring him.

Libby danced with Ted several times. They were good together. Jen tried not to look jealous as she pretended to listen to the professor telling about his research into nineteenth-century dueling customs, adjusting his voice to the volume of the music. "You mean dueling—like with swords?" she asked.

"More usually with pistols," he explained.

Toward the end of the evening, the DJ put on a slow number. Helen slid into Alex's arms. They danced close, making love through their clothes while he watched Libby over Helen's shoulder.

Alex didn't see Libby again for weeks. But he found himself listening for any mention of her name, thinking of her too often. Then one day, there she was at his apartment door. No smile. Just that same inscrutable look on her face.

"Well?" she asked.

"I can't screw you here," Alex told her. His voice sounded hoarse, like he hadn't spoken in days. "Helen sometimes comes on the spur of the moment."

Libby lifted her left eyebrow and said nothing.

"My folks have a cabin up near Rollinsville," Alex said. Sweat was gathering under his arms, in his crotch. His heart was thumping erratically. "Let me see if I can get someone to cover for me."

Had he already thought about it? Did he already know that,

given the opportunity, he would have sex with Helen's best friend? But years later, as he tried to explain it to his wife of nineteen years, he didn't remember his thoughts at that moment—just his actions. He spared Helen nothing. Almost angrily, he supplied every detail. She had wanted to know, goddamnit. For years. He would tell her and be done with it. Finally.

He had given Libby directions and met her at the cabin. He met her there seven times before the friends scattered.

That first time, Libby made him sit in a chair across the room while she explained very carefully what she was going to do. She planned to blow his mind—to fix him so that for the rest of his life, whenever he was having good sex, he would be thinking of her.

"I will always be there, between you and your darling Helen," she said, with no smile, no inflection in her voice. "Just call it Libby's revenge."

"What are you avenging?" Alex asked.

"Broken promises," she said, slowly rising from her chair, walking toward him, her body wondrously loose and fluid, like an exotic feline in the jungle.

She did a striptease for him. Libby was totally without inhibition. Her moves were erotic, but her body was innocent-looking—almost childlike—and that made her dance all the more lewd. She was lithe beyond belief, her breasts spreading to almost nothing when she arched her back or raised her arms. He wanted those tiny nipples in his mouth. To suck them hard until he hurt her.

Alex's clothes grew damp with sweat, his breathing ragged. He was cold and hot at the same time. He wanted her. Too much. Crazy wanting.

She set the terms. She was to be in control. Always. If he

tried to be the aggressor, to take the initiative, she withdrew and Alex found herself holding a cold statue.

He was not allowed to have a voice in anything. She said when they could meet. She set the scene, the pace. And she insisted on leaving marks on his body. Bruises on his neck. Fingernail scratches down his back. Teeth marks in his buttocks and thighs. She thought it was funny that he would have to hide them from Helen.

One time she stripped down to white-lace lingerie. Wearing only a half-cup bra, a garter belt, and white silk stockings, she masturbated, then gave Alex her fingers to lick. That time, he lost control and shoved her down on the floor. He wanted her then. That minute. That instant. None of her little games.

She fought him like a tiger. Then he realized that this was part of the game. He was behaving just as she'd planned.

But she was serious about her games and fought back with all of her surprising strength. She slapped at his face and made his lip bleed. She bit his neck and drew blood. She tried to jam a knee in his crotch.

He slapped her back, hard enough to make his fingers tingle, hard enough to leave a red hand print on her cheek. He had never hit a woman before. It made him angry that she had reduced him to that. And the anger made him hotter.

The blood from his neck dripped onto white skin and even whiter lace.

At one point, she almost got away, but he grabbed a stocking-clad foot and jerked her back down on the floor. She landed hard, with a scream and a thud. Using a knee, he forced her legs apart. They were both sweating, panting. Then, planting his knees to hold her legs open, pinning her arms above her head, he was finally able to enter her.

He was an animal. Grunting. Yelling. Not caring if he hurt her. Wanting to hurt her.

When he'd finally pumped himself to an orgasm, she tried to shove him off her. She beat on his back with her fists. "Get off me, damn it!" she screamed.

Alex laughed. *He* was in control.

And suddenly, he was hard again. He was able to go on and on. Her struggling and curses made it better. She dug at his back with her nails, tried to bite his shoulders. Their bodies reeked of sweat and sex.

It was the most intense sex he'd ever experienced, yet he could make it last. And last. When he finally came, he wondered if he was going to pass out. To die. Pleasure and pain all mixed up together.

Libby was exhausted and furious. Alex had broken her rules. "I hate you," she said, spitting in his face. "I hate you with all my heart."

"It's mutual, baby," he said, spitting back.

The next time, Libby was an innocent maid. She had her hair in long ringlets and was wearing a pristine white nightgown with long sleeves and a lace yoke. A tiny cameo hung from the pink ribbon around her neck. Her satin skin smelled of talcum powder. And Alex was tender. Exquisitely tender, with tears in his eyes.

Alex had never understood the love that Helen, Jen, and Bonnie had for Libby. Unquestioning love. When from the beginning, Alex saw something in her that none of them seemed to realize. Libby was the most egocentric human being Alex had ever known. She was calm and content only so long as she was the center of things.

Even Lenny and Ted accepted her domination. They made a joke out of it but mostly went along with her and even participated in Libby worship. Alex did, too. After all, she made things happen.

Alex was living two lives. At some level, self-loathing lurked. But he didn't deal with it. Other emotions took over. He was falling more deeply in love with Helen. Making love to her at every opportunity. Proposing marriage. Planning their wedding and their life.

And sneaking off to meet Libby. Or thinking about sneaking off to meet Libby. Almost constantly, it seemed, unless he was with Helen.

The last time he was with Libby was the day before his wedding.

That was the day he took the picture that Helen found. He had wanted a nude picture of Libby, but she wouldn't hear of it. "It wouldn't be the same in a picture," she said.

So they went outside, and she posed on the front steps, smiling over her shoulder.

Alex avoided Libby after that. He concentrated on his wife and marriage, on his upcoming induction into the military and their move to San Antonio. He labored at not thinking about Libby. Only Helen. Beloved Helen. The woman who would be his wife for a lifetime. The mother of his future children.

Libby left for New York before Alex and Helen moved to San Antonio, and when she was at last gone, he felt as though he were a convicted killer who had just gotten a stay of execution.

Alex got down on his knees and promised God he would be faithful to Helen for the rest of his life. Then he begged God to help him keep the promise.

He wanted to make his marriage work. He loved his wife. He had no doubt that she loved him. But he wanted to be gloriously happy. He wanted to be captivated by Helen. He wanted her to expel the memory of Libby. Helen didn't do that. Alex found himself blaming her. If she were more glamorous. More self-confident. More ambitious. Less domestic. She preferred cotton underwear to silk lingerie. Comfortable shoes to sexy ones. If Helen were a more exciting woman, Alex could leave his burden behind. If he could love Helen absolutely, he would be absolved of guilt.

Helen loved to cook. Alex hadn't realized how much during their frantic courtship, which was nourished by hamburgers and carry-out pizzas. But as a married woman, she put on an apron and began puttering around a kitchen—like a mother. The meals she prepared were delicious, but Alex felt cheated. And Helen couldn't understand why he wasn't more pleased with the wonderful meals she prepared. Other men bragged when their wives were good cooks.

When his orders came for Vietnam, Helen wanted to go with him. In those early days, dependents were still allowed. But Buddhist monks were burning themselves to death in the streets of Saigon, and already Americans were being wounded and killed in the mountains. A good husband would not take his wife to such a place. Helen's parents, of course, agreed with him. Their daughter could move in with them while Alex was gone.

Alex was grateful for the time apart. He planned to miss Helen desperately and return to her pure of heart. Distance would allow him to do that.

He was never tempted by any of the surprisingly beautiful Saigon prostitutes. But he would take out Libby's picture to look at while he masturbated.

When Helen wrote to him that Libby wasn't going back to New York after her brother's funeral, Alex felt physically ill. He even beat his head against the wall of his tiny cell-like quarters in the Saigon military hospital, where he was stationed. He already had been accepted in the residency program at University Hospital in Denver. It was too late to change course.

Or was it? He could write letters. Helen's physician father had a classmate who headed the OB/GYN program at Cook County in Chicago. Alex could arrange to take state boards in Illinois. Or in Arizona. Helen's parents were moving to Phoenix.

But he didn't do anything except wait, in a fog of euphoria and dread, for his own return to Denver.

For a time, nothing happened.

He was shocked to see Libby with the rest of the gang at the airport, but he was so genuinely caught up in the joy of homecoming, in the pleasure of seeing his darling Helen and sweeping her in his arms, that he was able to give Libby a one-armed hug and tell her she looked great with little more than a momentary tingle of uncomfortable awareness.

Alex was incredibly busy the first year of his residency. He and Helen were intent on having a baby. They skied and partied with friends. He fished with Lenny and Ted when he could. Life was good and getting better.

But deep down, he knew that when Libby beckoned, he would go. The waiting was agony. She wouldn't even give him one of those looks. At parties, he would wait all evening, his stomach in knots for her to give him a sign that never came. Afterward, he couldn't stand to talk to Helen. Conversation and booze made her high. She always wanted to make love after a party. That was when they had their most intense sex. No talking. Just sex.

He and Helen had yet to conceive a child. When that high, holy event happened, Alex didn't want to be thinking about Libby.

In the end, he went to her. Which was, of course, just what Libby wanted. He knocked on her door one night and told her she was driving him crazy.

She was dressing to go out. Her makeup perfect. Her hair in a sleek knot. Her satin dressing gown revealed her smooth, white throat.

"Sunday morning," she said, "at the cabin." And hurried him out the door.

The next four days passed in a confusing blur. Alex got through them on automatic pilot. He was in a perpetual state of arousal, aching with his need. He avoided his wife.

When he pulled up in front of the cabin, Libby was waiting on the porch, dressed in beige jeans and a man's white undershirt that revealed more of her torso than it covered. Her lustrous black hair was loose down her back, her skin white and devoid of makeup. And she was exquisitely beautiful. Alex wondered if he was in love as well as in lust.

She had the good grace to allow him to minister to her body as long as he desired. He had to have his mouth on every orifice. To touch his penis to her lips, her breasts, her belly, bury it in her wonderful black hair. She was wet with his saliva when he finally entered her. He didn't want to. He wanted to caress and lick and fondle her forever. But he wasn't strong enough to stop himself any longer.

His orgasm was immediate and painful.

Afterward, while they sipped straight bourbon, Libby made him describe in great detail what he had been thinking and feeling at each stage of the lovemaking. Talking about it made him want it again.

He went on endlessly. When he was about to come, Libby would make him stop. Take a sip of bourbon. Calm himself.

For hours, it seemed, he rode the roller coaster up and down without ever taking the final death-defying plunge. The end, when it came, was almost disappointing. Nothing could live up to that last climb to the summit.

"Do I love you?" he asked when he could talk.

"No. You hate me, remember."

"What if I want to marry you?"

"Marriage is for babies and keeping house. I will never be any man's wife."

"Will you be my mistress?"

She laughed. "*Mistress?* You've got to be kidding! I belong to *me*. That's why I make you crazy—because you know you'll never own me. I'd die first."

He leaned forward and bit her right nipple—hard. She screamed and smacked her hand hard against his ear. He had to shake his head several times to clear away the ringing, then he fell on her again.

On the drive home, he felt drained. He never wanted sex again.

The Rolling Stones sang "Satisfaction" on the radio. Alex turned it off and drove in silence. He hated himself. Hated Libby. And dreaded the evening ahead. But he knew that somehow, he had to act to normal around his wife.

It would end badly. He knew that even then, on the journey down the mountain. He took a tight curve and looked in his rearview mirror, hoping to see Libby in her red Thunderbird missing the curve and plunging to her death in the gully below.

Then he took back the thought. She couldn't die on this road. Not the road to the cabin. But the idea of Libby dead was a pleasing one.

Maybe she could be hit by a truck on the highway. Maybe her Victorian house would catch on fire. All that old wood would go up like a tinder box. Or maybe she would fall down the stairs to her upstairs apartment and break her neck. Her fine white neck.

The best times were after he'd just seen Libby, when he felt purged and could convince himself that had been the last time, that he despised her, that he would never go back. The day after, he'd be especially nice to Helen, daydream with her about how nice their life was going to be when they had a family and money and a nice house. And that night, they would make sweet, gentle love. Safe love.

He loved Helen. That was the irony of it. He really loved his wife. And wanted to have children with her. Build for the future with her. Grow old with her.

But he would find fault with her one day and treat her like a queen the next. At times, she looked at him with such pain and puzzlement that his heart turned over in his chest. His greatest fear was that Helen would leave him, taking his dream of home and family with her.

They both shed tears of joy when Helen found out she was pregnant. Alex cried again in the night, alone in the bathroom of their shabby Denver apartment, kneeling on the cold cracked tile, his folded hands resting on the side of the bathtub as he once again begged God to help him stay away from Libby. The God of his childhood. An old bearded man on a big gold chair who had the power to do anything. Alex didn't believe in that God anymore, or maybe in any other, but he had found no other image to replace him.

Eighteen

His daughter, Beth, was two months old when Alex found out the incredible truth about Libby.

Summer 1966—a time of nationwide protests against Vietnam. Which tore at Alex. Could the United States government be wrong? He and Bonnie argued about it constantly, Ted siding with Alex, Lenny with his wife. Helen and Jen weren't sure. Libby grew impatient and would leave if the war talk went on too long.

Alex felt his arguments grow progressively weaker as he became less sure about what young men were dying for. He both worried about being called back to active duty and thought about volunteering. His year in Saigon had been in many ways a respite from life.

But that was then. Wartime Vietnam wasn't the same. And when he came back, Libby would still be here, waiting to eat away his soul.

His unfaithfulness during Helen's pregnancy carried his self-loathing to new depths. Even impending fatherhood had not given him the strength he needed—even though his affair with Libby was less exciting than before. Even clandestine sex could become routine, he discovered. He thought constantly about ending it. Practiced the way he would tell her. Composed letters in his head. But when Libby sensed him pulling away, she would light candles, do her dances, play her games, leave marks on his body.

But it wasn't the same. Since the renewal of their affair, she had an orgasm only when he went down on her, and then it often took so long that all eroticism was gone from the act. And Alex found himself wondering if she'd really come during those first exquisitely erotic couplings when all was danger and mystery. Was it all an act? Did she really get that much satisfaction out of screwing Helen?

For that was what Libby's participation was all about. An act against Helen.

Libby wanted him to tell her that Helen didn't make him crazy, that Helen was less beautiful, less exciting. And Alex would confess that he thought of Libby when he came in his wife's body.

Libby wanted to come to his apartment when Helen was out and make love in their bed, but Alex refused even to discuss such a possibility. Once, when the group had gathered after a football game, Alex came upon Libby in the bedroom, lying on the bed, her head on Helen's pillow, eyes closed. He was stunned. Furious. What the hell did she think she was doing?

He was about to rush forward and drag her out of the room,

when Helen appeared at the bathroom door. "Libby has a head-ache," she explained as she handed Libby a glass of water and aspirin. He watched as his pregnant wife sat on the side of the bed in which they had conceived their unborn child and placed a wet washcloth on Libby's forehead. Shaking, Alex had backed out of the door, his fists clenched, hate twisting his insides. *If only Libby would die.*

When he held his newborn daughter in his arms, her body still wet from Helen's womb, he vowed to be worthy of his child's love and respect. And Helen's. *So help me God.* He would rather die than continue the lie his life had become.

The next morning, Alex was sitting by Helen's hospital bed when Libby arrived with an immense bouquet for Helen and pink-wrapped gifts for the baby. Alex had to turn away when Libby and Helen embraced.

"I've been by the nursery," Libby said, tears in her eyes. "She's beautiful, Helen. Just beautiful. I'm so happy for you and Alex. And for me. I'll be her Auntie Libby. I'll teach her to dance."

When he arrived home one evening the following week, Libby's car was parked in front of the building. Alex turned around and went back to the hospital, calling Helen to say he had an emergency.

"Oh, I'm so sorry, honey," Helen's voice said. "Libby's here. She brought our dinner. She and Beth are making friends."

The thought of Libby holding his baby made Alex feel ill.

Beth was two weeks old before Alex realized that "Beth" was a diminutive for "Elizabeth." He'd thought it was just a sweet old-fashioned name. He'd had a great-aunt Beth, who'd been his favorite relative as a child. He thought that was why Helen suggested the name. That's what he'd told his parents.

Surely Helen had explained to him why she wanted *that*

name for their baby. But sometimes he tuned Helen out. Sometimes he even tuned patients out and had to ask them to repeat
what they had just said.

He wanted to protest—to change the baby's birth certificate.
He couldn't have a daughter named for Libby. It was obscene.
But he couldn't say a word without explaining why. And Beth
was already Beth by then. Anyone who asked about his baby
was told that a beloved aunt had been named Beth.

Libby came by often over the next two months. And Bonnie.
They had two new mothers to visit, now. Jen had Mandy two
weeks after Beth was born.

Before, Alex had found it exciting to be around Libby and
his wife at the same time. At parties, after they renewed their
affair, he and Libby would indulge themselves with stolen
glances. Shoulders brushing. Living on the edge.

Now, he avoided her. He hated her. He wished she would
go away and never come back.

Beth was tiny and perfect. Already, she was responding to
his voice, trying to smile. But, even though he knew that new
fathers often felt a bit left out, even jealous of their babies,
Alex was unprepared for the disruption Beth brought to his
life and for how completely motherhood claimed his wife. Helen and Jen had daily telephone conversations discussing sched-
ules and rashes—a cult of two, with their own mothers hovering
on the periphery.

Alex hurt Helen's feelings when he asked one evening if
they could please talk about something besides the baby. But
for Helen, everything somehow related back to Beth—the
weather, the future of the world, the economy, Alex's health,
her own health, the health of their parents. The one time he
had been able to get her out of the house for dinner and a
movie, she called the sitter four times.

Alex welcomed summonses from the hospital. Deliveries were never boring. The lively bantering of the delivery room team was soothing. The family in the waiting room treated him like a god.

Postpartum sex with his wife had been disappointing. He had patiently waited the full six weeks, but even so Helen was tender and tense. And the presence of a baby in the bassinet by the bed was inhibiting. When Beth whimpered, Helen pulled away to jiggle the bassinet and pat their daughter's tiny back. He could sense her relief when he finally came. Alex wanted to rage at her, to warn her that she needed to do better than that.

Which was, of course, unfair. New motherhood was a special time. Normally Helen was loving and passionate. Not all the time, of course. Marriage wasn't like that. But Alex found himself reasoning that, if his wife were more sensual, he never would have strayed. He replayed that line of reasoning as his mind and body restlessly waited to settle into sleep.

The next night, he fell asleep waiting for her to finish nursing the baby.

In the days that followed, Helen would try to hurry him along so he'd finish before the baby started to cry. Beth was a restless baby, sleeping only in snatches, calm only when she was being held or nursed.

Then one night, they did better. Helen nursed Beth first— on both breasts until her little tummy was as round as a melon. Alex pushed the bassinet out into the hall and held Helen for a long time first. He knew his wife's body and her responses, but his ministrations worked only if she relaxed and let the sensations have their way. He could feel that happening, and his own body responding accordingly. Helen was wet and moaning before he entered her. And when he felt her shuddering in orgasm, he felt enormous relief. It was still there for them. With great tenderness, he held his wife and kissed her and told her how much he loved her. More than anything. And he meant it. More than baby Beth. More than the practice of medicine. And certainly more than Libby. But then, that was a given. He'd never *loved* Libby. He'd just wanted her more than heaven and earth.

An early morning thunderstorm had been predicted, and already the wind was intensifying, making the joints of the old apartment building creak. But the air in the bedroom was heavy and still. Helen had closed the windows, not wanting a draft on the baby.

Alex dozed a while and woke when Helen got up to nurse Beth. A lovely sight. His wife and baby. What he had always wanted.

I will not go to Libby again, he promised himself. It was over. Truly over.

And it was. Alex had been with Libby for the last time.

"No way," Alex said, loosening his tie and slumping down on his side of the high wooden booth. "Look, I'm dead tired, and I don't know who's gotten who pregnant, but I really don't want to be involved."

Alex glanced at his watch—already past six. Helen would be expecting him for dinner.

"But doctors do abortions all the time," Lenny was insisting, gesturing to the barmaid and pointing to his empty mug.

"Not really," Alex said, trying to decide if the beer was making his headache better or worse. "Not M.D.s anyway. We've got too much to lose. I've heard there's a midwife out by Lowry who does a good job."

"No. Nothing back alley," Lenny insisted. "I want you to do it."

"No way," Alex repeated. "I'd be risking my medical license, my whole damned future. Hell, I could go to jail."

"She says it has to be you."

"*She* who? Surely Bonnie doesn't want an abortion."

"No. Not Bonnie," Lenny said with a soulful sigh.

Lenny was having an affair. Alex tried to decide if he was shocked. Lenny was personable and boyishly handsome, already on his way to becoming a local celebrity, out and about a great deal. Here in the bar, people had recognized him. Women kept glancing his way. *The guy who does sports on television.*

Still, Alex felt indignant. Lenny shouldn't be screwing around on Bonnie. Bonnie would be devastated if she knew. Bonnie was a great gal, a loyal wife.

Like Helen.

Lenny looked so dejected that Alex reached across the table and put a reassuring hand on his forearm. "Look, good buddy, it happens. I know you've got all these cheerleaders and female sports groupies making eyes at you. Sometimes temptation gets the best of us."

"Have you ever been unfaithful to Helen?"

"Yes. Makes me feel like a real shit, too. I wish it had never happened."

"It's Libby," Lenny said.

Alex actually turned to see if Libby was coming in the front door of the bar.

He turned back to Lenny. "What do you mean—'it's Libby?'"

"I mean it's Libby who needs an abortion. She says if she has one, she won't let anyone do it but you. She doesn't want some butcher with a coat hanger. If she doesn't get an abortion,

I'm afraid Bonnie will find out. She might leave me, Alex. Hell, of course she'd leave me. How unfaithful can you be? Screwing one of her best friends. And I'm supposed to be the all-American boy. My career could go down the tubes. Hell, I can't believe this mess. Libby's crazy, you know. One minute she says she wants to have a baby, the next minute she's hysterical to get rid of it. She sure as hell wouldn't go through with an abortion if it wasn't safe."

Alex held up his hand to stop Lenny's onslaught of words. Libby *pregnant?* By Lenny? *No way.*

Alex didn't understand why Lenny would be saying such a thing? Libby was *his.*

"I don't believe you," Alex said. His voice sounded strange. His temples were throbbing. His gut felt like it was collapsing.

His tone made Lenny stare. "Well, I don't care what you believe," he said indignantly. "The fact is, the lady's pregnant."

Alex reached across the table and grabbed Lenny's necktie. "I say you're lying," he hissed, jerking hard on the tie.

"The hell I am," Lenny, raising his voice and shoving away Alex's hand.

The barmaid, carrying two beers on a tray, stopped short of the table. The people at the bar turned to stare. The burly bartender came out from behind the bar and started for the booth.

Lenny managed a smile for the waitress. "Everything's fine," he told her. He pulled a ten out of his billfold and held it out for her. "Keep the change."

Warily, she put the two mugs on the table and backed away.

And suddenly Alex found himself laughing. Everyone in the room was watching now. But he couldn't stop laughing. Such a joke. Such a big fucking cosmic joke.

Then, abruptly, without a word to Lenny, he scooted out of

the booth and headed for the door. He had to see Libby. To confront her. To smash her face. To do *something.*

She wasn't home. Alex pounded on the outside door to her upstairs apartment over and over. "Open the fucking door," he called. "I know you're in there." But he knew she wasn't. Her car wasn't parked in the alley.

By then Lenny had driven up and was standing below on the sidewalk, watching.

Finally, Alex gave up his pounding and sat down on the top step, his hands hanging between his knees. The street light had come on. Lenny looked yellow. "Where did you fuck her?" Alex asked down the steps.

"At the cabin. She had a key. She said Helen had given it to her. That Helen thought she was meeting that professor there. I didn't think anyone would ever know."

"In the bed up in the loft?"

"There. All over the place. You, too?"

Alex nodded.

Cautiously, Lenny climbed the steps. "Do you love her?" he asked.

"No. I don't think I do. Not now, anyway. But I've been obsessed with her. God, have I ever! Do you love her?"

"Yeah. At least, I thought I did. For a time, I'd even thought about leaving Bonnie." Lenny looked up at the closed door. "I wonder where she is."

"Probably fucking Ted," Alex said.

The two men stared at each other. *Ted?* Why not? The husbands of Libby's very best friends.

"I guess we'd better go talk to him and find out," Alex said.

Lenny sank down on the step below Alex, put his head against Alex's knees and softly began to cry, his shoulders shaking, his breathing ragged.

Alex leaned forward and gathered his friend in his arms. He was crying, too, tears streaming down his cheeks.

They found Ted at home alone, watching television. Jen and the baby were at her parents' house. Her dad wasn't feeling well. Lenny picked up Ted's shoes and handed them to him. "Put them on. We're going for a ride."

"Where?"

"To Libby's," Alex said, waiting by the door, his hand resting on the door knob.

"What the hell for?" Ted looked from Alex to Lenny, his eyes wary.

"Did you know Libby was pregnant?" Lenny asked.

"Oh, shit," Ted said, still holding one shoe. "Are you sure? She said that wouldn't happen."

"No, that's why we're going over there," Alex said. "To find out for sure. Put your other shoe on."

"I don't get it. How do you guys know she's pregnant? What the fuck's going on?"

In the car, Alex and Lenny tried to explain. Libby had been screwing all three of them.

"I don't believe you," Ted said from the backseat, angrily. "I don't believe any of this."

Libby's car was now parked in the alley. Alex parked behind it, and the three men climbed the steps.

When Libby opened the door, she didn't seem surprised to see them standing there, huddled together on her small stoop. She stood to one side to let them enter.

Her black hair hung loose and flowing. She was barefoot, wearing loose-fitting satin pajamas. Her face was devoid of makeup, her lips barely darker than the surrounding skin, her pale eyelids giving her eyes a childlike quality.

She could have been a Botticelli angel. Ethereal. Flawless.

But for once, her beauty left Alex unmoved. He grabbed her arm and pulled her into the bedroom. He threw her on the bed, jerked off her pajama trousers and peeled down white lace panties.

With Lenny and Ted watching from the doorway, Libby endured Alex's examination quietly, her face expressionless.

She was pregnant. About nine or ten weeks.

Alex wanted to reach inside of her and rip out the fetus with his bare hands. The last time he had been with her was the week before his two-month-old daughter was born. And he had no doubt that she also had been with Lenny and Ted that week.

She had planned it this way. One pregnancy. Three marriages ruined.

How could anyone so evil look like she did?

He refused to talk until they had left her apartment. He took big gulping breaths of air as the three of them walked toward his car.

Ted staggered. Lenny grabbed his arm.

"I still don't get it," Ted said. "You mean she's really been screwing all three of us? Christ! I've been going through holy hell, and she's been playing a joke. I thought she was in love with me. Really in love with me. I thought she was a saint. So pure and beautiful. I thought I was the first man she'd ever had. She told me that. And I believed her."

Alex roared with laughter. "Let me tell you two stiffs exactly what she is. Libby Ballard is a fucking witch. She is the most manipulative human being I've ever known. She set out to ruin our lives just for the hell of it. I wish I had the nerve to strangle her."

But Alex felt more pain than anger. He understood how Ted and Lenny felt.

261

Alex drove to a nearby bar. They ordered a round of scotch and water. Doubles.

"She has to have an abortion," Lenny said.

The three men nodded. Yes. Quickly. Before she starts to show. Before their wives start asking questions.

"I wrote her letters," Alex admitted. Explicit, incriminating letters. He'd refused to write them at first. But she insisted that he put on paper how it felt to make love to her, what his fantasies were. He got turned on writing them the first few times. But then the writing became a chore. And finally he was writing how despicable they both were. How he hated her and himself. How it had to end. Then when it didn't, he stopped writing.

"I wrote some, too," Ted said. "Love letters. Real heavy stuff about destiny and forever. Even while I was writing them, I thought how horrible it would be if Jen ever read them. But it was another way to make love to Libby."

Lenny nodded. "I'd never written letters to anyone in my life. Bonnie always takes care of the social stuff. The secretary at work does business letters. I didn't even write my parents from camp. But Libby insisted. Kinky stuff. What turned me on. Stuff I never told anyone else. Stuff I've never done with anyone but her. *Jesus.*"

"She could blackmail us," Ted said. He was smoking, the first time Alex had seen him smoke in months. Jen would smell the smoke on his clothes and give him a hard time. Ted had promised when she got pregnant he'd give it up. He was one of those men who'd be obese by forty and have his first heart attack by fifty if he wasn't married to a woman like Jen.

Alex called another resident physician to cover for him at the hospital. Then the three of them called their wives, claiming a late-night poker game with the guys, and drank on. When the bar closed, they drove up to Lookout Mountain with two six-packs.

The view was calming. A sprawling, golden Denver twinkled at their feet. The awesome bulk of the Rockies surrounded them.

"I came up here with Helen the night you and Jen got married," Alex told Ted. "We had been married a month—long enough to realize it wasn't going to be a fairy tale."

Alex dreaded the hangover that awaited him in the morning. But he couldn't give up the night just yet, even though the three of them kept saying the same things over and over. *How could she? What idiots they had been. Never had sex been more intense.* Letting out the secret felt good. Even jealousy was neutralized. She had duped them all.

She had begun her affairs with Ted and Lenny last summer, shortly after Alex had taken up with her again. Within the same month, they decided.

"Jesus," Ted said, sitting on a boulder, shoulders slumped forward, "what kind of game was she playing?"

"I actually proposed to her," Lenny confessed. "But Libby said she was afraid of marriage. She said it suffocated souls. And I really couldn't imagine living with anyone but Bonnie. I was beginning to feel like a real shit. But I couldn't bring myself to stop. If she called, I went. If I picked up the phone and it was her . . . Christ! I broke out in a sweat. There was no way I could not go to her. No way."

The other two men nodded silently. *No way.*

At 2:00 A.M., they were back at Libby's apartment. She put on a terry-cloth robe and rocked in her wicker rocker as she watched them methodically going from one room to the next, looking in, under and behind drawers; under mattresses; emptying cupboards; opening boxes; thumbing through books; looking inside record album covers, under rugs, everywhere. Ted took her car keys and went downstairs to search her car and the dance-school office.

For more than two hours they looked for the letters. Finally Ted demanded the key to Libby's safe-deposit box.

She gestured for them to sit down. "Why should I give you the letters?" she asked.

"Because we don't trust you," Lenny said.

"And I don't trust you—not any of you. The letters are my proof if I ever decide I need it—like proving to your wives that any one of you could have made me pregnant—like proving what shits you guys really are."

"You can't have this baby," Alex told her. "Too many people will be hurt."

"Alex has agreed to do an abortion," Ted told her. "Then we want you to leave Colorado. I can help you sell the building. You can use your equity to get started some place else."

"The bank gets the building," she said. "They've already given me notice."

"Then we'll give you enough money to tide you over," Ted promised.

She looked at each of them. Eyes moist. Chin high. "I had a life planned, you know. It would have been a beautiful life full of love and success. But the three of you took my girls away from me. You could have let them have a year or two. Or you could have come along. But no. You were *Colorado* men. Nothing would do but to stay near your beloved mountains. You owe me more than 'something to tide me over.' If you want those letters, you will have to pay for them."

"That's blackmail," Ted said.

"Well, do you have another suggestion?" she said, rocking slowing back and forth. "Right now, I'm broke. My father is a stingy old man with a hateful heart. I'm a failure at running a business. I was supposed to be a dancer, not a businesswoman. And I could have been a dancer if the people I loved had believed in me and helped me. New York is a tough place, and I needed my friends."

"Tell us what you want," Ted said.

"I want a hundred thousand dollars. I've already decided to leave. The abortion? I'm not sure yet. But whatever I decide, it will cost you that much to be done with me."

Alex listened as Ted and Lenny told her that much money was impossible, that they had no way to get it. Ted suggested fifty thousand. Finally they agreed on seventy-five.

Ted's family was rich. Lenny had inherited some rental property that he'd probably be able to sell or mortgage. But Alex couldn't imagine how he would manage his share. And how he could keep such a debt from Helen.

"But no letters, no money," Ted insisted.

"Where will you go?" Alex asked her.

"Back to New York, I suppose. I'll have Zubov come with me. Maybe try dancing again, but I don't think I have the heart for it. And the competition has gotten younger."

"We have no guarantee you'll leave here," Alex said. "Or that you'll stay gone if you do."

"No, you don't, do you?" She met his gaze. Alex looked away. "But I will," she said. "If I stay here, I'll die."

"The letters, Libby," Ted said anxiously. "We want our letters back."

"Not until it's all over," she said, her head resting against the high chair back, eyes closed.

"You give us the letters when we give you the money," Ted insisted.

"No," Libby said without opening her eyes. "Not until I'm

gone from here. That way, I know I'll leave alive—and with my money."

"Christ, Libby," Alex muttered. "What do you think we are?"

"I *know* what you are."

Nineteen

Lenny fixed coffee and sandwiches. The men ate at the table, while Libby remained across the room, in her rocker, sipping from a steaming mug of coffee.

Alex refilled his cup and went to sit on the window seat by Libby. "If you have an abortion, it needs to be done as soon as possible," he told her. Gently. But he didn't feel gentle. He wanted to demand that it be done. Tomorrow.

"I had one before. It was disgusting."

"When?" Alex asked, wondering if her first pregnancy was the result of their earlier affair.

"Before," she said, in a tone that indicated no other details would be forthcoming.

"Then I really don't understand why you took this game

of yours to such lengths. Why a pregnancy, for God's sake? Weren't the letters we wrote to you enough of a threat to hold over us?"

Ted and Lenny joined them, pulling up chairs. A cozy little grouping. Alex felt like he was trapped in the middle of a dream that seemed normal during the dreaming but bizarre on replay.

Wrapping her oversized terry robe around her legs, she pulled her knees up to her chest, bare toes hanging over the edge of the chair—a dancer's toes, distorted, with ugly calluses, the only part of her body that wasn't perfect. "Oh Alex," she said with a sigh, "I didn't want to threaten you. I wanted to ruin your marriages. They were a sham anyway. The way you were with me proved that. And the letters showed what sort of husbands you really were. But the letters were vulgar and cheap. They made me want to throw up. I couldn't imagine showing them to anyone. A pregnancy would be more dramatic," she said, pausing, making them wait for her next words.

"For almost a year, I'd thought about it," she continued, her gaze growing distant as she imagined what might have been. "I made up scenes in my head—how I'd explain to them that their husbands betrayed them. That their husbands really didn't love them at all. That one of them made me pregnant. Maybe I'd even wait until the baby was born to tell them—with a baby in my arms."

Then with a sigh, she rested her chin on her knees, her forehead creased in a frown. "I wanted them to be grateful when they found out the truth. That's very important. They needed to know their marriages were a lie. Maybe they'd offer to take care of me and the baby. A little girl we could all raise together. I wanted to see love in their faces. But no matter how many different ways I played it out, I couldn't find any love. They wouldn't understand. They'd blame *me*. And hate me."

She looked at Alex, her eyes black in the dim light. "Tell me, Dr. Alex, do you think I'm crazy?"

"No," Alex hedged. "Not crazy. Just mixed up. We've all been that way. For a long time."

"No, I've been crazy. Sometimes I'd look at myself doing all those disgusting things, and I'd think, 'That woman is crazy.' All my life, I'd had a plan, and when it fell apart, it was hard to find another. And hard to know who to blame. Was it their fault for abandoning me, or the fault of you men for taking them away from me? Then I thought of a way to punish everyone—*and* get my girls back."

"But you betrayed them as much as we did," Alex reminded her. "Doesn't that make you unworthy, too?"

Her frown deepened. She put her bare, knobby feet back on the floor, closing the robe carefully over her bare legs. "No. I wasn't doing it because I wanted to. I don't even like sex. It's just—control. I did like that. I liked making you men stupid and weak and submissive—so eager to do my bidding. It was all for nothing, though. Jen and Helen got those pregnant bellies and looked so happy. *Babies.* That's why they got married. That's who they really love. They love their babies more than any of us. And Bonnie wants a baby, too. She doesn't even know it yet. But she will. I see her looking at Beth and Mandy."

Libby leaned her head against the chair back again, her hands folded in her lap. "We were so happy, you know. Four best friends. I never understood why it had to end."

"It didn't have to end, Libby," Alex said. "Just change."

She closed her eyes again, her face smooth and lovely. "I'm afraid, Alex. I bleed sometimes. Food makes me sick. My head hurts. Stairs make me dizzy. I'm thirsty all the time. I have horrible dreams that wake me in the night. I dream about blood pouring out of me. Sometimes I have to turn on the light and make certain I'm not bleeding all over the bed. Then I'm dis-appointed that I haven't—that there's no blood and tissue and fetus to bundle up and throw away. I can't be a mother. I don't know what to do, Alex. I'm afraid no matter what happens. I lose every way I turn."

With Ted and Lenny listening, Alex explained to her how easy it would be to abort the pregnancy. His voice was soft, gentleness coming more easily now. No one need ever know, he told her. No one would be hurt. It would be an act of love on her part. She nodded when he said that. *An act of love.* No matter how angry and hurt she had been by Helen and Jen and Bonnie, she really didn't want to ruin their lives, did she? Wasn't it enough that she had left an indelible impression on their husbands?

"We've all three got you in our blood, Libby," Alex told her. "We will always be haunted by you. A part of each of us will always wish it was you in our arms and not our wife. But this has to end, Libby, or everyone will hate you. You don't want that."

They waited. Alex held his breath.

"After the anniversary party," she said finally. "I want us all together one last time."

They rose with her as she got up from her chair. She em-braced each of them in turn, then went off to her bedroom and closed the door.

Lenny mortgaged his rental property and borrowed the re-mainder of his share of the money from his grandparents. An investment opportunity, he told them. The grandparents said he didn't need to pay them back—that it would come out of his inheritance.

Ted tried the investment approach with his father. An opportunity for him and Alex. Fifty thousand dollars. Land for future development. Jason Echols demanded specifics. He wanted to see this land. Read the contract. Search the abstract. What about drainage? Ingress and egress? Mineral rights?

In the end, Ted admitted it was woman trouble. He couldn't bring himself to tell his father that he and Alex had both been involved with the same woman—with Libby Ballard, one of their wives' best friends. Instead, he told his father it was two sisters.

Jason called him every name in the book. But finally agreed to make the loan. And explained quite firmly that he and Alex would both pay every dime back plus interest.

"You get this mess straightened up," Jason Echols told his son. "Women are the heart of families, and don't you forget it! A man who messes up his marriage has to *visit* his children— and gets to see his grandchildren once a year on his birthday."

Alex took Libby the money, waiting until late enough for the evening ballet classes to be over.

She didn't answer his knock, but the door was unlocked. She was sitting in the wicker rocker by the window, wearing the same terry-cloth robe.

She held the money on her lap for a while, then rose and carried it into the bedroom.

When she returned to her chair, she said, "A baby would have been nice. I could have taught her to dance."

"Then don't have an abortion," Alex said. "Just take money and leave. Go to Zubov."

"Yes, we could teach her together," she said, staring out the window into the darkness, her profile so pure of line that it belonged on a cameo. "But what if she grew up and left me?"

Alex leaned close and took Libby's hand. Her skin was

clammy, but her pulse was normal. "Children leave," he explained. "They're supposed to. You can't own a human being,
not even your own child."

"I never loved my mother, you know. Never. I think she
tried to love me, but she didn't really. The only people I ever
really loved were Jen and Helen and Bonnie. I'm scared, Alex.
I'm scared to go forward and scared to go back. I'll do whatever
you want."

"No, it needs to be what you want," Alex said.

"Will it be big enough to bury?"

"No. Are you sure, Libby? I could help you find someone
to adopt it."

"No, I'm sure. I don't want some other mother with my
baby. Getting pregnant was a bad idea."

"All of it was a bad idea," Alex said.

"But you did love me some, didn't you?"

"More this minute than ever before."

She smiled. And Alex's heart turned over in his chest.

The morning after the anniversary party, Alex and Libby took
her car to his parents' cabin, medical supplies already stashed
in its trunk.

Their wives thought it was just another fishing trip. A two-
nighter. They'd be back Monday evening.

Ted and Lenny had picked Alex up early in the morning
and delivered him to Libby's apartment. They would come for
him at the cabin the next afternoon.

It was the first time he and Libby had gone in the same car
to the cabin. Libby insisted on driving and got a speeding ticket
on the way. "They'll have to find me in New York to collect,"
she said. "I'll miss driving when I'm back in New York. I missed

it before. Once I took the car upstate, just looking for a place to open up. But you have to drive forever to get away from the traffic. Not like out here."

At the cabin, she was like an obedient child, changing into her robe and waiting patiently while he laid out his instruments and supplies on the sideboard and covered the large picnic-style table with a plastic tablecloth and sheeting. He helped her up on the table, propped a cushion under her hips and used ether to put her under.

He paused for an instant, thinking of the fetus that would never be a baby. Maybe his baby.

During the three years of his residency, Alex had done D&Cs hundreds of times. A quick, simple procedure.

Libby started bleeding almost at once.

He gave her more ether and packed her uterus with wads of gauze.

Still the blood came. Too much blood. He tried more packing. Jesus, he must have severed an artery.

Sweat was dripping from his body. For an instant, he couldn't move. Couldn't think. Fear had turned him to stone.

Don't panic, he told himself. *Absolutely don't panic.* He stuffed several towels between her legs and wrapped her in a blanket.

She was coming to as he picked her up and carried her out to her car. He talked in a soothing tone. A small problem. He was going to take her to a hospital. She was going to be all right. He wouldn't let anything happen to her. Not to his Libby.

She put her arms around his neck. "I forgive you," she said, and kissed his mouth.

Frantically, he drove down the mountain with Libby slumped over against the door. With one hand, Alex would feel for a pulse in her neck. Faint.

He tried to think where to take her. Was there no hospital between here and Denver?

He was almost in Central City. Maybe the clinic there had an emergency room. His dad had taken him there years ago to have a fish hook removed from his finger. Alex headed there and hoped for the best. At least, they'd call an ambulance. Maybe have IV fluids.

The smell of fresh blood filled the car. The blanket around Libby was soaked with it.

Please, don't let her die. Please.

He felt for a pulse one last time as he pulled into the emergency room driveway.

She was dead.

Alex pulled into a parking place. He checked again to make sure, willing with all his might for a pulse to be there.

He pulled her body into his arms. "I'm so sorry, baby. So sorry. So very sorry." He sat there with her, sobbing, holding her as he felt the living warmth leave her body. Already her lips were cool when he kissed them.

Somehow, he drove back up the mountain. Crying. Calling out to God to make it not so. His emotions running the gamut between grief and fear. He had committed a crime that resulted in the death of another human being. He thought of his baby daughter who could grow up with a father in prison, a father disgraced, his right to practice medicine ripped from him like the collar from a defrocked priest.

He thought of Libby's parents with both their children dead.

He thought of Helen who would no longer love him if she knew.

And Libby. Gone forever.

He carried her back inside the cabin and stood there trying

to decide what to do with her body. The table was covered with blood. The blanket around her body soaked with it. He knelt and gently placed her on the floor. He wadded up the plastic tablecloth and took it out back to the incinerator where the cabin's trash was burned.

There were no paper towels, so he used dish towels to sop the congealing blood from the floor. His mother's dish towels. He'd worry about replacing them later. Then he scrubbed the floor with soap and water. The stains were almost invisible on the dark planks.

He unwrapped Libby's body and removed the blood-soaked robe and bloody towels from between her legs. With a sponge and a bucket of soapy water he gently washed the blood from her white skin, then dressed her in the clothes she had worn on the drive up. He kept talking to her, telling her he was sorry, that he hadn't wanted her to die. That she was beautiful. That he loved her. He couldn't stop sobbing.

He took a hairbrush from her cosmetics case and brushed her hair. Long, black, silky hair. So beautiful. The most beautiful hair he'd ever seen.

Then he reverently placed her body on the table and covered it with a clean blanket.

He removed his bloody clothing and took it, the robe, blanket, towels, and a trash can full of bloody dish towels to the incinerator and started a fire. The black smoke from the plastic tablecloth made his eyes sting. The burning blood-soaked clothing smelled like meat on a grill and made him gag.

Later, as he looked back, he supposed he knew at some level that he was destroying evidence, already planning to bury her body. But at the time, his actions were mechanical. Busy work. Getting all that blood out of his parents' cabin.

Then, there was nothing to do but wait.

He pulled his father's easy chair close to the table and Libby's blanket-covered body. He sat there all night, occasionally touching a strand of Libby's hair, drinking scotch until he threw up. Then drinking more.

Dawn's first light was coming through the front windows when he went into the back bedroom and fell across the narrow bed he had slept in as a boy.

He had no recollection of falling asleep but suddenly he was awake. It was raining. Gentle rain.

Then he remembered Libby in the next room and had to face the horror all over again. A scream of protest erupted from his lips and reverberated through the empty, lifeless rooms.

Lenny and Ted arrived in midafternoon. The rain had stopped. The birds were happy. The air was clear and crisp.

Alex was waiting on the front porch when Ted's Jeep came up the gravel drive.

"Oh, dear God," Lenny said when he saw Alex's face.

Twenty

Alex stood behind Ted and Lenny as they stared down at the covered form on the table. Lenny shuddered. Ted sucked in his breath.

What a tableau they made, Alex thought. Three stricken men in plaid shirts. A body on a picnic table. The blanket covering it was plaid, too.

A dog was barking in the distance. Neighbors. Not within view, but their sounds carried in the thin mountain air. Dogs and radios mostly. Occasionally a car backfiring or a door slamming.

The Radcliff cabin used to be the only one on this side of the mountain.

Alex ached with fatigue. And was dizzy with hunger and

dehydration. He reached for the back of a chair to steady himself.

Finally Ted stepped forward and lifted a corner of the blanket. Under it was a life-sized statue made of wax. Bloodless lips. Her head resting in a pool of silky black hair.

"Did she suffer?" Lenny whispered, as though he was afraid she might hear.

"Not with pain," Alex said, his voice breaking.

"Did she know she was dying?" Ted asked.

"Yes," Alex said, crying again. "She said she forgave me."

"Jesus," Ted muttered, his hand shaking as he carefully replaced the blanket.

Ted went out on the porch to do his sobbing. Lenny climbed to the loft. Alex sank into the chair by the table and leaned his forehead against the edge of the table.

His mother would expect him to come to the cabin again and again. Eat his meals at this table.

He couldn't do that. He'd burn the place down first. Maybe he should do it right now. A funeral pyre for Libby. He imagined it for a minute. A wonderful purging fire.

He must have dozed, or passed out, for suddenly there was Ted calling up the stairs to Lenny.

"Come on down. We've got to talk," he said.

Alex pulled himself to his feet and sank back down again. His legs were made of rubber, his head splitting open.

Lenny got him a glass of water and stood over him while he drank it. Then, he helped him to a chair in front of the fireplace.

Ted, the attorney, took charge. "We have to bury her. If anyone finds out what happened, we're in big trouble, Alex. You could be charged with murder, Lenny and I as accessories. Our wives would know. Our reputations would be ruined, our families disgraced. You'd lose your medical license. I'd be disbarred. Lenny'd lose his job. We have to bury her," he repeated.

"What about her parents?" Lenny asked.

"What about them?" Ted asked.

"They won't know what happened to her."

"That's the whole idea," Ted said, irritated. "No one will ever know what happened to her. It happens sometimes. People run away. Get lost at sea or in the mountains. Their car plunges down a canyon. Someone kills them and hides the body. No one ever sees them again. She's already dead, man. We can't do anything for her. We need to take care of ourselves."

"We couldn't just let her parents know anonymously?" Lenny persisted.

"Let them know what?"

"Just that she's dead. Nothing more."

"And they'd tell the police, who would then know that some-one was involved. That someone knows something. That there is a body. Probably foul play. It's best to leave it alone. A mystery with no clues."

"What about all that money and those letters we never got back?" Alex asked, rubbing at his forehead, willing the pain away. He needed to think, to plan with Ted. His whole life depended on it, but at this moment, the throbbing in his head was hard to navigate through.

"Christ. I'd forgotten about them," Ted admitted. "She's probably stashed the money and the letters in a safety deposit box." He paced up and down to do his thinking. "The money by itself wouldn't be so bad. No one could connect it to the three of us. No one would think for a minute that we were involved with her other than as the husbands of her best friends. The money could be part of an unexplained mystery. After all, without a body, there is no proof of a crime."

"But with the letters . . ." Alex protested.

"Yeah," Ted said, stopping in front of Alex. *"Motive."*

Ted started pacing again, thinking out loud. The body first. They had to get rid of her body. And her car. Then they'd have to risk looking through her building again. They hadn't gone down in the basement when they looked before. There was probably stuff in the attic.

"Remember what she said?" Lenny reminded him. "The letters were her insurance. Maybe someone has a package from her to be opened in the event of her death."

Ted stared down at Lenny. "No one is ever going to figure out she's dead," he insisted. But this time, he sounded less sure.

Alex didn't want Libby buried on his parents' property. Ted said they couldn't risk taking her someplace else. "We can't go driving around with a body in the car. What if we got stopped? What if there was a wreck?"

"But if I'm ever a suspect, the police might look for her up here," Alex protested.

"Hell, man, there's a lot of real estate out there," Ted said, exasperated. "You think they're going to dig up the whole damned mountainside? Besides, why would anyone associate you with Libby's disappearance—any more than Lenny and me? Or our wives? The men she dated? The dance professor? All those mothers with their budding ballerinas? All those debutantes she bossed around?"

Finally they agreed. As far back in the ravine as they could take her. Into the wilderness, well beyond the Radcliff property, where her body would remain forever undisturbed.

Before the digging, Alex took three aspirin with a warm Coke and forced down a handful of peanuts. Eating seemed like an obscene act with Libby lying dead on the table, but he needed to function, to do his part.

The three men took turns, first with an axe to hack through

the thick underbrush, then with the shovel from the cabin storeroom and a small camping shovel from the Jeep, digging a grave in the rocky soil at the bottom of the ravine. Back-breaking work—it was almost dark by the time they finished.

Alex carried Libby's now-stiff body out of the cabin, Ted following with her overnight bag and purse. Alex stumbled along, weak and panting, but he wanted to protest when Lenny took the body from him and carried it the rest of the way.

Ted jumped down in the waist-deep hole. Lenny knelt and passed Libby's body into his arms. Ted uncovered her face and kissed her lips. Lenny stared down at Libby's dead, white face, then reached out to touch her hair.

Suddenly Lenny leaped to his feet and jumped on Alex, knocking him to the ground, screaming. "Why did you kill her?"

Ted placed Libby's body at the bottom of the grave and scrambled out to rescue Alex. "Come on, Len. It was an accident. The whole damned thing was just one shitty accident."

The first shovelful of earth was the worst. It hit Libby's body with a thud. Alex felt like he'd been hit in the chest.

Then they hurried. Ted and Lenny shoveling, Alex pushing at the dirt with his hands, getting it over with as fast as possible.

They trampled the earth down and pulled branches and brambles over to conceal the bare spot.

Filthy and panting, sweaty bodies shivering in the cool evening air, they stood beside the camouflaged grave. "Don't you think we should say some words over her?" Lenny asked.

His voice quivering, Alex began the Lord's Prayer. The other two joined in. But they couldn't finish. The words themselves meant nothing. But the act of saying them, standing in this wild, lonely place at Libby's grave was overwhelming beyond belief, the horror of what had happened too much to bear.

Alex wanted to dig her up. To take her someplace nice. He

sank to his knees and placed his open hands on the ground. "God, Libby, I'm so sorry," he kept saying. "So sorry."

Ted pulled him to his feet, and Alex threw his arms around Ted's fleshy body. Ted's arms came around him. And Lenny's. They were locked in a three-way embrace. "Oh dear God," Lenny kept whispering against Alex's cheek.

Arm in arm, they staggered back to the cabin.

Ted and Lenny each opened a can of beer and carried it to the living room, avoiding the table.

Alex tried another glass of water but had a hard time swallowing.

They went outside to look at the Thunderbird. The seat was covered with dried blood. Coagulated blood was pooled on the floor.

They would have to take the car out of state, Ted decided. New Mexico. Kansas. Nebraska, maybe.

Alex drove the Thunderbird, carefully adhering to the speed limit, with Ted and Lenny following Alex in the Jeep. He covered the bloody seat with a blanket and kept the windows down to ease the heavy smell of congealed blood.

Just past Idaho Springs, Alex saw flashing red lights in his rearview mirror—coming up fast. He was overcome with sheer panic. Ditch the car. Take off and run. Hide out in the mountains. The blood was just as incriminating as a body.

Frantically, he adjusted the blanket covering the seat and pulled onto the shoulder.

The highway patrol car sped on by him. Alex slumped over the steering wheel, weak with relief. Ted's face appeared at the window. "You okay?"

"No. But give me a minute."

Alex took several deep breaths to calm himself, then waved to Lenny and Ted and guided the car back out on the highway. He dropped his speed still further.

For no reason, Alex turned south at Englewood, frequently glancing at the rearview mirror for the reassuring headlights of Ted's Jeep. They stopped at a highway truck stop near Monument for coffee and doughnuts, then pushed on. Alex drove mindlessly through the darkness, not knowing how he finally ended up at dawn looking down at a deserted, isolated farm pond.

Lenny waded out to make sure it was deep enough. Ted nudged down a section of fence with the front of his Jeep. Then Alex released the Thunderbird's emergency brake.

It only took one good push to send the car on a roll. They watched as the little car entered the water and gently settled out of view.

They woke early Monday afternoon in the motel room they'd rented, agreed on the story they'd tell their wives and called home. Car trouble. They were stuck in the mountains, in Fraser, waiting for a new fuel pump to be sent up from Denver and would be late getting in.

"You okay?" Helen asked.

"Yeah, fine," Alex said. "Just pissed about the delay."

"Catch anything?" she asked.

"Not much luck. I'll get home as soon as I can. I love you, honey. A lot."

Alex made another call, checking in with the physician who was covering for him, informing him he'd wouldn't be back in town until late tonight. Then they cleaned up, ate, and took their time getting back, arriving in Denver after dark, parking the Jeep several blocks away from Libby's building, cutting through dark alleys.

Ted tried several keys on the ring he'd taken from Libby's purse before he found the one that opened the door to her apartment. Not daring to turn on the lights, they searched by moonlight and flashlight—one from the Jeep's dash, another from Libby's kitchen—finding a surprising number of assorted keys, none of which appeared to be to a safe-deposit box, but keeping a few that might be. But they found no letters, no money. For hours, they searched throughout the entire building, checking every inch of flooring for a loose board, crawling about in the space under the rafters, pulling the front panel off the furnace, looking in cereal boxes, under the burners on the stove, turning the furniture over, taking everything out of drawers and cupboards, then carefully putting it all back just like it was.

Ted stopped on the Eighth Avenue bridge long enough to throw Libby's car keys and the keys they had confiscated at her apartment into the river.

In the months that followed, the three men lived in cloud of perpetual dread. *The letters. The damn letters.* Did they dare hope Libby had destroyed them? If not, they were out there waiting like a time bomb to destroy all their lives.

Alex dreamed of Libby—all manner of dreams from the two of them holding hands in a mountain meadow to images of her about to chop off his daughter's head with the axe from the cabin. He would wake up from the bad dreams with a start, his heart jumping in his chest, his body drenched in sweat. He would wake up from the other kind crying. He began to rely on sleeping medication so he could sleep without dreaming. Helen fretted. He was working too many hours. The hospital treated its resident physicians like slaves.

The men saw each other only in the company of their wives, and then only when they couldn't avoid it—the women's endless speculation about Libby was too disturbing. No fishing trips. No golf dates. By not being together, they didn't have to decide if they should or should not talk about what had happened.

Either way was too painful, the ghost of Libby too fresh, the possibility of impending disaster too real.

But passing time began to lull some of their fears—if the letters were going to be found, wouldn't they have turned up by now? And they had secrets that could never be shared with anyone else, that bound them together. They were brothers in a bizarre fraternity, and their friendship became as deep and strong as the one their wives shared. Libby had done that for them.

And over the years, Libby's hold on their wives loosened. If her car had never been found, they would have continued their satisfying lives full of family, friendship, successful careers with only an occasional painful memory to mar their peace.

Alex told the story to his wife late into the night, her impassive face illuminated by the lamp on his side of the bed, her side in shadows.

When Alex finished his tale, Helen asked only one question.

"Are you sure her death was an accident?"

"No. I close my eyes and imagine inserting the curette, paring away the endometrium. Did I apply too much pressure? Did I want it over that much? I don't think so, but sometimes I wonder."

Then there was nothing to do but sit side by side in the oversized, unevenly lit bed and stare at the wall of family pictures across the room. Babies. Parents. Vacations. Helen as a bride. School pictures. The life of a family—a family he had violated.

He wanted desperately to gather his wife in his arms, to ease his pain and guilt with the comfort of her love. But he dared not.

The room was silent.

"Did you read those letters?"

"No. Libby's mother destroyed them years ago."

"We searched for them. God, how we searched for them. I had nightmares about you finding them. Reading them."

Helen said nothing. The room fell back into silence.

"Would you like me to go to the guest room?" he asked. She nodded.

At the bedroom door, he paused, "I love you, Helen. You and the kids are my life."

"Why didn't you break our engagement?" she asked. "Why didn't you marry her? You wanted to, didn't you?"

Helen

Twenty-one

Don't tell Bonnie and Jen, Alex begged his wife. *Please.* No
need for them to suffer what Helen had suffered. No need to
drive their marriages into the shallows alongside theirs.

Helen both wanted to protect her friends and to scream at
them not to be so damned smug. Their husbands were not
without blame. Her knowing this separated her from them.
Isolated her.

She didn't return their calls and cut conversations short
when they did reach her. She was always on her way out the
door or expecting an important call.

"No, I don't want you to call me back," Jen finally said. "I
want to talk to you *now*. You've said you'll call me back the last

three times I've called, and you never do. And you've been giving Bonnie the same runaround."

"I really am on on my way out the door," Helen lied. She was still in her bathrobe. Sitting at her kitchen table. She had mornings like that sometimes—when functioning seemed like too great a challenge. "What is it you want to talk about?" she asked, already knowing that whatever it was, she didn't want to discuss it with Jen.

"You," Jen said. "Why are you doing this? And what about the anniversary party? It's your turn, you know. Are you just going to let twenty years of tradition die? This was supposed to be the year for a cruise. I realize you're not in a cruise mentality, but short of that, don't you think you should at least have us up for hamburgers and beer? We miss you, honey."

The anniversary party! Helen held back an irritated sigh. Carrying the phone with her, she began pacing nervously between the refrigerator and the kitchen table. A party to celebrate three marriages that weren't what they seemed.

"You guys go ahead and do something without us this year," Helen said. "As soon as I tape the last show of the season, I'm taking the kids to my folks for the summer."

"For the *summer?* Since when? What about the kids? I thought Beth was going to pitch this year. And Ben was going to take tennis lessons from the CU coach."

Helen twisted and untwisted the telephone cord around her finger as she marched up and down. "I need to get away," she said. "It will be good for us all."

"Helen Jane Donaldson Radcliff, what the hell's going on with you? Bonnie and I are your *friends,* remember? Your *best* friends. It's like you dropped off the earth after Bonnie found out about that damned traffic ticket. But it didn't prove anything. And no matter what happened between Alex and Libby, it doesn't change our friendship. Don't you know that?"

"Sure. I just need to spend some time with my folks."

"They came to see you in March."

"Okay then, I'd like some time to do a little writing. Alex always said I should write a book. Is that a good enough reason?"

"You know something you're not telling us," Jen said. "We all decided the truth was better than not knowing, and now you've gone and changed the rules."

"Look, Jen, I know you're trying to be a good friend. But I just can't deal with you and Bonnie right now. I've got stuff to figure out on my own. And Phoenix seems like a good place to do it."

Yes, Helen thought. In Phoenix, she could take comfort in being the beloved daughter. She needed that. And she needed to get away from a marriage with separate bedrooms and an uncertain future.

"What about Alex?" Jen demanded. "Are you going to abandon him for the whole summer?"

"He'll manage."

"What about your business?" Jen asked.

"I've had an offer from Pioneer Bakery. I may sell. Or not. I have pretty good help."

"Sell your business! Just like that? Look, Bonnie and I will drive up and see you before you leave," Jen said firmly. "At least let us tell you good-bye."

"No, please. I'm really busy. Take care. Tell Bonnie I said hello."

Helen spent the rest of the day in a panic. Doing laundry. Pulling suitcases down from the attic. Canceling appointments. Making an uncomfortable phone call to the station. She'd have to miss the last taping. She was sorry. But this was a personal emergency. Maybe they could repeat an earlier show.

The children would miss the last day of school, but she knew Jen too well. Helen wanted to get out of town before Jen and

Bonnie drove up here. Eventually, she would have to see them, she supposed. But not yet. She wouldn't know what to say. They might see the truth in her face. *Don't feel sorry for me! Your husbands did it, too.*

Beth refused to pack her clothes and threw a stack of freshly laundered underwear on the floor. She screamed at her mother that she wasn't going anyplace. She wanted to play ball. She wanted to hang out with her friends. She didn't want to leave her boyfriend.

"I'm not going. And you can't make me," she said, folding her arms under her bosom—high young breasts that she probably wanted her first real boyfriend to touch during the long warm evenings of summer.

"I need for us to go," Helen said wearily, sinking on the edge of the bed beside her angry daughter. Beth moved away from her. "I have to do this, Beth. And I need your cooperation."

"Why do you *have* to do it? 'Cause you and Daddy can't get along? Is that any reason to ruin my life? Why can't I stay here with Daddy?"

"You know why. Your dad is gone all hours of the day and night. I don't want you here alone."

"You don't trust me," Beth accused.

"No, not altogether."

Alex appeared in the bedroom door. "Don't give your mother a hard time, Beth. She's not doing this to be mean."

"You don't want her to go either," Beth told her father. "I heard you asking her not to go. Why can't you just *tell* her not to?"

"Because she has the right to do what she thinks is best. And I honor her decision."

"I hate you both," Beth screamed, shoving the lamp off the

bedside table. The pottery base broke with a crash. Alex started for her.

Helen shook her head at him.

Ben was worse. He cried.

Alex did too, closing the bedroom door, begging her not to go. What could he do or say to make her stay? "Christ, Helen, it happened so long ago! And I can't change what happened, but why can't you believe me when I say I'd do anything on earth to make it up to you?"

"Just help me load the station wagon," she said, folding clothes into an open suitcase. "And don't forget to call your mother on her birthday."

"Just tell me what you want, Helen," he said, following her to the closet. "Do you want me to turn myself in? Go to jail? For God's sake, talk to me."

"What is it you want me to say?" she asked, grabbing clothes down from hangers. "That the statute of limitations has run out on straying husbands? That it's okay now that you stayed married to me because Libby wouldn't have you? Because Libby turned out to be crazy? That it's okay she's buried in an unmarked grave? That it's okay the whole affair turned into a tragic, sordid nightmare? That it's okay that you kept me in the dark all these years? Well, if I said those things, I'd be lying. Nothing is okay. And I know it all happened a long time ago. But the truth is brand-new. Maybe if you'd told me before, I'd have healed by now."

"And maybe if I'd told you the truth years ago, you'd have left me back then. Can you honestly tell me that you wouldn't have?"

"No, I can't honestly tell you anything except I'm very confused, and that's why I have to go away."

Helen's parents guessed that trouble with Alex was the reason for their daughter's sudden visit and curtailed their busy schedule of golf, bridge, art classes, and ballroom dancing to hover. Every time they looked at her, it was with concern in their eyes, and this made Helen want to cry. But then tears sprung to her eyes these days at the slightest provocation. Simon and Garfunkel singing "Bridge over Troubled Water." The picture on her father's bookshelf of her standing beside Alex in his cap, gown, and doctoral hood after his graduation from medical school. She was looking at his face. She remembered how she felt. So proud. So in love. So eager for the future.

Beth and Ben pouted in front of the television set and couldn't say two words to each other without an argument. They punished their mother by rebuffing their grandparents' attempts to organize excursions, games of Monopoly, golf lessons.

The second week of her visit, Helen cooked a special meal for some of her parents' friends. It was late when they finished cleaning up the kitchen.

"Thanks, honey. The food was terrific. We brag about our famous daughter. It was fun to show you off," Maxine said with a hug.

Then it was her father's turn. He held her a minute. "Alex isn't running around on you, is he? If he is, I'll . . ."

"No, Daddy. Nothing like that. We just needed some time apart."

Helen wasn't ready yet to crawl into the bed she was sharing with her daughter and poured herself a finger of brandy to carry out onto the patio. The desert air was cool and dry—like in the mountains, but different somehow. The smells weren't the same. The night sounds. The distant ridge of low mountains didn't compare with the Front Range. And tall silhouettes of alien-looking cacti marched across the strip of grassless sand that separated her parents' yard from the abrupt edge of the lush green golf course that was the focus of her parents' existence in the expensive retirement community.

She didn't realize she was crying until she felt tears rolling down her cheeks. *Damn.*

Coming here hadn't been a good idea. She missed her own home, her own kitchen, her own bed.

The next day, Helen called Alex and asked him to move out of the house. She was bringing the children home.

She told Beth and Ben on the drive north that she and their father would be living apart for a while.

"How come?" Beth demanded.

"Because we aren't getting along."

"No kidding!" Beth said, arms across her chest.

"Well, if he's not living with us, how are you going to start getting along better?" Ben wanted to know from the backseat. Sweet, earnest Ben with his freckles and braces.

"Has he been having an affair?" Beth asked.

"You watch your mouth, young lady."

"That's the reason most parents get divorces," Beth said, refusing to back down. "If he's going to expect Ben and me to start spending weekends in an apartment with him and some bimbo, I'm not interested."

Helen had to laugh. She reached over and patted her daughter's arm. "No, honey. There's no bimbo."

"You guys are going to try and get along better, aren't you?" Ben asked.

Alex tried to court her. But Helen didn't want flowers or expensive gifts. She didn't want promises of extravagant vacations. She could not endure his phone calls with attempts at small talk. Of course, her day wasn't all right. How stupid of him to ask. How could her day be all right when her life was falling apart?

She tried to decide if she still loved him. She didn't hate him. She still felt like he occupied a permanent place in her life. They were married. Connected. By the years, by their children.

The time she missed him most was at dinner. No matter how wonderful a meal she prepared, it seemed like a snack to be hurried through when Alex wasn't there. Dinnertime only counted when the whole family gathered about the table, when one of the children asked the blessing, when she and Alex quizzed them about school, friends, and life, when family business was conducted, announcements made, trips planned, good news shared.

At night in bed, Helen tried to imagine making love with him. She wanted to want him. But instead, she closed her eyes and saw him with Libby. And now Helen had this hideous new image of blood and dying. For all those years, she had wanted Libby to be dead. But now, the reality of that death brought confusion and guilt. And repulsion that her husband had been the executioner.

Libby had poisoned their marriage. Alex had warned Helen that would happen if she didn't leave things alone.

Was it her fault, then, for not choosing to remain in the dark?

Could she ever get over the truth? If she allowed him to come home, their marriage would never be the same. He would remain in the family and in their marriage through her good graces.

Jen and Bonnie knew that she and Alex were living apart. When they called, Helen would say she still couldn't handle talking to them, that she'd call them when she was ready.

Helen doubted if that time would ever come. A chapter was

over, and with it, their friendship—their wonderful friendship that had sustained her for most of her life. Without her husband, and without her friends, she felt lost.

But she still had her children, and she was determined to make the most of their last few years at home. And she was tired of managing two jobs. She sold her cheesecake business without a backward look. Amazing how unemotional she was about it. But the cheesecakes had served their purpose. She'd proved she could create and run a business. She was no longer just a housewife who baked.

The Pioneer people wanted to keep her name and picture on containers and use them in advertising and would pay an annual fee for the right. And Pioneer would become one of the sponsors of her television show. Helen would forever be associated with Helen's Heavenly Cheesecakes. The company would even pay her to create new recipes. Not a bad deal at all. And Helen had negotiated it, her lawyer sitting at her side.

Bonnie and Jen drove up one morning. Helen saw them pulling in the driveway. The doorbell rang and rang. She wouldn't let the children answer it. She held her hands over her ears, Ben and Beth looking at her like she was crazy. Finally, the ringing stopped. And the car drove away.

Helen knew that Jen and Bonnie assumed Alex had confessed to something. They couldn't know to what, but they had made the same assumptions she had. Libby had been going to the cabin to meet Alex. Alex was doing a residency in OB/GYN. Libby was pregnant. And never seen again.

But of course, Jen and Bonnie thought that only Alex had betrayed his wife. That only Alex had a hand in Libby's death —or disappearance. And Helen would not be able to endure the horror and pity in their faces. She would hate them for it and want to scream the truth at them.

The days she didn't go into Denver, Helen was restless.

With a cleaning woman and a yardman, she didn't do much housework anymore. She still cooked on the nights that she and the children were at home to eat together. But that was only two or three nights a week.

She began compiling the cookbook she'd always said she would write, and ironically she started writing the mystery that Alex had always wanted her to write. Her protagonist was a famous female chef who ascertained the character and background of suspects by their food habits and manners. She knew how and where they were raised, where they had traveled, how sensual they were, and even their character flaws and strengths just by observing them at mealtime or in the kitchen.

Beth and Ben usually endured their mother's constant hugs and pats. Helen wondered what was going to happen to her when her children grew up and left.

She worked hard at not thinking about Libby. The past had exhausted her.

Twenty-two

Alex came to dinner on Beth's fifteenth birthday.

Without being told, Ben arrived at the table with his hair combed and his shirt tucked in. Beth did not pick her usual dinnertime argument with her brother. Both were too polite and anxiously watched their parents' faces.

Alex's gift to his daughter was a diamond-encrusted heart on a gold chain. Beth's hands shook as she took the necklace from its velvet case. Alex's shook while he tried to fasten it around Beth's neck. Helen had to help.

And then he told them about his great idea for a family trip. To Katmai National Park in Alaska to see the grizzly bears. A real adventure. He'd buy each of them a good camera.

Helen slipped on her coat and walked Alex to the car afterward. "Shut up about trips, will you?"

"Why? Don't you think we'll ever take a family trip together again?"

Helen didn't answer.

They stood at the curb, Alex leaning against his Ranger. "Good dinner," he said.

She nodded and started to back away.

"Lenny called," Alex said. "He and Bonnie have been approved by an agency offering Korean orphans for adoption. They've asked for a girl about three or four years old. Lenny said they're too old for nighttime feedings and toilet training."

A little girl for Bonnie. Helen felt a knot of pain in her stomach. Bonnie would have told her and Jen over lunch. They would have wept for joy. Together.

"You okay?" he asked.

"Yes," she said, starting to cry. "I'm just very sad not to be part of the excitement. Bonnie and Lenny will paint and paper the world's most adorable little girl's room. Jen will have a little girl shower. They'll all go to the airport when she arrives, with balloons and toys."

"You wanted the truth," he reminded her.

"Don't," she warned.

"When can I see you again?"

"I don't know." She brushed away her tears with the back of her hand.

"Well, I guess I'll be going," he said, reaching for the door handle of his vehicle.

"What about the cabin?" she asked. "The children miss it."

"You have the key."

"You wouldn't care?" Helen asked.

"I used to think I'd burn it down. But it's just a place. Evil comes from people, not places."

"You aren't evil," Helen said softly. "I don't think Libby was either. I want you to show me where she's buried."

"Why in God's name would you want that?" Alex asked.

"I don't know. I just do."

"I want to come home, Helen. I can't stand not having a home." He started to touch her arm, but didn't.

They embraced instead. Politely. Helen almost wanted to cling to him, but not quite.

Helen read the announcement of Evelyn Ballard's death in the *Post*. Such a short obituary.

. . . after a long illness . . . preceded in death by her husband, son, and daughter . . . survived by a sister.

Helen had been back to the nursing home only once after Evelyn told her about the letters—to take her the apple crisp. Evelyn had been watching birds out the window with binoculars. "I saw a yellow-bellied sapsucker yesterday," she announced proudly. "Birds are so beautiful. I get pleasure from watching them." Evelyn had been like Jen—determined to squeeze all the good there was out of life.

The graveside services were scheduled for day after tomorrow. Jen would be there, of course. Probably Bonnie, too.

Helen considered not going, but she wouldn't like herself very much if she didn't. She would arrive late and leave immediately after the last prayer, she decided.

She couldn't sleep the night before. Jen and Bonnie probably hated her now. She had broken the bonds of friendship that had tied them together for more than thirty years. Yet, she still loved them. And missed them so acutely it felt like a part of her was missing. Their friendship had been more intimate even than a marriage.

It sleeted on the way down to Denver, the roads turning to

a sheet of ice. And more bad weather was predicted. Helen would have been justified in turning back, but she kept going. Evelyn's funeral was giving her a reason to see her friends again. She felt as though she were about to ski down an uncharted mountain. Taking a risk. A frightening, thrilling risk.

Only six cars were parked behind the hearse, a handful of people huddled under the canopy. Jen's parents were there. And a few people Helen didn't know.

When Helen saw Jen and Bonnie standing apart from the others, waiting for her, she began to cry. The tears froze on her cheeks. She didn't think her legs would carry her across the frozen grass.

Wordlessly, they linked arms with her.

And they stood arm in arm as the clergyman quickly read a bit of Scripture and committed Evelyn's remains to the ground. Tiny particles of ice beat against Helen's face.

They went to offer condolences to Evelyn's sister, whose leathery tan skin looked out of place in the middle of a Colorado winter. "Oh, yes. Libby's friends," she said, even her voice shivering. "I'm trying to dispose of Evelyn's things. Would one of you like Libby's portrait?"

"Why don't you send it to the CU School of Dance?" Jen suggested. "Libby was something of a legend there, you know."

Helen touched Evelyn's casket in farewell, then hurried toward her car, shivering inside her fur coat. In spite of fur-lined boots, her feet felt like ice.

Bonnie and Jen caught up with her, once again linking arms. "You're coming with us," Bonnie said.

"But my car," Helen protested.

"It will wait for you," Jen said.

"No, I'd feel better with my car."

"But will you follow us to Bonnie's?" Jen asked.

Helen nodded. She would go. But she had to have her car parked outside so she could leave when she needed to.

At Bonnie's apartment, their greeting was careful—light hugs and cheek kisses. Bonnie bustled about making hot toddies. Jen lit the logs already stacked in the fireplace.

The room was different. The sofa recovered. A new oriental rug.

Bonnie showed Helen a lovely white and pink bedroom with toys already in place. Their daughter would arrive any day now. Her name was Kim Song. "We've already started calling her Kimmie," Bonnie said. Helen had to fight back tears.

Back in the living room, Jen wordlessly handed Helen an envelope and left her alone by the fire. The letter was addressed to Jen. It was from Evelyn Ballard—handwritten by a tremulous hand.

My dearest Jen,

First of all, I want to thank you for being my surrogate daughter these past years. And yes, I accept your offer to be here with me at the end. The nurses have written on my chart that you are to be called. At first I thought no, that's not fair to that darling girl. But I would like your hand to hold, your presence. I don't want to be alone.

You told me once that you were just standing in for Libby, doing the things she would have done had she still been with me. But I think we both know that isn't true. Libby and I had our problems. I'd like to think that deep down she loved me and that someday we might have become close. But maybe I was simply spared more pain by her early departure from my life.

I sense that the end is very near. My mind wanders more than not. I saw my sweet Carl last night, sitting there in the chair by my bed. Wouldn't it be nice if there were a Hereafter, and I could be with him once again?

See what I mean? My poor old mind does wander. It's time to write this letter while I'm still able. I hope it's not too hard for you to read. I haven't written anything in so long, and my fingers seem to have forgotten how to hold a pen. Or maybe it's just the cold. I'm cold all the time, now.

Last summer, I told Helen something I probably never should have. And I have regretted it every day since, especially when you told me that she and her husband are living apart and that she has severed her ties with you and Bonnie.

But you see, Helen knows a terrible secret. And she can't face you and Bonnie because of it.
Do two wrongs ever make a right? I'm not sure. But I am about to commit a second one.

Helen has tried to protect you and Bonnie from the knowledge that your husbands were also involved with Libby. All three men got caught in her net. Libby had some scheme to punish you girls for not loving her enough—which for Libby meant more than anyone else—and to prove you all made terrible mistakes by throwing your lots in with three unworthy men. But oddly enough, I think she was also fighting to get you girls back. My poor Libby. She was so very confused.

I think Libby realized she'd lost the fight when you and Helen had babies. I remember when she took me to see your new baby, Jen. On the way home, I said what a good little mother you were and how much you loved your baby. Libby said, "Yes, like you loved Carl. I can't fight against that kind of love."

She was pregnant then. I know that now, but at the time I only suspected. And I was afraid to say anything. How I regret that! Maybe if I had told her how happy I would be to help her, to have a baby with her, maybe I would be a grandmother and Libby would not be dead.

So, you see, there is much guilt to go around—mine, Libby's, her father's, your husbands', perhaps even you three girls'. Libby wasn't an evil person, but she did do some evil things. Whatever happened to her, she brought upon herself, but maybe one of us could have stopped her.

But then, how could any of us know it would end so badly?

I never told Fred or the police or anyone until Helen about the letters Libby had given to me for safekeeping—three packets of them, one from each of your husbands. She destroyed her own life, and I didn't want to see other lives destroyed because of her.

And now, I pray with all my heart that you and Bonnie won't judge your husbands as harshly as Helen has apparently judged her Alex. The only reason I told her the truth was to show how determined Libby was, how ruthless. The men were no match for her. Surely you can see that.

I don't know the whole story of what happened to my daughter. Perhaps only your husbands know that. But I don't want to die without doing something to get you girls back together again. Your friendship has as much right to survive as your marriages.

I'd like to think that Libby's lasting legacy is the

friendship she brought into existence so many years ago. I can see you four little girls with skinny legs skipping down the sidewalk just like it was yesterday.

Let Libby die, but keep the friendship she created alive.

Be happy, sweet Jen. And love your husband. And see if you can't help Helen find some forgiveness in her heart for Alex.

Much love,
Evelyn Ballard

"There," Helen said, pointing to a place at the bottom of the ravine directly below a twisted pine tree that leaned outward from the steep hillside. "Alex said that pine tree was just a sapling then, but he was pretty sure this is the place."

The three women scrambled down the steep incline, the ground still wet from the recently melted snow, then stood and stared at the tangle of briars and branches that covered Libby's grave.

"It's still hard to believe she's dead," Jen said, "I think of her dancing. So beautiful. So alive."

"And it's hard to imagine our husbands digging a grave and burying her here," Bonnie said. "Jesus. How could they do that? Put her body in a hole in the ground and throw dirt on it?"

"They were afraid," Helen said. "They were afraid of losing us, losing everything. They wrapped her in a plaid blanket. And said a prayer." She looked around, trying to imagine that scene—to feel their horror and fear and sadness.

"I've tried to figure out what would have been the right thing for them to do," Bonnie said. "Turn themselves in? Tell us what happened? Take her body someplace where it would have been found? It's hard to imagine how all our lives would have turned out if they'd been arrested and stood trial—maybe even gone to jail. But burying her here like this seems wrong. So very wrong."

"Does it bother you that they were never punished?" Helen asked.

"Oh, I think they were punished," Jen spoke up. "And I don't think anything would have been accomplished by their turning themselves in."

"But she died," Helen said.

Jen and Bonnie nodded, staring down at the ground. Yes, she died. Her bones were down there someplace. All that was left of Libby. Who was to say what should have been done all those years ago? And the passage of time itself made rectifying any wrongs all but impossible. Maybe it had been impossible from the very beginning.

"The four of us are together again," Jen said. "What a strange ending for our little band." She was crying. Bonnie reached for her hand.

"I used to think of her as dead and buried," Helen said, "in a silver casket, her black hair on a white satin pillow. I wish I could hate her. I wish I could hate Alex. Everything would be easier. Cleaner. But God help me, I feel so sorry—like it's our fault somehow for not realizing how seriously she took all that sisterhood stuff."

"I take it seriously," Bonnie said. "You guys are my sisters. My friends for life."

They walked for a time, puffing more than they used to as they trudged up the hill to Blind Man's Bluff. Buster, the old Lab, only went partway and turned back. "I remember when he used to wait for us at the top," Jen said.

From the bluff, they could see the next ridge. And cabins where there didn't used to be any. But the cabins were for other people who loved the mountains.

On the way back down, Jen asked Helen, "Will you let Alex come home?"

"I suppose. Eventually. When I want him to make love to me. Right now, I don't want that."

"I know what you mean," Jen said. "I want Ted, yet I find myself wondering at the wrong time if he was in love with her. But it was so long ago. And he's still my Teddy Bear. I could forgive anything as long as he stays with me."

"That's the catch," Bonnie said. "We'll never know if one of them would have left."

"Alex said she wanted Zubov to live with her in New York," Helen said. "But you're right, we'll never know what was in her heart or theirs."

"I always knew something had been going on," Jen admitted, "but I was too proud to admit it. I wasn't sure it was with Libby—in fact it petrified me to think that it might have been. I knew Ted was suffering through something. The whole time I was pregnant with Mandy, he didn't sleep well and told me every five minutes that he loved me."

"Lenny even confessed that he'd had an affair," Bonnie revealed. "But he said it was with someone at the station—or at least he didn't deny it when I assumed it was someone at the station. He said he wanted us to start over—to fall in love all over again. That he knew more than ever before how much he loved me and needed me. I felt like our marriage had survived the ultimate test. Now, I don't think I'll ever love him as much as before. But I wanted our Kimmie. I needed him to get her. And it's lovely—seeing him be a father. That makes up for other things."

After dinner, they put on their jackets and gloves and went back down to the ravine. It was dusk. The night noises were beginning in the underbrush. The low, mournful hoot of an owl signaled the beginning of the night's hunt.

Jen knelt and cleared away some of the underbrush. Bonnie found two sticks and tied them with her bandana to make a cross.

"I loved you, Libby Ballard," Jen said as Bonnie stuck the cross in the moist earth. "We all did."

"I hated her, too," Helen had to say. But there were tears in her eyes.